Just Like a Fairy Tale

Cameron James

SRL PUBLISHING

Just Like a Fairy Tale

Cameron James

SRL Publishing Ltd
London
www.srlpublishing.co.uk

First published worldwide by SRL Publishing in 2023

Copyright © CAMERON JAMES 2023

ISBN: 978-1915-073-23-5

1 3 5 7 9 10 8 6 4 2

A CIP catalogue record for this book is available from the British Library

SRL Publishing is a Climate Positive publisher offsetting more carbon emissions than it emits.

To celebrate all the queer happily ever afters in the past and present, and the many more to come in the future

And for L, my own happily ever after.

Luca's
Pronouns

Luca Madison-May – he/him
Queen Beau – she/her
Mateo – xe/xer
Alistair Madison – he/him
Rory May – he/him
Connor Madison-May – he/him
Riley May – he/him
Kieran May – he/him
Oakley May – he/him
Skylar Reynolds – they/them
Enzo Madison – zie/zir
Caleb Madison – they/them
Emma Madison – she/her
Marley Madison – they/them
Quinn Madison – they/them
Phil Potter – he/him
Queen Lime – she/her
Felix Potter – they/them
Queen Lemon – she/her

Jackson's
Pronouns

Jackson Bennett – he/him
Queen Madison – she/her
Reed McDonald – he/him
HRH Queenie – she/her
Jason Baker – he/him
HRH Queen Jasmine – she/her
Jesse Baxter – he/him
HRH Queen Daisy – she/her
Jamie Bennett – he/him
HRH Queen Cherry Blossom – she/her
Dylan Bennett – he/him
Rosie Bennett – she/her
Evan Bennett – he/him
Eloise Bennett – he/him
Avory McAllister – he/him
Queen Robin – she/her
Milo Anderson -he/him
Chandler Duncan – he/him
Jonathan Lawrence – he/him
Charlie Franklin – he/him

Luca

I've always wanted to be a Drag Queen.

My first experience of the art of drag was accidental, mostly. I was small, and it was the night my brother, Connor, was born. My Dads were otherwise occupied with the whole birth thing and I was being babysat by my Dad's twin, Enzo. We sat up on the couch awaiting the call to tell us both that Connor had arrived safe and well. I'd never seen the TV this late. We'd watched the news together than multiple comedy shows where the jokes went over my head.

Enzo left me to make some toast to get us through and suddenly there they were.

The screen was full of fierce and loud Queens. All of different shapes and sizes, different colours and creeds. All unapologetically themselves.

According to Enzo, zie had watched me for a few minutes. Smiling to zirself at how besotted I was at the screen. I'd barely acknowledged zir when zie passed me the toast.

The call came during the runway and I was livid Enzo was about to talk over this marvellous display on our screen, even if it meant I was getting a new baby brother.

Enzo took the call out of the room and waited for the show to finish before telling me Connor had come into the world.

After that, my obsession just grew. I idolised any and all Queens I came to know. I adored the art, the commitment. The wigs, the clothes, the heels. I wanted to be in that world and every damn person knew it. I was Luca Madison-May and I loved Drag Queens.

I had never thought myself good enough. Not really, but then I saw it on the notice board at Rainbow Connection.

HIRING DRAG ARTIST at THE ROSE QUARTET
MUST BE 18+
NO PIOR EXPERIENCE NEEDED

And I went for it. I decided I had to. Opportunities like these did not come around often enough for me to look my dream in the face and think *later*. I took the poster.

It was only afterwards I found out it was my uncle Oakley who'd put it there.

And now I was auditioning.

I was stood on a stage, in a club. All the lights were on but it wasn't any less exquisite. The tables were dressed in rose red cloths and individual lamps. The stage itself had little individual bulbs along the perimeter and a big LED screen.

There were two men sat in front of me.

Both were more sophisticated. The one who'd spoke to me the most was beautiful, he wore half rimmed glasses, his hair styled and white. His eyes so kind.

The other man was older than me, too, but younger than the first. He carried a little more weight, his hair blonde. He wore a floral shirt, and he wore it well.

They both seemed to like my song.

"Luca?" the first man asked. I nodded slowly, confirming my name. "I like Luca," he told the man next to him, who instantly laughed.

"Jason, you like any Queen with a pretty face."

Jason looked at me, crinkling his nose. "That's true and you are a very beautiful Queen."

"Thank you," I replied as I played with the microphone because that had embarrassed me.

"Still modest, huh, we'll knock that out of you," the other man said.

I laughed, "Wait, am I hired?"

They conferred with their eyes.

"Luca, have you done drag before?" Jason asked. I looked down at my feet. "No?" I shook my head slowly. "That's okay. Jesse had never done drag before either."

"And now I'm the Queen," he intoned.

Jason laughed. "Was..."

"*Was* the Queen," he grumbled then stood from where he was sat and climbed up onto the stage walking towards me. He lifted my chin. His eyes examining me a quiet smile on his face.

"I stood on this stage at eighteen and told George, a man who you will learn all about, that I wanted to do Drag." He looked at Jason then laughed, "I had never set foot in a drag club before. I had never even thought about it, but I had taken a job as a lighting technician up there." He pointed towards the lighting box. "I saw the Queens. I decided I wanted to be one of them. Simple as."

"Just like that?" I asked.

"Just like that. It takes work, yes, but if you're willing, we can help you become the Queen you wish to be. Do you have a name?"

"Yes," I replied without thinking then I sighed.

"It is?" Jason asked.

"A bit pretentious," I said.

He laughed. "I'm HRH Queen Jasmine…" he tilted his head. "I wasn't very creative at seventeen, Jason, Jasmine. Poor really but whatever." He waved towards Jesse.

"HRH Queen Daisy," he said as he curtsied.

I curtsied back as if it were a reflex. "Beau," I said quietly then shook my head. "It was stupid. I was playing about with names and Beau just sounded good, I guess."

"And it's accurate," Jason said nodding. I laughed as I tugged on my fingers.

"Beau, I like that," Jesse agreed. "You're hired, Beau."

"Is it just Beau?" Jason asked. "I feel like you should have a last name."

"My last name is Madison-May."

"First of all, I love that," Jesse said.

"But you can't have Madison."

"Oh no, definitely not. May though, Beau May." Jesse said.

"Beau May," Jason repeated as I grinned. We all turned as laughter came through the door.

"Speak of the Princess," Jesse said in a laugh as two boys came through the door. One was tall, very tall, blonde, with tortoise shell glasses. He, I would imagine, would have an incredible hourglass figure when in drag. The second was shorter, his hair and eyes dark. He was petite, almost feminine although I guess he'd take that as a compliment, he also wore glasses, rounded and large.

"I present our current Queen," Jason said waving his arm with a flourish. "HRH Queen Queenie…"

"Queen Queenie," I repeated.

The taller of the two laughed. "Yeah, that so doesn't work," he said, his Scottish accent wrapping around his vowels. "Maybe just HRH Queenie. I think I prefer that."

"Queenie is a musical theatre Queen," Jason informed me, "and Princess Madison."

"Madison," I repeated as the petite boy waved.

"Queenie, Madison, meet Beau, our new Queen."

"Oh," they chorused.

"Beau," Madison replied, as I looked away.

"You're only a wee Queen, aren't you? How old are you?" Queenie asked as he walked towards the stage, stepping up onto it in a singular fluid movement. Jesse groaned beside me, muttering something about how he wished he was still that young.

"Nineteen," I answered, although I didn't sound all too sure.

Queenie laughed looking over his shoulder. "Still the baby Jackson."

"Reed," Queenie reintroduced himself.

I smiled. "Luca. When they say you're the Queen, what do they quite mean by that?"

"Ah..." he shrugged as if he was coy. "It's just a title mostly. We're currently in Queenie's reign. Before that was Daisy's," he nodded vaguely towards Jesse. "Before Daisy, was Cherry Blossom's, Jasmine's Crystal's... Rose's..."

"Of the Rose Quartet, huh." I said, then smiled. "So you're the headline."

"He's the headline," Jackson confirmed.

"But Queen sounds far more fancy," Reed pouted; I laughed before looking away when I caught Jackson grinning at me.

"Our Queens will help you create Beau." Jason told me from where he was stood at the end of the runway, his hands flat on the stage, *he* wasn't making any attempt to join us up here. "They'll teach you how to pluck, tuck..."

"I've been learning how to tuck since I was thirteen," I informed him *totally* unnecessarily. I looked down as I felt my cheeks flush. He laughed it was soft.

"Queen after my own heart," he said. "You'll fit in just fine Luca and as I say, our Queens will help you out. They're always up to lend a helping hand." He rose an eyebrow at them, Reed laughed.

"Jackson can teach you how to walk in heels," he informed me as he walked down the stage. I turned watching as he walked towards Jesse who'd sat himself at a piano.

"Jackson's good at that," Jesse agreed as Jackson walked pass me, his cheeks pink.

"Or have you been doing that since you were thirteen, too?" Jason asked. I scoffed at him, he rose an eyebrow at me.

"Please, I was nine."

He laughed behind me as I joined Jackson and Reed at the piano.

"Let's do some scales, Queens."

"You're not working tonight," Jason interjected quickly, "don't worry, baby, we're not just going to throw you out on the stage."

"I just want to see how you sound together," Jesse told me.

My Pa picked me up from the club, as he'd offered his services to me when I was halfway out the door. I'd *completely* forgotten until my phone vibrated in my pocket asking me when I would be ready for my taxi.

Jason had excused me when he had arrived, telling me he wanted me in on Wednesday for my first *lesson*.

I'd agreed without asking for any clarification, because I didn't *need* clarification. In fact, Jason could probably tell me to do *anything* right now and I'd bend over.

Pa looked stricken I didn't share the afternoons events with him the *moment* I got into the car.

"Luca," he gasped.

"Is Oakley visiting?" I asked, smirking at him.

"Not tonight, he and Sky have date night."

"That's a shame," I said softly.

"He'll be round Dad's tomorrow."

I nodded turning to look out of the window. He hadn't pulled away yet so I could still see the emblem of the rose that hung on a wooden plaque above the staircase leading down towards the club.

"Good." I nodded then bit my lip so I wouldn't laugh too loud. "I must thank him; *you* know for getting me a job."

"Shut up."

I turned, "*I* will not."

He laughed a squawk of a sound before wrapping his arms around me. "I am *so* proud of you; oh, you have no idea, Luca," he said straight into my ear. "What do we need to get you? What do you need?"

"I…" I laughed shaking my head, "I don't know. Jason, my *boss*," we gasped excitedly at the same time, "said he wants me in on Wednesday for my first lesson, so I guess I'll find out then."

"What's your first lesson?"

I shrugged back at him; he mirrored me almost perfectly.

"Oh, just wait until you tell your dad, and my Pa and…"

"I'll tell them tomorrow," I told him. "Grandad and Grandpa, I mean. I'll tell Dad tonight."

"We can get pizza," Pa said enthusiastically. "From that place where the gluten free base *isn't* too bad, deal?"

I nodded. "Deal."

"Because we're celebrating, Luca."

I laughed as he turned the engine on and pulled away from the club.

He didn't even look at me as he took his hand from the gearstick and onto my knee. Squeezing gently before shaking my leg.

"So proud," he whispered gently whilst checking his mirrors.

Jackson

I've always wanted to be a Drag Queen.

There had always been something within me that wanted to be a Queen. When I was younger, I'd sneak down to our basement, fondly referred to as the Queens Lair because my Grandad has been a Queen, and not just a Queen but the Queen. HRH Cherry Blossom who ruled The Rose Quartet and was fondly remembered in *every* damn anecdote that were to come up.

He'd never hidden that from me, taking me down to the lair before I was old enough to walk and when I could, he'd find me there. Just sat admiring his dresses or looking through the pictures trying to figure out how those captured moments felt, how they smelt, how they sounded. Prides, events, holidays, and shows. I envied his memories. I wanted to make my own.

Through his pictures was how I found out I was a descendant of not one but two Drag Queens. When Grandad Avory began to appear in photographs in his skyscraper heels and afro hair to match.

From then, my desire just grew because it was fate. Right, it was just fate being a descendant of one Drag

Queen was enough but two? There was nothing else I could ever become.

And I had become it. I had been hired, *finally*. Under Jason's management and Jesse, Queen Daisy's reign, I was crowned a Queen, my dream was becoming a glittering technicolour reality.

And I was *loving* it.

I stood in the wings to watch, I *always* stood in the wings to watch, but especially for our Queen. Chandler, her technician at my side, us both infatuated by her performance, by her stage presence, by *her*.

"I'm so glad you're not wearing wings this week," Chandler murmured between Queenie's songs. I began to giggle quietly holding my hand over my mouth, so the sound didn't echo around backstage.

"You should've ducked," I told him, we glanced at each other. He looked bemused until it almost became mean.

"Saw that, New Queen."

"What?" I whispered.

"Didn't catch his -"

"Luca?" I asked, then caught myself, biting the end of my tongue, he rose an intrigued eyebrow at me, I shushed him with my finger.

"The *Queen* is on stage. Have some respect," I hissed, turning away from him hopefully quickly enough that he couldn't see what I'm sure was a furious blush on my face.

He laughed behind me, with no attempt at being quiet before talking into his comms. I took a step closer to the stage, just short of peeking my head around the curtain. I *would've* if I didn't know Jason and Jesse were sat just to the left of the stage, and they'd *both* lynch me if I did such a thing.

Queenie was into at least the second chorus of her

highly energetic *Six* finale, wherein she'd opted to wear a Catherine Howard inspired dress – made by *yours truly* – she looked *incredible* and I was eating her up as much as the audience was.

She caught my eye when she turned to face the wings, winking at me, blowing a kiss to me which I caught holding it against my heart as she grinned.

For as long as I can remember I've had a piano lesson with Jesse on a Sunday. *That* had started long before anything else. As much as I'd been besotted with the Queen Cherry Blossom and everything Drag, my grandfathers mutually refused to allow me early entry in the club and I knew, the only way I was getting in was through Jason, or the easier option, Jesse.

Jesse played the ukulele, the guitar, the drum, and the piano. I, when I was much younger, had asked after lessons on all his musical expertise. He'd refused most knowing my motive *until* I asked after the piano.

By then he had decided to call my bluff. Telling me he would teach me the piano on a Sunday morning – because amongst all of Jesse's other roles in The Rose Quartet, he also did the Payroll. Which he for *some* reason opted to do early on a Sunday morning.

He genuinely believed I'd back out the moment he uttered Sunday morning.

It turned out he severely underestimated my tenacity, so I turned up *early* to all our piano lessons.

"Good morning, lovely," Jason said as I walked in twenty or so minutes before I should've. "He hasn't finished the accounts yet." He continued looking up towards their office, I followed his eyeline up. "Given he has to add our new Queen to the payroll."

"Is Luca here?" I asked.

Jason smiled at me. "No baby, he's not."

I nodded, hugging my sheet music closer to my chest.

"Speaking of Luca, though, you'll show him how things work here right?"

"Of course." I replied lightly, "always happy to help a new Queen out."

"I'm sure."

"Why are you smirking at me?"

"I am *not*," he said in a gasp. "I'm merely smiling at my Godson, of whom I deeply love."

"You're full of bullshit," I said in a laugh.

"Ah, ah."

I covered my mouth, he grinned then turned as Jesse leant on the door to the office, closing it with a click.

"Good morning," he said fondly, "just give me two minutes, okay?"

"Okay." I replied walking around the stage and up onto it to sit at the piano. I glanced at Jason as he watched me with interest. "What?"

"Nothing, my darling, *nothing*. I've got some work to get on with."

"Then I'd suggest you do in *fact* get on with it."

He chuckled fondly, picking up his folder and taking it towards the office. Crossing paths with Jesse as he returned.

"Ready, lovely?" Jesse asked as he walked around the stage so he could climb up the steps. I nodded as I stroked my fingers over the keys. "Take it away, you don't even *need* me anymore."

"Not true, Jesse," I said as I began to play a scale. "I'll always need HRH Queen Daisy in my life."

"I'm not going anywhere," he said softly as he reached for my sheet music. He flipped through it before settling on one of the pieces. "Although our new generation of Queens is making me feel my age."

"You're still young at heart," I informed him as I

began to play from the sheet music.

"You're sweet," he told me as he leant on the body of the piano. "Or you want something?"

"I don't," I laughed.

"Really?"

I glanced up at him, grinning at him innocently to ensure he knew I was telling the truth and I *was*, mostly; I knew *anything* I wanted Jesse to give me he wouldn't be able to.

He examined me closely before deciding to believe me.

"I was twenty-six when I became Queen. *I* had to wait until your dad was born and Jamie finally decided to leave to…"

"Be a father to my dad," I offered; Jesse smiled.

"I paid my due what did Reed do? Hop over here from Scotland, sing a few theatre numbers and get made Queen by his twenty-first birthday."

I snorted lightly.

"Didn't *you* make him Queen?"

"*Yes*," he stressed, "but that's not the point." He said then, "wasn't that supposed to be a G sharp?"

I bit my lip.

"Do you want to take your Grade Eight?" he asked.

I laughed. "Because I played F sharp instead?"

"No," he laughed tapping towards me. "I'm *just* asking. You're a Queen now, you don't have to use me to get into the club."

"If I were using you Jesse I wouldn't be here."

"You were using me *once*, though."

"Yes," I admitted. "I was young then, Jesse, I didn't realise how playing the piano could get me … all the penis." I said.

"Jackson," he gasped. "I wasn't expecting you to say that."

17

I laughed with him, until the door to the club opened. Jesse turned as I silenced.

"Xavier?" he asked sounding confused.

"Called in by our Lord and Master," Xavier, our Stage Manager said but I wasn't looking at him, I was looking behind him at one of our ASM's Charlie.

I swallowed deeply, then gasped when I felt Jesse's hand on mine.

"It's okay," he whispered, squeezing my hand. "Keep playing," he added nodding to me, so I nodded back, holding my fingers over the keys then fisting my hands because I didn't like how they shook. I took another deep breath, glancing up as Jesse left the stage to retrieve Jason. I met Xavier's eyes. He nodded to me waving delicately so I smiled back. Making sure it was bright and undeniably happy. I winked at him then began to play.

"That's still meant to be a G sharp." Jesse heckled as he came back downstairs with Jason behind him.

Luca

My family were loud. Completely organically loud *but* they didn't mind I was quiet. Sunday was family day and had always been and that meant come three o'clock we were expected to be present at my Grandparents house for lunch.

This was usually achieved, or at least I hadn't failed to attend yet. I guess it helped my boss was my Pa. He always managed to write my rota around this three o'clock call.

My relief came in as I served an older couple. Two men who I wished to know better. They'd come in every week, or at very least every Sunday I'd ever worked. They'd order a pot of tea and a singular slice of cake – whichever was the new flavour that week and took their seat on the old cosy couch at the back.

I, however, was never around long enough to ask them any questions.

"Hey sweetheart."

"Hello," I whispered back as I reached around my back to undo my apron. I turned as I did, smiling and kissing Mateo's cheek as xe kissed mine.

"Busy morning?"

"Rushed off my feet," I said raising my eyebrow at xem, they smirked. "I didn't even have time to update the board," I added nodding behind xem to the blackboard.

"Because we were so busy."

"Obviously," I teased, as xer tied the back of xyr apron. It was littered with little badges like my own. Xer name written in chalk on the little blackboard we wore as a name badge, it was alongside our required pronoun badge and flag. Mateo had chosen the genderqueer flag after much deliberation between xer sexuality and gender flag. It was proudly alongside a button badge that demanded 'No More Plastic', and another with an adorable rainbow dinosaur that stated, 'Sounds Gay let's do it'.

"Could finally ask Milo to do it," Mateo said.

I shook my head. "Who's Milo?"

Mateo nodded behind me so I turned looking at the old couple on the couch.

"He, Avory used to work here, years ago, I think before your Pa did."

"Really?" I whispered.

Mateo nodded lightly. "He was a Queen," Xe flourished, "at the Rose Quartet of course…"

I looked back towards the couple.

"His husband Milo was a makeup artist. Incredible artist."

"Wow," I whispered; Mateo grinned. We *both* jumped when my name was crowed. I sighed.

"*Oakley*," I sang turning towards my uncle as he stood leaning on the countertop.

"Come on baby, you don't want to be late," he sang at me then pointed at the rainbow cake. "Two to go?"

"You'll have to pay."

"Get off," he laughed, "*my* brother wouldn't make me pay."

"Oh, he definitely would," I told him as Mateo stepped around me to put the cake into a polystyrene box. "Seven pounds," I told him.

"Daylight robbery," he informed me. "How did your audition go?" he asked as he tapped his card to the machine.

I touched my lips. "Wouldn't you like to know."

"Audition? For what?" Mateo sang at me as xe placed the polystyrene box in front of me. I bit my lip turning towards xem so Oakley couldn't see my face.

"The Rose Quartet," I said.

Mateo gasped reaching for my hands and shaking them together. "Are you a Queen?" xer asked, I smirked mouthing *yes* to xem, Xer *incredibly* composed xemself, only their eyes showing the barest amount of glee at my success, I winked at xem. Xer looked behind me towards Oakley.

"I'll be in on Tuesday."

"Well, I will see you then. Enjoy lunch," Xe said. I nodded taking my apron off over my head and hanging it where my coat resided.

"Come on, Peanut, Sky's in the car," Oakley said holding his hand out to me. I took it, squeezing tight as Mateo laughed fondly.

"Goodbye, Peanut."

I shushed xem then waved as Oakley walked me out of the café and towards Sky's car.

Sky turned cheerfully to me when I got into the car.

"Hello gorgeous," they said. "How did your audition go?" they asked, I touched my finger to my lips. They nodded. "Got it," they smirked at Oakley, "must be really pissing you off that he won't spill the beans?"

"You're correct," Oakley muttered, then added, "I didn't get him any cake."

I squawked when I laughed.

"I'm *coeliac* you idiot."

He turned to look at me as Sky smirked.

"I love you kid; you have no idea."

My Uncle Oakley had essentially hit the motherlode and ended up dating their best friend, Skylar Reynolds, the person who thoroughly pissed off my Grandad Kaiden in the effort to form Rainbow Connection Nonbinary.

They had won. There was now a Rainbow Connection Nonbinary.

They then went on to piss off our Secondary School in the fight for more gender-neutral language to be used.

They had won that also; my entire school career was had with very gender-neutral language. I idolised them a little too much and I fully acknowledged that as they were who encouraged me to dye my hair purple *and* get my nose pierced.

They were a bad influence *really*.

But I'd also complimented their electric blue hair from the moment I'd lay eyes on it, much like Oakley's candy-floss pink hair.

I'd *apparently* continued a treasured family tradition as my Grandpa also had a certain love for bright coloured hair. Although right now, he was white. He'd been a bright, clean white since I was born – when he was officially named Grandpa.

He answered the door when we knocked. The noise of life flooding out of the door as he opened it. He smiled at us, bright and warm before grabbing Oakley into a hug.

"Hello baby," he said fondly, as Sky crouched to pick up Sonic in their attempt to escape. They lifted her to me, smiling as she pawed at me, purring contently in Sky's arms.

Sky followed Oakley into the house, Grandpa

scratching Sonic between the ears as they passed.

"Hello, Peanut," he said turning back to me, I smiled cuddling him as his fingers threaded through my hair. "How did your audition go?"

"Not yet," I whispered, he nodded against me.

"Okay darling. Come on in out of the cold. Your Pa is cooking today; I believe he said shepherd's pie."

I hummed as I walked in with him.

"That sounds good," I told him before sitting myself beside my brother. He glanced up at me, nodding once as a greeting. I nodded back then turned as Peach prowled the back of the couch. She purred at me jumping down the back to curl up on my thighs.

The table was by far the *loudest* part of the entire day. Everyone spoke over each other, whether it was asking for the potatoes, or the gravy boat. Asking if there was wheat in anything on the table, to asking if there's more wine.

Questions flew and conversations flowed.

And then, when the plates were piled and taken away, Grandpa connected his knife with his wine glass and the table fell silent.

Like it did every single week. I lifted my own wine glass, barely drinking from it as Grandpa looked around his family, a quiet smile playing across his face.

"I declare Vent It Sunday, open," he said raising his glass.

Vent It Sunday, a May family tradition wherein you can declare anything, whether it be news or nerves without the possibility of being told off. It gave us *all* a chance to sit and listen, to celebrate or help each other where needed. It gave us a chance to talk freely and honestly without fear.

"Well, I'll kick it off," Grandad said, glancing at

Grandpa with a slight smirk on his face before lifting his half full pint. It was mostly foam now, *mostly* drank. "As of Friday, I am *officially* retired." He smiled; it looked content. "From my job, *and* from the club."

"Wait? What?" Pa said, "I didn't know you were leaving the club, too?"

Grandad nodded. "I started in RCT when I was sixteen, that club has been my life, I'm the first to say it. I wouldn't be here today without that club..." he looked at Grandpa, "and of course Riley." They squeezed hands on the table, "I've seen so many boys pass through, like Alistair." He nodded towards Dad who smiled back at him, "I've seen them become men and fully embrace who they are. It was something that was rewarding *every* single day.

"I will never regret a second of being in that club, of giving so much of my time to it but it's been sixty years. I think, now, I'm ready to rest."

"Hear, hear," Dad said raising his own pint, we all raised our glasses.

"My turn?" Oakley asked, Grandpa nodded to him, as Oakley glanced at Sky. They smiled back weaving their fingers around each other's.

"Sky *and* I have set a date for our wedding," he said, the table went to *implode*, each and every one of us itching to scream, or squeak or squeal with delight. "Just a small ceremony," Oakley added quickly.

"The party will be big, though," Sky laughed; I grinned as they winked at Oakley.

"We think we're ready to have the ceremony. We think it's the right time, too."

"And now that Frankie's had the baby, I'm going to have him as my witness," Sky added, "Frankie and my Dads."

"I want you guys to come," he said to Grandpa and

Grandad. "I can't get married without my dads there."

I turned to Grandpa, watching as he wiped away a tear running down his cheek. I had to look away before I too started crying.

"And Rory, I want you to be my witness," he said to Pa.

"Of course," Pa gasped, squeezing Oakley in a hug.

"Is the position of flower boy taken?" I requested; Oakley laughed into the hug with Pa.

"Not by you," he said, "we must go by cute factor. You have *so* many competitors."

"Marley and Quinn for example," Dad intoned, I gasped *but* agreed because Enzo's six year old twins are cuter than me, they're probably cuter than I ever have been.

"And Sydney," Sky helped.

"They named the baby Sydney?" Grandpa asked.

Sky nodded. "Theybie, raising them neutral, Sydney Addison-Bruno."

"That's adorable," Pa said.

"But *that* isn't the news I'm bringing to the table, that doesn't count right?" Sky asked.

"That doesn't count." Grandpa told them. "What's your news Sky?"

"I've been talking to Kaiden…"

"*Just* talking?" Alistair asked.

Sky laughed. "For once, *yes,* I didn't piss him off at all, he's also retiring as I'm sure you know." He said to Grandad, he nodded back because Kaiden had been at Rainbow Connection for at least sixty-three years since he was a transitioning teenager himself.

"He said he was struggling to find someone to take over the club, he'd had so many interviews, over and over and none of them seemed right.

"We met up for a coffee and I thought *that's* it I'm in

for it now, but he started talking about the club and guys, I think it was the first time I've thought of him as *human*."

I snorted into my wine glass as Grandpa, Grandad, *and* Dad laughed openly – we were all a little bit sure Grandad Kaiden wasn't human.

"He loves that club *so* much; he doesn't want to give it too just anyone."

"Is this going where I think it's going?" Grandad asked.

Sky smirked as they drank the bottom of their own wine. "He offered me the club."

"What?" Dad laughed as Pa shook Oakley.

"He said I obviously cared about the club; I've made that evident since I was fourteen. He said I didn't have to take up his offer but he thinks I'd be the best fit." They shrugged lightly as they played with their glass. "I took the job."

"You own Rainbow Connection?" Grandpa asked, Sky nodded slowly biting their lip as they laughed.

"No way." Grandad said, "that's so *right* but you're twenty-five isn't that like, a *lot*."

"I guess so, but also not, there's an amazing team there and it's not like I'm going in blind. I took over RCNB when Riley left."

"That's true," Grandpa said softly, "and you did an incredible job. I'm so proud of you Sky."

"I'm excited," They said. "Oakley's excited."

"Oakley is," he assured us. "I'm even more excited about the funding that Sky is going to get that can be given to Queercuts to provide more free haircuts for the kids…"

Sky rolled their eyes amused.

"Congratulations Sky," Grandad said. We all cheers again. His eyes met mine as we lowered our glasses and I definitely was prepared to go next.

I glanced at my dad's.

"You're very quiet," I offered.

Pa shook his head amused as Dad did. "We have no news this week, nor worries."

"And how exactly can we compete against retirement, marriage, and new jobs," Dad said. I laughed then turned to Connor.

"Nope," he said. "It's your turn, Luca."

"Well, *okay* then," I said finishing my own wine. "I went for an audition at The Rose Quartet, yesterday." I turned to Connor, "that's a drag club."

"Oh," he said before turning to Grandad. "I didn't actually know that."

Grandad chuckled fondly.

"I got the job," I said nonchalantly, shrugging at them. It took a moment for my words to drop, *and* I saw it, I watched as it dawned on Grandpa what I'd said, the smile growing almost instantly as Dad covered his mouth with a gasp.

It was only Oakley who broke the Vent It Sunday rules by leaping out of his chair and running around the table to wrap his arms around me and kiss my cheek.

"I knew you'd do it," he gasped at me, so I cuddled him back. "Remind me to tell Chandler to look after you. I do *not* want to hear my baby nephew isn't the star."

"I'm definitely not the star," I laughed, "but Beau May is *officially* the newest Queen at The Rose Quartet."

"Finally," Grandpa sighed. "It's been *what*? Thirteen years?"

I laughed.

"Thirteen years, yep," Dad said. "Every single year he hasn't been a drag queen has been a travesty."

"Good word travesty," I said.

Dad laughed nodding to me. "You don't seem nearly

27

as excited as you should be?" he replied.

I bit my lip. "I am *so* excited. Ecstatic but also nervous and apprehensive."

"Very *Luca*," Grandpa said as Oakley stroked through my hair.

"I know," I moaned, "it'll be amazing. I know it will, I'm just nervous."

"Of course, you are baby," Oakley said, I looked up at him, "dreams don't come true every day."

"But you're lucky, because from now on everyday your dream will come true." Sky said, I turned to them, they winked at me.

"Thank you." I whispered.

Jackson

My family were loud. All the damn time and I kind of loved it. We, my parents and twin sister Rosie, lived with our grandparents and there was *always* something going on in the house regardless of the time or, in fact, day.

My grandparents were long retried. Jamie having retired from The Rose Quartet and having enough in his savings to do so comfortably and Dylan who retired from teaching Drama in Kingsbury High School when he started showing the symptoms of Alzheimer's. He'd been diagnosed six or so months after leaving his job. I had been fifteen.

This, of course, meant they were home most of the day.

I *presently* worked from home.

Reed was one of my best customers, *and* primarily my best friend.

He was sat on my bed beside me looking through my swatches to decide what this week's dress was going to be made from. The brief I'd gotten was Beetlejuice Dress. Reed didn't make many alternations.

"Luca's cute," he said.

I stopped drawing to glare at him, he smirked back at me. "I'm choosing to stay single, right now."

"That decision has been made for you, Jackson," he told me. "*You* know, I wouldn't have…"

"Are you about to tell me a really romantic origin story about yourself and Quinn, because I *know* the real version."

"What real version?" he whispered.

I laughed. "That he was in your lecture, and you were *afraid* of him because he was an…" I paused, touching my chest and looking into the distance, "Adonis."

"Shurrup," he laughed pushing me to the side, his Scottish accent heavy, rolling the Rs that didn't exist in those two words. "He *is* an Adonis."

"You were paired together so you had to talk, and it was *fate*."

"You're a wee shit."

I grinned at him.

"I *still* think he's out of my league."

"You're beautiful," I told him.

He cooed at me touching his chest. "Baby, I might very well be, but Quinn is *still* out of my league. I'm keeping hold of him as long as I can. *You* just need to be brave."

"No," I said laughing, "*no*. I met him and found him visually attractive. *Once*. I can't jump on him and bring him into…" I waved my hand above my head. "This."

"What's wrong with *this*?" he asked. I shook my head back at him as I tapped the end of my pencil against my pad.

"Where do I begin?" I muttered then cleared my throat, "*besides* that, I'm asexual. That's not fair to him."

"Ah, no. We've talked about this, stop condemning yourself. You deserve to be loved as much as the next person."

"*Yeah*, but I'm not going to get that fairy tale ending, am I?"

"*What* fairy tale ending is that?" he asked.

I shrugged. "You know, finding the girl who the glass slipper fits, kissing her out of a sleeping curse, climbing up her hair to rescue her."

"You don't want *that*," he said, I scoffed back at him. "You don't, glass slippers would be useless, and I bet they only make them in wee girl sizes anyway. Kiss out of a sleeping curse, ever heard of consent?" he said, I laughed quietly knocking my head against his arm, "and climbing up the hair, *Jackson* your wig would fall off."

"I love you," I told him.

"I love you too." He kissed my forehead.

"Quinn's your fairy tale prince, isn't he?" I asked.

He laughed. "*No*, he's my boyfriend. I love him deeply, but putting fairy tale prince on somehow is a heavy title to carry."

We looked at each other.

"Fairy tale ends don't exist. I'd go as far to say happily ever afters don't either…"

"Why not?" I whispered.

"Because *what* counts as the end? When you guys get together, no you're only just getting started, marriage? Definitely not. Death?"

I shrugged meekly.

"You're meant to enjoy the journey *not* the ending."

"That's prolific, Reed," I informed him. He smiled then looked behind me as I heard distorted noise from downstairs. I sighed as I stood, putting my pad on my bed behind me and leaving my room.

Reed following me closely as I weaved through the house trying to find the source of the noise. It was in the kitchen. I saw Grandad Jamie first as he looked at me over Grandad Dylan's shoulder.

"It's okay," he assured me.

"What happened?"

"Just dropped a mug. He got a fright," he said then pulled away from the hug he was giving Dylan. Resting his forehead on Dylan's and talking quietly to him. I looked at Reed.

"This, too." I offered.

He hit my shoulder lightly. "This is *life*, Jackson," he whispered then cleared his throat so Jamie looked at him. "I'll grab a brush."

"Thank you, darling," Jamie said softly as he sighed and walked Dylan around the counter so he could sit him on one of the chairs. "I only went to the toilet," he told me even though he wasn't actually looking at me. "Decided to make himself some tea." He looked up at me, "lucky it was a mug and not boiling water." His smile was delicate.

"I'm sorry, I should've been down here."

"No, no, Jacks no. This isn't you fault in any way, it's no one's fault," he said. "I'm not blaming myself for needing the bathroom, *you* shouldn't blame yourself for needing to work."

I nodded lightly as he sighed. "I'll make some tea," I offered.

"Good plan," he said as he stroked over Dylan's palms, he seemed to decide something. "Escaped without injury this time, Mr Huddersfield."

Dylan smiled back at him. "You're a very beautiful man," he told Jamie.

"You're a very cheeky man," Jamie told him, his voice soft. I stepped closer to the counter as Reed began to brush around my feet.

"Jamie, would you care to weigh in on our conversation?" Reed sang.

"Shut up," I said.

Jamie laughed. "If its upsetting Jacks this much, definitely."

"Fairy tale endings? Do they exist?" Reed asked, Jamie hummed glancing towards Dylan as he reached for the magazine on the countertop.

"No," he said gently. "Sometimes it can *feel* just like a fairy tale, but do you know how many evil Queens and curses are in fairy tales. *Why* would you want that?" he asked.

I laughed. "You're an evil Queen," I informed Jamie.

"I was…" he paused, "*actually,* yeah I was," he smirked at me as I raised an eyebrow at Reed. He laughed as he leant on the brush handle.

"All hail Queen Cherry Blossom." Reed said.

"Daisy started it, she would've happily assassinated me for the crown *and* Jasmine, don't get me started on the Queen Bitch of all."

"Jason's so nice," Reed said in a gasp.

Jamie laughed. "*Now.* When we were younger, he had a sharp tongue," he smirked lightly. "You Queens are far too nice to each other."

I laughed as Reed did. "This is evident, didn't you hate Grandad Avory?" I asked.

"Loathed him," Jamie smirked. "We did not get along and it wasn't just Blossom and Robin didn't get along. Avory and I didn't either. Then I left when we had Evan."

"Evan," Dylan repeated quietly, I glanced at him as Jamie did.

"But didn't Avory leave when he had Mum?" I asked.

Jamie glanced at me, "No," he laughed. "But Avory was doing one twenty-minute slot a week when they had your Mum. When I had your dad…"

"Evan," Dylan repeated.

"Evan," Jamie agreed. "I was the Queen. I did

33

Wednesdays show and an hour on a Saturday night. I had to take a step back," he looked bitter for a moment, "when I returned when Evan was three, Daisy was the Queen. I got pushed to second billing."

"Excuse me, I'm second billing," I said.

He smirked. "Yes, but baby you'll become the Queen one day," he said eying Reed as he gasped.

"What are you planning on doing, killing me?"

"You think if I start whispering about babies to Quinn, he won't bite?" Jamie teased.

Reed shook his head. "Don't," he said. "*Oh* don't. We're twenty-one we don't need *that*."

I laughed as I passed the tea to Dylan.

"Thank you," he said then he looked at me, I could see something calculating behind his eyes as if he was searching for *something*. "Evan?" he asked.

I swallowed deeply. "Jackson."

He nodded slowly. "Jackson." He repeated softly then turned to Jamie. "Evan?"

"Evan's our son," Jamie said softly. I admired how his voice didn't even quiver, given my entire body was wobbling. Reed came up behind me, wrapping one arm around my shoulders. I took a deep breath. "Evan is Jackson's Dad."

"Evan is our son?" he repeated.

Jamie nodded slowly. "Yes, Evan is our son," he sighed as I passed the second cup of tea to him. "Thank you darling. You should get back to work, huh?"

"Yeah," I said slowly then I cleared my throat, "*yes*." my voice somehow sounded less sure.

"Let's get a Starbucks." Reed suggested.

I hummed against him. "I've just boiled the kettle."

"Jackson," he said softly.

I nodded. "Starbucks. Let's get a Starbucks."

There was a rat-a-tat kind of knock on my bedroom door that I almost missed because my music was *so* loud. I was aware it was. It was *purposely* loud.

Reed's dress now had a skirt, or *mostly* a skirt but I lifted my foot from the sewing machine when I *thought* I'd heard a knock. When it came again, I welcomed the knocker in.

"Smart speaker, turn down," Jamie said from the door, I turned to look at him as my speaker compiled. "I figured you needed a hug."

"Yep," I said quietly as he came into my room.

"I know it's hard," he said gently as I stood, he wrapped his arms around my head, kissing the top of my head as I wrapped my arms around his stomach. He was unnecessarily tall. As was Grandad Avory. I almost felt cheated that I came in at five foot five and a half, but it meant when I hugged Jamie, my head just about reached his chest.

"So hard. How do you cope?" I whispered.

"I don't," Jamie laughed. I looked up at him as he swallowed. "I really don't, Jacks, but we get through day by day because we *have* to. Some days are better than others, *we* both know that, but nothing quite prepares you for…"

"Him forgetting who you are," I said into his stomach. He squeezed me a little tighter.

"I don't think he's forgotten who we are," he said quietly as I stepped away from the hug. He sat on the end of my bed. I sat back in front of my sewing machine. "I honestly don't. Sometimes there's this little bit of recognition, it's there and it's Dylan and it hurts *more* than when he's not here."

"I get that," I said quietly, "it's hard to I don't know, *connect* him to *Grandad*. Is that bad?"

"No, no sweetheart. It's not bad. It's hard, I agree.

It's been like that for a long time. I struggled to see the seventeen-year-old Dylan as the twenty-year-old I knew, or the twenty-year-old as the thirty-year-old man, who was a father. People change and sometimes they're not the person they used to be, that's why memories are so important."

"Like, how he built my bed," I said, he grinned stroking the nearest poster to him, that I'd wrapped baby pink fairy lights around. They weaved all the way to the canopy at the top and did so on all four posters.

"I remember the night before so well," he said quietly, "you were thirteen, right?"

"Right, and Mum and Dad told us over tea that we were getting our own rooms. After we'd shared for*ever*."

"Exactly, your dad told us Rosie was getting the bunk bed. He was going to buy you a new bed, *but* when we were in bed... Dylan told me he was going to build your bed. He knew *exactly* how you'd like it, there was no debate, and he had this wild sense of determination in his expression.

"I knew not to tell him no and when he told Evan the next morning before you had gotten up, Evan knew not to deny him either.

"He didn't tell us a thing about the bed, not *one* detail, he'd barely let any of us in either, except when I brought him coffees and *ogled* him in his work jeans."

"Grandad," I laughed.

"He worked on it all day."

"I remember because I didn't think it'd be done for me to sleep in it that night."

"But it was," he whispered.

I nodded. "It was but..."

"The mattress hadn't come," We said together. I laughed as he smiled at me.

"I remember you came in here with Dylan when he

was done…"

"I told him I loved it," I said.

He shook his head. "You made his… *life*. You jumped on him, telling him over and over how much you loved it and thank you, *thank you*, thank you Grandad."

I nodded slowly.

"He regularly reminded me of that, *because* sure Jackson wanted to be a drag queen like me, but *he* had built you a bed you loved."

"I didn't think it was that… prolific of a memory," I said quietly.

"He was proud of himself. You and Rosie, when you two were born you became his whole world. He adores you both, and he was delighted he knew you that well that he had no doubt this was what you'd want.

"I mean, sure I'd told him time and time again that *I* wanted a canopy four poster bed, but did he ever build one for me? *Nope*."

"He loved me more," I proclaimed.

Jamie smiled lightly. "Loves."

I nodded sighing deeply as I closed my eyes. "Loves." I agreed then sighed.

"This design is beautiful," Jamie said.

I turned to look back at the sewing machine. "I thought I'd make it look like Beetlejuice's suit, *but* a dress," I explained even though that was totally clear from my drawing. "Especially as Reed, *well* Queenie's more of a diamond shape so there's an empire line and the jacket *looks* like a jacket but is attached."

"Beautiful," Jamie said squeezing my shoulders. "I wish I still did Drag so you could make me a dress."

"I seem to remember Blossom wore crop tops and super short skirts," I said.

"I had the body for it," he whispered before kissing my cheek. "You want to talk anytime Jacks; you know?"

"I know," I turned more towards him, "*and* Grandad if ever you want to talk."

"I know, darling," he said. "Feed the rats," he added. "Goodnight, don't stay up too late working on the dress."

"Goodnight," I replied lightly, he nodded blowing me a kiss from the doorway. He left it open, *hinting* to me to go and feed Sugar and Spice our rats. So, I did.

Luca

The club was alive even though it was mid-afternoon on a Wednesday. There were people *everywhere*. Technicians running around all in black doing multiple jobs at once.

There was a piano being played.

And numbers being shouted across the room.

There were spirit bottles clanging as they were replaced at the bar.

Reed, HRH Queenie was stood on the stage, in a big warm looking hoodie and a pair of ripped jeans. His hands buried deep in the hoodie pouch as he spoke to someone off the stage. I followed the direction he was talking in with my eyes. Smiling lightly when I saw Jesse leaning on the end of the stage talking with his hands.

Jason was sat at a table behind Jesse, a folder open in front of him as he chewed on the end of a pen.

It was Jackson who was playing the piano. I probably focused on him for far too long.

"Luca."

I jumped when Jason said my name.

"So glad you made it," he said softly, a quiet smile on his face so I approached him. "Reed's about to start his rehearsal. Well, he *should* be." He sounded amused as he watched their conversation. Jesse tapped the stage nodding as if fully agreeing with whatever had been said.

"Jackson, sweetheart, rehearsal is about to begin." The piano stopped and Jackson walked down the stage. Squeezing Reed's arm as they passed each other before jumping off the end.

He stumbled forward a few steps, looking up towards me so I smiled warily.

"Hi," he said.

"*Hi,*" I whispered back.

Jason laughed beside me. "Let's get this rehearsal going hey."

Jackson sat on the opposite side of the table. Jesse sat on the table behind me.

I turned my attention towards the stage.

The lights went out around us, the stage dark. Until a rainbow travelled around the stage. A simple chase light going around and around until it began to build, strip after strip. The entire edge of the stage a rainbow growing brighter and then it just turned *off*.

I glanced at Jason then at Jackson as they both just watched, neither of them at all phased by the mini light show we'd just witnessed.

The stage turned green. Glowing as brightly as the rainbow had. The music began before the rest of the stage came to light and I knew it, I'd *definitely* heard it before.

Beetlejuice.

I jumped when the stage came to life. Reed stood at back. He looked up, smirking at us and then, he began to sing.

Wow.

He was incredible.

Wow.

I couldn't take my eyes off him.

Wow.

There was no-way I was anywhere near *this* standard.

Wow.

"Stay for the show, Luca. You can see him do it in heels," Jesse said in a laugh as he stood at the end of the rehearsal walking towards the stage because *apparently* there was notes for Reed, there was actual notes for the Queen of everything.

"Hey."

I glanced up; Jackson smiled at me from where he was stood in front of me.

"*Hi?*"

"I'm the lucky Queen on the sandwich run today. Come with me," he held his hand out to me, I frowned at him. "Come on. I need to know what kind of sandwich person you are, too."

"I… don't eat sandwiches," I said.

He laughed. "Well then you definitely need to come with me, what will I get you?"

I took his hand. He led me towards the door of the club, turning just before we stepped through. He laughed as he waved towards the stage.

We walked up the staircase out of the club in silence but *still* holding hands. He realised when we got to the top, glancing up at me before opening his hand. I figured I should probably let go.

"Don't let Reed intimidate you," he said as he began to walk.

I frowned walking a little quicker so I could walk on step with him. "What do you mean?"

"He's a musical theatre Queen."

"Like dramatic?" I asked, blushing and looking away.

He smiled at me, "Like Musical Theatre. He literally studied it in university. He's amazing. Don't get me

41

wrong, he is *actually* incredible, but I'd suppose that's why he's the Queen, but we're also Queens which means *we* must be *also* that incredible."

"How did you get to *that* conclusion?" I whispered.

"The Rose Quartet has standards. Very, very high standards. I have old videos of the past Queens. George, the man who was Jason *before* Jason recorded every show. He liked to have a record of performances.

"When he died a few years ago he left the videos to me in his will. He wanted me to watch them, to learn from them. They've been invaluable but the key thing I learnt from them was that The Rose Quartet only hires Queens worthy of that title."

"I've never done this before," I told him as he stepped through the automatic door.

"That's okay too," he replied as we walked towards the sandwich fridges. "Jesse hadn't. Look where he is now. You just have to... I guess put on your face." A smile quirked on his face. He glanced at me; I must've been frowning. "It's something my grandparents say, a lot. That sometimes you just have to put on a face to get through things. Whether that be faux bravery, or a sunny disposition."

He went to walk on, choosing sandwiches as he went. I reached for his hand again. He stopped.

"Will you help me?"

He turned to me, not letting go of my hand. "You've never seen me do drag. You don't know, I might be terrible."

"You're not," I told him confidently, he rose an eyebrow at me. "Well, you've been hired by The Rose Quartet haven't you, *that* implies that you're incredible."

His smile was definitely embarrassed but he still nodded. "I'll help you out, Luca."

I smiled at him, big and unreserved until I

remembered I had braces and covered my mouth. He touched my wrist lightly.

"What?"

"Nothing…" I replied, "I just don't normally you know… show people my…"

"Brace?" he asked, I nodded. "I don't normally let people see me wearing my glasses, so I guess we're even."

"You were wearing glasses when I saw you on Saturday."

"I normally wear contacts. I guess."

"Your glasses suited you," I informed him because I thought that'd be helpful even though it probably wasn't.

He paused. "You shouldn't be embarrassed by your braces."

"That's easy for you to say," I said as I reached for a little tub of sausages and tomato sauce. "You've never had to deal with something stuck in them," I continued as I flipped over the tub to read the back.

Wheat.

I put it back on the shelf.

"Okay, that's fair."

We looked at each other again, he appeared to be watching me as I read the ingredients. I picked up a bag of chicken.

Contains Gluten.

I put it down sighing deeply as I rubbed my eyes.

"Struggling?" he whispered, I nodded. "Jamie doesn't eat bread… didn't when he was a Queen anyway, he always speaks very highly of the salads." He pulled me towards them before I could reply. "I assume you don't eat pasta either?"

"No."

He reached for one of the little pots, read the top then passed me it. I flipped it over almost instantly.

"Perfect." I told him.

43

"You should get used to that," he winked.

I nudged against him gently. "You being perfect?" I asked as he picked up bags of crisps.

"*Yep.*"

"Or Drag Queens egos?"

Reed's boyfriend was gorgeous, *and* I didn't hide this fact as I took his phone from him to ensure I got a closer look at the Hollywood Movie Star who apparently resided in close enough proximity to just drop in on our average look's life.

Except Jackson. *He* was also gorgeous.

"Quinn?" I repeated, Reed nodded taking his phone back, lying it alongside his sandwich. "I have a nibling called Quinn."

"Nibling?" Jackson repeated.

"Nonbinary niece or nephew. Twins, Quinn and Marley, they're being raised neutrally, so they're my niblings."

"I kind of love that," Reed said although he still appeared to be thinking about it. "Are you?"

"Nonbinary?" I asked.

Reed nodded. "Sorry, that was quite forward I shouldn't have asked that."

"It's okay. I'm not, I'm cis but there's a lot of nonbinary and trans in my family."

"My grandad is trans," Jackson said, *almost* absently. "Sorry, that sounded like I was *trying* to be interesting. He is trans, though. I didn't make up a fake grandfather to progress a conversation."

"Jackson," Reed laughed. Jackson turned to look at him, I however didn't take my eyes from Jackson as his cheeks flushed. "You're word vomiting." Jackson mumbled something as he reached for his sandwich. "Moving on, swiftly. Does Beau have a look?"

I turned to him.

"Oh, I… don't know."

"Well, do you plan on Beau having your hair?"

"Purple?" I asked.

"Curly." Jackson said, "completely changes the wig."

"Purple and curly would look incredible." Reed added.

"There's a few from Avory. From Robin. Some are crimped afro; I think there was one curly. One was definitely coils."

"I didn't know there were so many different names for curls," Reed said.

"Not curls," I corrected, "afro. I got my dad's hair. *Luckily* otherwise that'd have made me ginger."

Jackson's laugh was quiet. "I wish I'd gotten my Mum's hair. I feel genuinely cheated out of gorgeous afro hair. Like yours."

"We grew it out when I was really small," I told him, "a full natural afro. Dad put cornrows in when I started school, but we soon cut it…"

"Because of school?"

"Mostly. I didn't want the cornrows all the time, and Dad advised that I keep them in. I went against him only *once* I was in year two, seven years old and it was an own clothes day, so I played that angle."

"What happened?" he whispered.

I looked down at the table, picking at the remaining polish on my little finger. "I got upset pretty quickly because the other kids kept pulling on my hair, and just *touching* it without asking. I started crying. Of course. Cried so much I got sent home. *None* of the kids were told off. I remember that upset me further.

"When my teacher asked me when I was crying, I told her, and she said I'd just have to get over it. My hair is different and I should let the other kids touch it so they

45

can learn or whatever.

"Dad picked me up. He didn't work Fridays when I was small, Connor, my brother was only one, so he was on Daddy duty. Still sobbing in the car, I asked for my hair to be cut off. Dad, he *really* tried to change my mind. I was adamant, so he took me."

His hand touched mine. His thumb stroking over the back of my hand. I swallowed.

"Sorry, that was *really* personal," I forced a laugh.

Reed squeezed my hand. "Don't worry this place does that to you."

I jumped, turning to look at him because I'd completely forgotten he was there.

"You've never grown it out again?"

"No," I said clearing my throat, "I got a fade, it's only since I left school that I let the curls grow back in."

"Your hairs gorgeous," Jackson told me, "I *am* dying to see a picture of you when you were small."

I laughed nodding before squeezing his hand. "I will find one for you."

"You don't have to wear an afro wig, if you don't want to."

"I love it. I'm sad that its always stopped me growing it out so I'd love to try them out. *If* Queen Robin gives her blessing of course."

"Of course," he winked.

"I'm intruding right?" Reed asked.

"Reed, darling. Time to get ready," Jesse said.

Reed nodded standing from our table, taking his drink by the lid as he left.

"I think we might have to dye the wigs, if you want them to be purple," Jackson said as he watched Reed walk away.

"I shouldn't think that be a problem."

He turned back to me. "No?"

"No," I repeated, "I know a guy." I added grinning at him.

My phone buzzed again. Rattling the entire tabletop. I went to reach for it, meeting Oakley's eyes in the mirror as he played with the comb.

"What?"

"Someone's texting a lot."

I shook my head. "It's work," I informed him as I reached for my phone.

He squeezed my shoulders. "Work," he said excitedly like I knew he would.

Text Message

Luca Sent a Picture

Jackson ♡: GORGEOUS

Jackson ♡: Your hair is beautiful, and you are adorable! I'm so glad you found that picture!!

Luca: I got it from Grandpa. I'd barely finished asking before a photo album was in my hands.

Jackson ♡: Are you telling me there's more pictures??

Luca: There might be

"Work," Oakley laughed so I turned my phone over underneath my cape. "Okay, okay. Got it. I'm doing your dye right?"

I nodded.

"Want a cut?" he asked snapping the scissors above my head.

I looked at them in the mirror before tilting my head back so I could look at them directly. "No."

"Really?"

I tilted my head further so I could look at his face.

"Don't get me wrong, Luca, I *love* that I'm just surprised... you know..."

"I know..." I said slowly, "I still want the sides shaved, I think but the top..."

"Your wish is my command," he said reaching past me to put the scissors back on the tabletop. "Okay?" he asked softly, I nodded then leant my head into his hands as he ran his fingers through my curls. "Now tell me about the Queens."

"They're phenomenal."

The audience had one hundred percent been there for Queenie during her show. They screamed and shouted, applauded and threw flowers.

They completely adored her, and I fell in love with her.

Everything about her was immaculate, a long shiny black ponytail was her wig of choice, a green beetle barrette near to the bobble of the ponytail.

Her face painted like a doll.

But her dress, her dress was like something off Broadway itself. The iconic black and white stripes of the Beetlejuice suit, a blazer that cinched at the waist, the skirt large, aided with a black petticoat.

And her boots, Jackson and I had obsessed over her boots for most of the night – after I'd given him my number at least. They were at least four inches black, suede and lace ups.

I wanted them.

Jackson wanted them.

Reed *wasn't* giving them over.

We'd talked about that in the other text thread of a

group chat called *The Queens* that I'd been added into practically seconds after I'd given over my number to Jackson.

Just before we all signed off to go to sleep, I'd been added into another group chat, *The Rose Quartet* that also had Jason and Jesse in.

I hadn't gone straight to sleep because I'd just sat, looking at the chat because I was *officially* a Rose Quartet Queen.

"Do you start Saturday?"

"I believe so. I've got to be there at ten. There's a technical rehearsal before lunch then hair, makeup, wardrobe. *Then...*"

"You're on?"

"Yep."

"Sky and I will be there," Oakley told me as he continued to wrap my hair in foil. I met his eyes in the mirror again. "What? You doubted that? You'll have to physically ban us from the club before we don't turn up."

I laughed, he winked at me.

"I'm sure Pa..." he waved his comb, "Grandpa will be there soon too. Actually, your Pa too."

"I don't want *everyone* there too early; I think that'd make me nervous."

"This is a good point, but I can tell you Grandpa and Grandad *never* missed any of my orchestra concerts." He leant a little closer to me, so his head was on line with mine in the mirror. "Except when they were too hungover of course."

I laughed, "Because Grandpa's a lightweight."

"The lightest," he agreed.

"Like Pa."

"Like you," he said.

"I don't drink."

"In public because you're such a lightweight."

"You're mean to me sometimes."

"It's in the description," he said then kissed my cheek. I laughed as he stood back upright so he could continue with my hair. "As Uncle who is within the correct age gap to be a sibling."

"I think you made that up."

"Probably."

Jackson

The club was alive even though it was mid-afternoon. Backstage was even busier. Technicians moving between jobs with their head buried into their comms.

They were not to be disturbed and I didn't plan on it as I sat in my dressing room unrolling my makeup bag on the table. I was second billing, *just* before Queenie graced the stage. I didn't have to be ready for hours yet.

A knock on my dressing room door.

"Enter," I sang towards the door, it opened slowly. "Come in, Luca."

He did until he was hovering awkwardly next to my dressing table stool. That was when I looked at him.

"Hi," he said meekly.

I stood from the stool, "Take a seat lovely." I put my hands on his shoulders. "You're here for a colour match today?" I teased, he smirked at me in the mirror.

"I am," he teased back.

"Ever been matched before?"

"No, I actually never have."

"Well, you've come to the right dressing room," I told him as I turned to search for a second chair. I found one by the door. "If you'd gone to Reed, you'd have made a big mistake."

"Yeah?" he asked as he watched me carry the chair back to the table.

"Well, yes. He is Scottish for a start," I said as I reached for the bag underneath my table. "He doesn't just use light makeup, Luca, he uses fair."

He laughed covering his mouth as he did.

"He wouldn't have *nearly* the shade of foundation you'll need. I on the other hand…"

I opened the bag. "Why do you have so many?"

He laughed, I laughed with him as I began to stand them on the table.

"It took me far too long to find the right shade. I've got from the darkest tan, *Mocha* to the middle deep, *Tiramisu*," I said the name jokingly.

Luca smirked lightly as he lifted the nearest bottle to him. "They're like thirty pounds a bottle."

"*Right*," I sighed.

"Did you find your shade?"

"Chai," I answered with a slight inclination. "I started too light then went to dark," I continued before stretching my arm out in front of me. He copied me without instruction. I hummed at him; he almost retracted his arm. "You've done makeup before, right?" I asked as I held bottles against his arm, painting a line onto his arm when I thought the shade matched his skin.

"I've… dabbled," he replied. "I've tried, and I can do things like lipstick and eyes, but I'm not stage standard yet. You do your own?"

"Learnt young," I told him. "I've practically been raised here. My Grandad Milo is a makeup artist, I was taught to draw by him and once he found out I wanted to do drag, he started teaching me makeup. Jason too, I always idolised Jasmine, revered her almost. Her makeup was flawless. I was lucky enough to learn from her for the last few years."

Luca nodded, I smiled at him.

"Spiced Rum," I said. "Your shade is Spiced Rum, or at least it is in *this* brand."

"Spiced Rum," he repeated his eyebrow raised.

I laughed. "I didn't name them. If it helps, Reed is Porcelain."

"That does help," he laughed.

"Are you ready?" I whispered. Luca nodded pushing his lips together, his Adams apple bobbing precariously.

"Ready." Luca smiled back then laughed when I dabbed his nose with the foundation.

"Have you chosen your outfit?" I asked as I continued to dab the foundation around his face.

"I have…" he replied quietly.

"Do I have to guess?" I teased.

"Yes."

"Beau, she doesn't feel like a leotard Queen."

"That's because she isn't," he informed me.

I smiled. "I don't even think she's a short skirt Queen."

Luca smirked ever so slightly. "You think I can't pull off a short skirt?"

"Oh, I never said that," I stated, "on the contrary, I'd love to see you in a short skirt." I paused, "that sounded creepy."

"No," Luca whispered. "I'll take it as the compliment it was intended to be." He smiled. I smiled back before clearing my throat and looking away. I reached for the concealer.

"Jumpsuit?"

"No, but that's just a no I'm not wearing one tonight."

"So, a dress?"

"A dress," he confirmed as I tilted his head back by

the chin dotting concealer under his eyes.

"One from the wardrobe?" I asked, he nodded lightly. "Okay, so I know that wardrobe inside out."

He smirked as I wiped my hands with a baby wipe.

"There's only Queens of past dresses in there. Those of which they donated anyway. You're not a short dress person so you're not wearing any of Jamie's, nor Avory's. Maybe Daisy's?"

"No, it didn't say Daisy on the hanger."

"At least tell me what colour it is?"

"Red," he confirmed. "Red wine, red."

"Sexy," I said.

He laughed lowering his head as if he was embarrassed. "I'm using the opportunity of the wigs not yet being dyed to wear red."

"You don't have to dye the wigs," I reminded him as I opened my eyeshadow palette. "It isn't a requirement."

"Maybe just one," he whispered holding a finger to me as I held the palette next to his eyes. "I've already mentioned it to Oakley."

"Your eyes are *very* pretty," I told him as his met mine. I bit my lip.

"Two compliments, this is going well."

I chewed on my lip as I picked up an eyeshadow brush.

"Your brush has a bowtie."

"Close them. I have deduced you're wearing one of Jasmine's dresses."

"Correct."

"I wouldn't have you down as a Princess dress type."

"But it's so pretty," he moaned. "I honestly didn't think I'd wear a Princess dress either, but I saw it and I just... fell in love."

I blew lightly against him. He didn't flinch.

"Heels?"

"Yes."

"Have you worn heels before?"

"Yes," Luca laughed. "I've worn heels for years."

"Excuse me?"

He opened his eyes. "When I went on nights out with my uncle and his partner, or in fact just went out. I usually wore heels, heeled boots."

"I adore you."

"Gender stereotypes…" he said. "My family point and laugh at gender stereotypes."

"Look up," I whispered.

"Didn't you?"

"It never occurred to me, *ironically*."

"I've just changed your world."

"You could say that," I said as I recapped the mascara. I cleared my throat, "are you going to tuck?"

He nodded slowly.

I smirked. "Are you prepared for that?"

"I think so. I've been practicing. Can I get ready in *here*?"

"Yes," I said without thinking, although my answer was still yes after I thought about it.

"Thank you."

"I'm not going to do your lips yet," I told him, "otherwise we'd just have to keep reapplying it. I'll do your blush, though," I said as I held my blusher against him. "Are you nervous?" I asked as I stroked the brush over his cheeks.

"Terrified." He let out a long breath, "so, so nervous but I was talking about it with my Grandpa and he told me it was good I was nervous because that meant I cared about it, and that I would do an *amazing* job because I cared. Still terrified though."

"I get that. My first show, *well*, I had been preparing for my first show since I was old enough to talk but when it came to the day, I was almost sick to the stomach with worry. I realised I was a legacy. I had the weight of Queen Cherry Blossom and Queen Robin on my shoulders and *let* me tell you, they were *heavy*. I told George…" I paused.

"*Jason* before Jason," he said nodding, I bit my lip as I nodded back.

"I told him I didn't want to do it; I didn't want to go on. I wasn't ready."

"What happened?"

"He said *fine* and left my dressing room."

"What?" he squeaked.

I laughed. "Just like that. I called after him, he didn't come back. I realised I wanted him to fight for me to perform. I wanted him to stand there and tell me I was amazing, and I was going to do a good job and I shouldn't give up before I'd started *just* because of my grandfathers, so instead of making someone else tell me, I made sure I persuaded myself that all of those things were true.

"Sure, I get compared to Jamie a lot, but I soon learnt how to take that as a compliment because he was an *incredible* Queen and I should be *so* lucky to be in his league. Okay?" I asked as I brushed over his nose.

He grinned at me. "Okay."

"Look in the mirror," I said as I stood from the chair, *"don't* forget you've not got your lips on yet."

"I look beautiful."

I turned back to look at him.

"Thank you," he breathed.

I smiled. "Beau."

"Beau May," another deep breath.

"I'm going to order some food before the show. Want in?"

Luca turned to look at me as I fished my phone out

of my jeans.

"I *was* thinking McDonalds."

He shook his head, then he paused. "Actually, can I have a large chips?"

"Just?" I asked.

"And a diet coke."

"And a diet coke," I repeated examining him as he glanced at me before looking back in the mirror. "Will that be enough?" I asked.

He nodded to me in the mirror. "It'll be fine, perfect even especially with a nervous stomach."

I nodded, opening up the app to order.

"How do you feel about a McFlurry?" I offered because he definitely wasn't eating enough. He hadn't for lunch either when Reed had gone on the sandwich run and returned with the same potato salad he'd had on Wednesday, but that was all. He hadn't partaken in our snacking on mini brownies and shortbread during the afternoon as we were to do on show days.

I *remembered* Jamie talking to me about it, not long ago. Telling me how he'd strived for Blossom to have the perfect body, to be perfect all the time and that had led to him not eating properly. Cutting out breads and pastas, anything remotely sweet or indulgent. He'd said the need for perfection overtook any other of his needs and it was a *bad* time.

But he'd also told me how he'd snap when anybody commented on it. If Grandad made a comment on what he'd eaten that particular day they'd row. It was worse if another Queen mentioned it.

"What's in a McFlurry?" Luca asked.

I waved my phone in the air. "Ice cream. I usually get smarties."

He nodded. "I think I can work with a McFlurry."

Jamie had gotten help in the form of George. When

57

George had taken him up to his office and spoke to him. Jamie was forever thankful for that day.

Luca's eyes met mine. "Are you going to do your face?"

"Not until the foods come," I replied as I sat on my chaise lounge. "Someone needs to answer the door."

"True," he whispered, I beckoned him towards me. He *unsurprisingly* came. "*Until* then, tell me how your first show actually went... please?"

My dressing room *stunk* of food when I walked back in after throwing the bags away. Luca was stood by the chaise lounge emptying his backpack onto it until he found a pair of shorts.

"Shapewear?" I asked, he nodded meekly, "*you're* well trained."

"I've been preparing for this for *years*," he said as he pulled on the shorts.

"I fully recommend just *one* thing," I said holding a finger to him, he nodded looking back up at me. "Go to the toilet," I said pointing towards my ensuite, "because I can *guarantee* the moment you're tucked and in your shorts, you'll want to go."

"Have you been there?"

"*Yep*," I replied as I sat on my stool, "and I don't wish to talk about it."

Luca laughed happily nodding as he went into my ensuite. I turned on the stool to put my foundation on.

I was dabbing my concealer under my eyes when he came back out.

"I'm going to attempt this," he told me picking his shorts back up and a bag.

"Break a leg," I said, crossing my fingers before watching his reflection step behind my room separator.

I was applying my false eyelashes when he stepped

back around the separator.

"Wow," I offered, he appeared pleased so I turned to him properly. I stood, walking towards him, then around him. "It's not often I circle another guy checking out his crotch... just so you know." I said as I stopped back in front of him. "I'd say you've definitely been doing this for years."

He winked at me.

"My turn, I guess," I added before turning towards the bathroom. He was sat at my dressing table when I walked back through, a dressing gown on as he painted his nails. He glanced at me in the mirror as I stepped behind the separator. I waved at him, all fingers as I did. I heard his soft laugh it made me grin.

I hung up my own shapewear, a lacy leotard that spawned from a discussion with Jason when I'd commented shapewear was the true glamour of Drag.

He'd laughed and asked me why I couldn't be glamorous all the way down to my shapewear. I'd left the conversation confused then fell into a Google search that ended with me buying three different lacy leotard shapewears *and* never going back because Jason was right, why couldn't I be glamorous all the way down to my shapewear?

I stepped back around the separator as Luca stood to retrieve his dress. He stopped. He stared, mouth agape and I laughed, hiding my face behind my hands.

"What?"

He shook his head *not* taking his eyes off me until he swallowed deeply.

"I *like* your leotard," Luca said.

"Thank you," I purred reaching for my robe, a totally unnecessary long satin thing. I didn't tie it shut right away. "Dress?"

"What?" he asked, his eyes downcast, I smirked as I

tied off my robe.

"Dress," I repeated, my voice gentler. He nodded pointing towards it, so I went to it, lifting the skirt out of the protective bag. I gasped when I did because the dress was *stunning*. I had no doubt that it had belonged to HRH Queen Jasmine.

I helped him into it, holding the waistband as he lifted the bodice up and placed the straps onto his shoulders. The dress itself was stunning, an elegant red wine ball gown, the skirt mid-length. The feature of the dress a simple bow that covered the zip at the top of the skirt. The bodice backless.

I ran my fingers down the straps flattening them against his back, he shivered under my touch. I smiled lightly, securing the zip, fixing the bow so it was hidden then I walked around him.

"How does it look?" he asked.

I nodded and I must've smiled given his smile in response. "Gorgeous." I said, "you wear it amazing too, *it* doesn't wear you."

"Yeah?"

"Yeah," I breathed, "take a seat." I gestured towards my dressing table. He went, pausing before the stool. He looked at me over his shoulder before lifting his skirt so it covered the entire stool when he sat.

"I've always wanted to do that."

"Make you feel like a Princess?" I asked.

He nodded as he reached for his wig. It was one of Avory's, a curly afro wig that resembled his hair.

He closed his eyes as I pinned the wig into place, taking deep breaths in and out.

She opened them when I started to fluff out the curls.

"I'll just top up your mascara, do your lips," I said, she nodded both of us looking towards the little clock on the dressing table at the same time. "It's almost time."

She turned to me. I did her mascara.

I did her lips.

She stood, going to the chaise lounge to put on her shoes. Red stilettos. They gave her an extra four inches or so, making her a whole head and shoulders taller than me.

She laughed at this, I gasped pushing her back by her shoulder.

"Shut up. You're already taller than me it isn't fair."

"You're just…" she waved her hand as if trying to catch the word, "petite."

"That's not the first time I've heard that," I told her as I shrugged off my robe, lying it over my chaise lounge and reaching for my own dress bag.

My dress was a dusty pink, a corset like bodice with over the shoulder straps that crossed at the back and a mini tulle skirt. My platform heels silver and sequin covered.

I ensured I stood in front of Beau when I put them on, pulling my tongue at her as I stood face-to-face with her.

She pulled her tongue back.

I sat at my dressing table.

She helped with my wig. A long black wig, which stopped around my hips, with a full fringe. Her fingers threading through my wig as I painted on my lipstick.

"You look beautiful, Madison," she said softly.

We both turned when there was a knock on my door.

"Yes?" I asked, it opened.

"Ah there you are," Charlie said to Beau. "This is your call to the side of the stage."

She nodded taking a deep breath. I took her hand.

"Break a leg darling," I said softly, kissing the back of her hand, "I'll be watching."

She nodded, taking a deep staggered breath in before

standing up straight, a smile on her face as she stepped through the door and continue towards the stage.

"You're not supposed to be here," I said to Charlie.

He turned back to me from watching Beau. "What do you want me to do? It's my job."

"Leave."

He scoffed. "I didn't know she was going to be in here."

"Chandler is *my* technician. Chandler should've knocked."

"And *I'm* Beau's. I'm just trying to do my job, Jackson."

I glared at him.

He sighed. "Madison." He shook his head, "why was she in here anyway, you guys... something."

"I think you'll find that's none of your business." I said as I left my dressing room past him.

He mumbled something after me that I'm sure was less than complimentary, so I chose to ignore it, opening the door to backstage and stepping into the opposite wing to where Beau was stood.

I squeezed Queenie's arm when I was stood next to her. She grinned at me, taking my hand and squeezing back.

We both blew a kiss across to Beau as she stepped out onto stage.

She smiled back at us, almost looking relaxed as she lifted her microphone and she began to sing.

Luca

The sun was going down and Mateo was joyful as xe sat on the tabletop opposite me. The brush between xer legs because xe was *meant* to be brushing up.

Xe wasn't, but neither was I *and* the café was empty. It'd been empty for three hours; we could've closed up. Pa had told us we could assuming it was after the dinner rush and we'd done all the little jobs like cleaning, and covering the cakes.

We hadn't even thought about it, the thought of closing never crossed our minds because Mateo had asked how my opening night had gone and I'd started talking.

And talking.

And talking.

"What did you sing? What did you choose?" xe asked as xe swung the brush.

"Get Happy…"

"Judy Garland, *gorgeous*," Xe nodded.

I nodded back. "And Edge of Glory."

"Wow," Xe laughed, "all of it?"

"All of it," I confirmed. "Jason stopped me as I left, laughing because he was very impressed I took his two songs and made one of them five minutes."

"They're keeping you?"

"I hope so. They haven't fired me yet." I said, stuttering. "I *hope* they don't."

"Did you get any pictures?"

"I… did," I told xem as I stood from the table, I turned my phone before I reached xem who took it straight from my hand.

"Excuse me, *why* are you so gorgeous?" Xe gasped as they zoomed in on the picture. "Your face is immaculate."

"That was *all* Jackson's doing," I told xem, xyr rose their eyebrow at me so I swiped to the next picture, a selfie of Jackson and I before either of us had started getting ready.

"That's Jackson?"

"Yeah," I answered quietly then swiped to the next picture, of Madison and Beau *after* we'd gotten ready.

"No-way, *he's* gorgeous too, oh wait, no, is it *she* when you're in Drag?"

I nodded once.

"He's gorgeous. Is he single?"

"No," I said quickly, even though I didn't *actually* know the answer to that.

"Telling," Xe sang at me as I frowned. "You like him."

"I hardly know him," I said, because it was true. I didn't know anything *important* about him. All I really knew was his foundation shade was chai, his grandparents were Drag Queens, or at least two out of the four were and that was… it.

"Oh no, did you just have a startling realisation?"

"No," I stated.

"Good. Then we need to go out."

I laughed shaking my head.

"We *do*, if you will not allow me to pursue Jackson,

you should help me have some fun." Xe pointed behind me, I didn't turn as I knew xe was pointing towards the bar opposite the café.

Its shutters were always coming up as ours went down.

"Come on, Luca. We close the café, have some drinks."

"I don't drink," I reminded xem, I got a dramatic sigh back as xe passed my phone.

"You don't have sex either," Xe teased. "Come on, Luca. Come have some fun. If you have drinks that don't come in pint glasses, you'll be fine."

I sighed as I laughed because that was the reason I didn't drink – in public. Grandpa had told me one too many horror stories of glasses that had beer in them not being washed properly.

Beer was made with hops, water, grain, *and* yeast. It can have up to fifty percent wheat. Not worth the risk, *not really*, but when glasses haven't been washed properly, the wheat can contaminate your pint of coke, or lemonade or *whatever*.

Being coeliac was such a bother…

"Okay," I said to Mateo. "Okay, okay fine but we're *not* getting drunk. We're not doing that, one or two drinks that's all. Okay?"

"Whatever you say, Luca."

Glitter rained from the sky and, given it was a Tuesday, although technically it was actually Wednesday morning, I was suitably impressed at the Sailor Bar we'd ended up in.

It shouldn't have been Wednesday morning.

It had been five o'clock Tuesday when I'd crossed the street with Mateo.

I had a vodka and coke, just *one*.

Two.

Four… and a half.

Then Mateo had whispered directly into my ear about the Sailor Bar, and it'd just be rude to say no.

Which was how it ended up being Wednesday morning, and I ended up with a wine glass raised above my head, catching some of the glitter that rained from the sky whilst wearing Elliot's – a Sailor of the Sailor Bar – cap.

Elliot was particularly friendly.

He's given me my last wine for free.

Maybe I liked Elliot.

I *might* even let Elliot kiss me tonight – this morning. Mateo had found someone, xe had made it look easy. Xe had prowled, pounced, and got up to promiscuous behaviour before I'd even drank my first wine.

Xe had disappeared during my free one, whilst I was talking to Elliot and taking his cap from him.

I'd turned back and Mateo was no-where to be seen.

So, if it was that easy for xem then surely it would be as easy for *me*. I mean, Elliot *was* willing.

Right?

Or had I been completely misreading those signals.

No.

It turned out, I had not.

He grabbed my hand, weaving me through the bar towards a quieter corner although the music was still loud and ringing in my ears.

He pushed me back against the wall.

That was thrilling.

I began to feel hot. My skin pricking as my temperature soared, was this what people meant when they said *hot under the collar*.

Was this what being turned on felt like.

It wasn't what being drunk felt like, I'd been drunk

before. I knew what *that* felt like, and I'd felt that two hours ago.

I was sweating, now. My stomach jumping as he played with the ribbon from his cap, twirling it around his fingers as he got closer to me.

He whispered something I couldn't hear into my buzzing ears.

He kissed my neck. His stubble prickly against my skin. I slid my hands up his back wanting *more*, trying to figure out how to get *more*.

The buzzing in my ears got louder, thumping almost like a heartbeat in my head. My skin slicker, my body at boiling point.

He stopped kissing my neck, raising his head to look at me, he was going to kiss me. This was it. This was going to be my first kiss, with a Sailor called Elliot, covered in glitter.

Which honestly wasn't that far off what I thought it'd be.

He smiled, I smiled back, he moved forward in an attempt to kiss me.

I threw up.

Shit.

Shit.

I was surprised it wasn't Thursday when I woke up. The sun was bright, my curtains not drawn, but it was *my* room and that I was thankful for as I rolled over in a groan to hug my pillow. Burying my head deeply into it, stroking it from side to side as if trying to shake away my headache.

I was still in my clothes. *Still* covered in glitter although now so was my bed and what looked like most of my carpet.

I rolled onto my back, rubbing my eyes before

looking down myself. My jeans were undone, the zip low and my boxers showing through them. I was proud of myself for managing *that* action even though I was still wearing my shoes.

I sat up. Kicking my shoes off by the heel before getting out of bed.

I changed into pyjamas, picking my blanket off the end of my bed and wrapping it around my shoulders before venturing downstairs.

I *hoped* I'd be alone.

Connor was almost definitely in school; Pa should've been at the café. Dad... was stood in front of me in the hallway.

"Afternoon..."

I moaned, lifting my blanket so it went over my head like a hood.

"Two thirty is impressive..." he said as he turned away from me so I unwillingly followed him into the kitchen. "Especially on a Tuesday night. Meet someone?"

I sighed.

"Mateo," I told him as if that was all the explanation he needed. "I did meet someone. He was nice."

"Oh yeah?"

"I threw up," I said. I hid further underneath my blanket.

He laughed. "Because you were drunk? Or?"

"Drunk," I agreed. "It was so embarrassing. I came home then because I was so embarrassed."

"How did you get home?"

"I walked," I answered as he rose his eyebrow at me. "What?"

"You were on Stanley Street, right?"

I nodded.

"You *walked*, drunk from Stanley Street. Half twos even more impressive."

68

"Not when I left at half six."

He laughed. "When you say you threw up?"

"On him, he came in for a kiss and I threw up... on him. Congratulations you conceived *this*."

He rose his mug to me. "You must get that from Rory." He told me. "Although Rory never threw up on *me*."

"I'm a special kind of human."

"You sure are Peanut."

Peanut. A baby is the size of a peanut when it is a nine-week-old foetus. *This* was one of the first facts my Pa had learnt after finding out about me. He affectionately called Dad's stomach it when he was nine weeks pregnant. I guess it stuck.

But it was better than Connor who was known as Spud. Eighteen weeks, or *when* my parents found out they were in fact pregnant with Connor. I don't know which of us it was the biggest surprise to, honestly.

"You..." I said then looked at Dad. "You're working from home?" I changed tact.

"I'm going to pretend that's what you wanted to say," he said. "I *am* working from home."

"Is that all you're giving me?"

He shrugged gently. "I guess so. Is *that* all you're giving me?"

"I'm hungover," I informed him; he went to walk past me. "You did embarrassing things when you were..." I paused because I couldn't really call what I was doing dating.

"Yes," he said. "I *never* vomited."

"Dad."

"We all do embarrassing things," he sat on the seat opposite me.

"You've been with Pa for*ever*."

"Yeah," he sighed. "So there was plenty of teenage

absurdity that could cause embarrassment. I mean, your Pa was thirteen when we got together and *honestly*, we were a mess. We were just kids, and really all we were doing was holding hands, kissing, and making fools of ourselves."

"Everyone makes it look so easy."

"Who?"

"You and Pa..." I said. "Oakley and Sky, *Grandpa* and Grandad. Connor and *every* girl that comes through here."

"Connor aside," he said in a laugh. "Your grandparents have been together for *half* a century."

I laughed. "You're not even exaggerating. Couples like them will *never* show you the hardships. I mean, take away that they're your grandparents and it's not your place to hear about issues they might have."

"Their relationship is private, all relationships are private. Your Pa and I aren't going to involve you or Connor if we're having an issue because it's *not* necessary."

"You have issues?"

"Yes."

"But you're happy."

"Yes," he sighed. "You can have issues and be happy at the same time. We had an issue this morning when Rory wanted to wake you up for your shift."

"Shit," I moaned. "I forgot I told him I'd work today."

"Exactly," he said. "That's what I said, and somehow persuaded Rory to let you sleep and go to the café."

"Sorry I caused an issue."

"You missed my point."

"I'm sure."

"We all have stuff going on, not everything is perfect all the time. I know how it *can* look, especially with

70

Oakley and Sky, but you don't live with them."

"That's true," I replied quietly. "I just don't think I can get it right."

"You will. You'll find the boy who loves you because of who you are and you will love him for the exact same reason. It'll be easy with him, because *if* it's hard it isn't love."

"What?"

"People talking about *always* knowing and shit, like that's not true."

"It was true with you and Pa."

"Yeah, but we're overachievers," he said. "You won't feel like you're jumping through hoops to get them to like you or that you have nothing to talk about.

"It'll be easy, and comfortable and even if you do embarrassing things they won't care because they like you."

"As simple as that?"

"As simple as that," he repeated.

I nodded taking in a deep breath then looking towards the clock. "I'm going to get a shower, get to the café for the afternoon shift." He was smiling when I turned back to him. "Apologise to Pa."

"Good plan Peanut," he said as I stood, "and Luca, don't dwell on a boy at a bar." I stopped turning to look at him. "It'll do you no good and you'll likely not see him again. Okay?"

"Okay," I sighed. "Okay." I cuddled my blanket tighter as I left the kitchen and went into my bedroom. I paused as I walked in crouching and picking up the sailor cap. I laughed brushing some glitter off the top with my hand as I stood and hung it on the back of my door.

Pa was brushing the floor when I stepped into the café after Mateo, and I had thoroughly neglected it the

71

night before – but we *had* covered the cakes. He stopped brushing to look at me as the door dinged.

"I'm sorry," I started. "I'm the worse son in the world."

He laughed. "Thank you for apologising, Peanut. What are you doing here?"

"The afternoon shift."

"Luca you don't have to."

"I *want* to be paid." I joked.

"Okay. Grab your apron," he said, smirking. I nodded walking towards him and kissing his cheek before getting my apron. He gave me the brush when I walked back towards him. I nodded chewing on my lip as I began to brush. "So, your dad did call," he continued. I frowned glancing up at him but not meeting his face, instead I focused on his chosen pin badges. The bisexual flag, he/him pronoun pin, a smiley face, and a little 8-bit of him and Dad that Dad had made at some point near the beginning of their relationship. It was cute. "You threw up on him then."

I sighed. Pa laughed so I met his eyes.

"Did I ever tell you about the time I did that in university?" he said as he sat on the table behind him. I shook my head. "It was a guy I wanted to sleep with, finally got him back to my flat."

"What happened?" I whispered.

He laughed, "Turns out I have a gag reflex."

Jackson

The sun was going down as I walked from the Chinese takeaway to Reed's flat, *or* more appropriately, Jason's flat. When Reed was going into his second year at university and had shared his dislike of the shared accommodation, Jason had noted he was living alone after the passing of his partner and, if Reed wished to, he could live with our King.

It was the perfect arrangement apparently; Reed was going to graduate this year and I knew he wished to stay with Jason as long as he could at least before he planned on moving in with Quinn anyway and Jason wasn't quite ready to lose his flatmate just yet.

Reed answered the door when I knocked. He smiled at me, resting his head on the door.

"Jason's entertaining," he said.

"I brought Chinese," I told him.

He moaned. "Did you get spring rolls for Jason?"

"Of course," I replied while he stepped aside welcoming me into the flat. "Who is entertaining today?" I whispered as I put the bag on the countertop.

"Jonathan, *but* he did stay the night."

"Have you seen him this morning?"

"Yeah, they came out, had breakfast…" he turned so he was leaning on the counter. "Went back in. Not going to lie, he's *kind* of my idol. If my sex life isn't as active as his when I'm in my sixties I'm suing."

I laughed, he knocked against me we both stood upright when Jason's bedroom door opened.

"Good evening, Jackson," he said fondly.

I waved then, "Good evening, Jonathan," I sang with a wave.

Jonathan smirked at me. "Long time no see," he said hugging me. "How is my Chandler treating you?" he asked.

I looked up at him from within the cuddle. "Like a Queen, although he's still bitter about that week with the wings."

"He mentioned that," Jonathan laughed.

Jonathan Lawrence, Chandler's grandfather *and* the widower of George.

Reed had whispered to me late one night when I'd slept over that Jason had admitted to *always* fancying Jonathan. He'd known him for *years*, but he'd always been George's husband and, for a brief few years, Jason's teacher. He was off limits. *So* off limits he wasn't even a passing thought.

But that was okay because Jason was in a relationship with a man called Parker, who treated him like a Queen. Parker had passed away when I was twelve, from lung issues after many years of smoking.

George then passed away when I was sixteen on the night of Pride.

A year later, Jason and Jonathan started *entertaining* the idea of them, because apparently the lust for each other was a mutual thing.

Jonathan wasn't Jason's only conquest. He entertained a *lot*.

74

"How's Dylan doing?" Jonathan whispered to me.

I sighed as he squeezed my arms. "Not too bad, he's not getting any worse or at least Jamie doesn't think so, so I guess that's good."

"That *is*. I was going to visit but I didn't know if it'd confuse him, or…"

"Sometimes he remembers," I said then shook my head. "It's unreliable."

Jonathan hugged me again. "Sorry, I didn't mean to upset you."

"You didn't," I assured him because he hadn't, not really, it was unfortunately something I was used to.

"Promise?" he asked. I nodded smiling at him, he still looked wary, "I had better go, Chandler's on tea tonight, gets upset when I'm late." His smile was fragile. "I'll see you soon," he said kissing Jason lightly, "and I might drop by your house, I'll give Jamie a call." I heard Reed let out a breath behind me, so I turned to him.

"Want a drink?"

I laughed. "You know I don't."

He nodded looking thoughtful then he opened one of the bags. "Prawn toast?"

"Yes," I laughed taking the piece of toast from him.

"Do you mind if I drink?" he asked.

I waved my hand. "Please enjoy, what's lined up for tonight?"

"Apparently Hello Dolly!" Reed said as he got a beer bottle out of the fridge. He waved it at Jason who nodded.

"I will be continuing your Musical education young Queens," Jason told me as he walked towards the couch.

"I quite enjoyed My Fair Lady last week," I informed him as I helped Reed plate up the food. "Not as much as Funny Girl, though, I really enjoyed Funny Girl."

"You like Barbra," Reed said.

I nodded touching my heart.

"Well good news, Barbra is Dolly," Jason told me then hummed appreciatively when I passed him a plate. "Thank you, darling."

"Is Hello Dolly! The Trolley song?" Reed asked as he took a seat on the floor in front of the couch.

"*No*, that's Meet Me at St Louis'."

"Judy Garland in fact," I said sitting behind him.

Reed gasped covering his mouth as I grinned. "That's sacrilege."

"It is," Jason added. "I'm going to add another hundred pounds to your rent for that."

Reed laughed hitting Jason's leg lightly.

"One must know their Judy from their Barbra from their Julie," Jason said dramatically.

Reed nodded. "Strip me of my degree."

"Strip you of your Queendom," I stated, he looked up towards me the laugh clear in his expression. "Can I be Queen now?"

"Definitely," Jason said nodding. "Although…"

"Although?" I repeated. "I'm hurt, I'm definitely next in line, are you Prince Charles-ing me?"

"Luca… is a spectacular Queen."

"That's true," Reed said. "I vote Queen Beau." He rose his hand; I kneed the back of his head. "What don't you like Beau?"

"Shut up," I murmured, they gasped in unison. I believe Reed's was more fake aghast at my telling him to shut up, I dare *not* think what Jason's was for. I still looked at him. "What?" I whispered.

"We should invite Luca to our Musical Parties," Jason said. "I *think* he'd enjoy that."

"Maybe," I said quietly. "I don't even know anything about him, not really," I said *because* I didn't. I knew his foundation was Spiced Rum and he *really* didn't eat enough – in my opinion – but other than that my knowledge of him was *surprisingly* minimal.

"He sang Judy," Reed said, "and I don't think he'd say no to spending time with you."

I turned to him as Jason laughed. "Shouldn't we start the film?" I whispered; they both mocked me as if I'd told them off.

Luca had sent me a text whilst I was brushing my teeth. A question he could've asked in the Queens group but instead he asked *me*. I tried not to think too much into it, nor smile too much as I walked from the bathroom into Reed's bedroom.

"There's only one bed."

I looked up startled at Reed as he stood pulling back the covers of his bed. I laughed when I realised what he'd said. "Shut up. We've shared a bed loads."

He grinned back at me as he got into his bed.

"Who are you smiling at?" he whispered.

I bit my lip shaking my head as I put my phone on his bedside table and picked up my lens case. He moaned and squirmed at me the entire time I took my contact lenses out.

"I don't know how you do that," he shivered.

"You wear contacts for Queenie," I laughed.

"Yeah, but you do it *every* day. I *couldn't*."

I smirked at him, placing the case back on the bedside and picking up my phone.

"So, go on, who were you smiling at?" he asked again.

I sighed. "I thought I distracted you by taking my eyes out." I said.

He laughed taking his own glasses off then lying so he could face me. I looked at him, *him* being close enough I could see him clearly.

My phone lit up on the bed between us. He looked

down towards it.

"I wish I could read that," he murmured.

I laughed swiping away the screen and reading Luca's message. "Luca," I confirmed, then rose my head, "but you cannot tell *anyone*."

"I wouldn't," he said, I hummed at him. "I swear, Jackson, I won't tell anyone."

"I think I like him," I whispered, "which I shouldn't, and I hardly know him and…"

"Jackson…" he cut off my rambling. "Stop shunning yourself for having feelings for, *all* things considered, a really beautiful boy."

"He really is, isn't he?" I sighed. "It's stupid right. Love at first sight doesn't exist."

"No, but he's beautiful and wanting a beautiful thing you've seen is completely valid…"

"I don't know him."

"You're getting to know him. Jackson it won't happen again."

"You don't know that for sure."

"No," he agreed. "I don't know it for sure but I'm pretty confident that it won't."

"I think I need to talk to Jesse," I whispered.

"Oh," he laughed.

I smiled. "But I can, I guess, gossip with you."

"You guess."

"Best friend rights, I can gossip and fantasise with you, and you won't judge me."

"Never," he whispered back, "and if you want some ammo, there's always Quinn fantasies."

"Deal," I whispered then looked down as my phone vibrated again.

"We need to talk."

Jesse physically jumped backwards. "You need to not

78

shriek at me."

"I'm not shrieking." I was *totally* shrieking. He rose his eyebrow at me. I moaned, burying my face into my hands. "I have an issue."

"Jackson," he said, his voice soft as he warily approached me. "What's wrong?"

"I'm having feelings," I moaned. He laughed attempting to hide it in a cough when I looked up at him. "I shouldn't have feelings."

"Why?" he asked slowly, rolling his eyes as I scoffed. "Are you aromantic?"

"I don't even know what that means."

"Don't have romantic desire. Aren't romantically inclined."

"I don't know. I guess no, I'm not aromantic. I was romantically inclined with Charlie but we also slept together, but I'm asexual, like I'm definitely ace."

Jesse took my hands. "Jackson. It's okay."

"But ... feelings."

"Having romantic feelings is different to sexual, okay? Romance *doesn't* equal sex. Just like sex doesn't equal romance."

I nodded slowly taking a breath.

"We talked about Charlie, remember? How you developed sexual feelings for him, but you'd known him a long time and your feelings for him were deep. You told me you thought you were demisexual." Hearing him repeating it back to me, it made perfect sense.

"And he cheated on me," I muttered.

Jesse sighed. "That had nothing to do with your asexuality."

"How sure can you he about that? Because I definitely think it was a component. I mean, it might not have been the forefront of his mind, but..."

"But that's the past and it doesn't matter anymore."

"Isaac," I said, then closed my eyes. "How does Isaac deal with it?"

"Mostly, masturbation," he said, I felt the corners of my mouth try to quirk into a smile. "Isaac…" he sighed, "we've been together a long time, Jackson. You come to compromises when you've been together so long. We talk about everything, always have. I've become more, I guess, flexible as I've gotten older as our relationship has grown."

"I'd imagine marriage and two kids does that," I said.

"Grandkids on the way," he told me. "Before we got married, we didn't have sex. We did other things. Like, sensual things, but also things like, he'd masturbate and I'd help him out or I'd do it for him. But I'm asexual, Jackson. I'm homoromantic. You're demisexual."

"There's a chance of sexual feelings to emerge."

"Right," he said. I nodded taking a staggered deep breath out. "Your feelings…" he said slowly, "does Luca feel them too?"

I opened my eyes to glare at him.

"Its obvious, Princess. Neither of you are discreet."

"Neither of us?" I repeated, Jesse shook his head. "You think Luca likes me back?"

He pursed his lips, as if he thought he'd spoken out of term. "Our trip is coming up," he changed tact so I narrowed my eyes at him. "Can you tell Luca about it?"

"Why can't you?"

"I can. I'm very capable of it, and I can text him if you want."

"No no, I will," I swallowed. "Where are we going?"

"This year, London. They're hosting Winter Pride."

"Winter Pride sounds exciting."

He nodded as he continued through the club. "It looks like an amazing event, it's a fundraiser *mostly*, they do it every year. Jason's been trying to get us an invite for *years.* I'll text you the details and you can pass them onto Luca, okay?"

I nodded once.

"Now go home, Jackson. Stop worrying," he said gently lifting my chin.

"Can I request *one* thing?"

"In what capacity?"

"As my boss?" I said, he nodded again, "can you change Beau's technician?"

"From?"

"Charlie," I said as he sighed. "Beau got ready in my dressing room this week; Charlie came knocking, it…"

"Okay," he said nodding. "I can sort something out. Beau has her own dressing room, you know."

"I *know*," I said quietly.

"Rest your head, Jackson," he said, smiling. "Liking someone isn't the end of the world."

"I don't think I'm ready to put myself out there like that again."

"You don't have to do anything you're not ready for, Jackson. If you want to be his friend be his friend, if you want to see where it can go, do that. Just make sure it's what *you* want to do."

I nodded.

"And tell him about the trip," he added.

"I'll tell him about the trip," I laughed.

Luca

I glanced down at my phone as I waited to do my makeup. I could hear Jackson's rehearsal as I sat in my dressing room, the gorgeous romper I'd found in the wardrobe with a long detachable skirt and *Robin* written on the label hung up on my room separator.

I was staring at it when there was a knock on my dressing room door. I turned then smiled *far* too widely when I saw Jackson stood in my doorway.

"That dress is gorgeous," he said coming into my dressing room.

"I believe it belong to your grandfather," I said nodding.

He frowned as he walked towards it. "Jamie?" he asked then lifted the label with his fingertips. "Avory, that makes far more sense."

"You don't talk about Avory as much…" I said.

He turned to look at me, his expression was definitely amused. "You've known me for three weeks."

"Sorry," I whispered.

He shook his head. "Don't be sorry. I *guess* we'll just have to talk more."

"I guess so," I said quietly narrowing my eyes at him

ever so slightly because of his smirk. That smirk had far more behind it. What, I didn't know but it was something.

And I liked it.

Shit.

"Avory…" he let out a long breath. "Avory was the first black Queen here."

"Really?"

He nodded. "Hired under George but it was risky…"

"Because he's black?"

"*No.* No, because of his background. He'd been a Queen on Brick Road; I don't know if you know it…"

I shook my head slowly.

"It's the next street over…" he pointed vaguely. "Full of backstreet clubs, they sell drugs there, there's always fights, and the police are *always* being called to it. Avory worked in almost every Drag club there from when he was, I think, nineteen. He jumped from club to club, getting fired or leaving or whatever. It's a dangerous street. Still is.

"Avory got drugged, he was working and the club owners paid them more if they went on high, or drunk, or *whatever.* Avory refused, one of the other Queens drugged him. He blanked out, woke up in George's house."

"What?"

"George used to visit the other clubs, poach essentially, get good Queens away from shit deals. He walked past when Avory was blacked out, he took him home."

"Offered him a job?"

"An audition, when he came around. He aced the audition, *then* when he offered him a job the other Queens were a bit wary…"

"The other Queens…" I repeated then I frowned.

83

"Jason, Jesse, and Jamie?"

He nodded then shrugged. "We're a straight club. No drugs, no illegal acts, no sex, no money throwing and Queens actually got fired if they go on drunk. Avory wasn't used to it but he adapted. He learnt and well, Robin is prolific."

"Never Queen though, never the headline?"

"No," he said quietly. "I wouldn't like to speculate the reason. I mean, I know when Robin was hired Blossom was the Queen, then Daisy took over. Queenie was who took over from Daisy…"

"That recent."

"Yeah," he shrugged lightly. "I'd love to redeem Avory, to become the Queen one day… but I'm mixed, it would still be a big deal but not a redemption."

"I have no doubt you'll be Queen one day," I said. "You'll be an amazing Queen."

"Thank you," he whispered then looked over my head.

I turned. "Beau you are on second tonight," the technician, who I *think* was Chandler, said. "Madison is opening."

"Oh," Jackson said.

I frowned. "You're not my technician."

"No," Chandler agreed. "I'm not but I'm still telling you this information."

I laughed as he grinned. "Madison, you have two hours."

"Thank you, beautiful," Jackson said then touched my hands. "I better get ready."

"Can I come with you?" I asked then gulped. "Wow that sounded needy, let me assure you I did not mean for that to come off that needy."

His laugh was breathy as he stood holding his hand out to me.

"Come on, then," he said as I took his hand. "But don't forget your dress."

He laughed so I tugged on his hand pulling him towards my dress.

I watched him as he put on his makeup, sat on his chaise lounge and *not* even preparing not to watch. He smiled at me occasionally an almost shy thing through the mirror until he turned.

His face done except for his lips. He chewed on his bottom lip thoughtfully. "What's your favourite colour?"

I frowned; he waved his hand at me.

"Lavender," I answered.

"Really?" he replied.

I nodded pointing to my hair, he looked away, I caught the barest of blushes on his face. "My Uncles pink right. My uncle and his partner are known for their hair because he's pink, and his partner, they're blue. Have been since they were like thirteen and I've always loved it. Oakley's six years older than me, so I was seven and constantly bugging my parents to let me dye my hair."

"Did they cave?"

"No," I mock-pouted. "Not until I was sixteen and I'd left school, then they let me do it because they had to bleach my hair. Oakley does it for me now he's a barber, but he told me it was my grandpa who started it.

"He's been dying his hair since he was a teenager, and he went white when I was born as I officially made him a grandpa."

"That's amazing," he whispered.

"What's *your* favourite colour?"

"Red," he answered. "The colour of strawberries kind of red." He turned to his dressing table picking up something. He grinned when he showed me the lipstick. "My Grandad Milo is so annoyed at me because all I wear

85

is this, he wants me to try all kinds of different colours but, *no*, this is my favourite colour."

"Milo…" I said. "Wait Milo and Avory? Is Milo a makeup artist?"

"He used to be, yeah. He taught me how to draw."

"Really?"

"Yeah, when I was very small, we used to just sit and draw together. Why?"

"They come into our café."

"Our café?" he repeated amused.

"I work in the café across the street. *LGBTea*…"

"Avory worked there," he laughed. "Do they still give out condoms?"

"Yeah, we've got a big basket of them by the door."

"That was his fault, because he couldn't be bothered changing the basket back to crisps after World Aids Day then it became famous for it."

"They come in on a Sunday, right?"

"Yeah, every Sunday without fail they go and get a pot of tea and some cake."

"I always serve them," I said.

"Inevitable then," he said grinning. He pointed between us. "We were destined to meet, sooner or later."

"You never come to the café with them?"

"No, I don't see Avory and Milo as much. Given I live with Jamie."

"Oh."

"We live with my grandparents. Always have, I also live with my parents and my twin sister."

"You're a twin?"

"I'm a twin."

"Does your twin…"

"We're *not* identical," he interrupted me.

I rose my eyebrow at him. "Does she look like Madison?"

He laughed so much he snorted, then gasped covering his mouth but not actually touching his face.

"No," he answered. "We couldn't look any more different, actually." He moved back on his dressing table stool. "Come, I'll do your makeup."

I went without hesitation. Sitting opposite him on the stool, we were *really* quite close. He didn't make any effort to move back, so neither did I.

He reached for my foundation without having to check. I let out a slow breath because, *why* did that give me butterflies? *Why* was I feeling so weird?

Why was Jackson making me feel weird?

I didn't have time to unpack this right now.

"Is she at home?"

"No. University in Manchester. Studying to be a sports therapist. Do you have?"

"A twin? No," I interrupted him as he pulled his tongue at me. "I have a little brother. Not so little, he's thirteen." I closed my eyes without his request. "Why all the questions?"

"I realised I didn't know a thing about you, and I wanted … to learn about you."

As I opened my eyes he winked at me.

"You like him," Mateo suggested. I groaned shaking my head and refusing to turn to look at xem. "You do, tell me about his shapewear again."

I turned to glare at xem, xe smirked back at me. "If you'd have seen it."

"I'm sure. He's gorgeous with his clothes on, never mind off."

"Mateo."

Xe bit xer tongue, crinkling xer nose at me. I wanted to hit xem, *if* we weren't on shift I likely would've.

"Back off?" xe asked.

I nodded. "Quickly."

"You're just proving further you like him, you know."

"Shut up," I muttered. "What should I do?"

"Tell him," xe said with a shrug, "you won't ever know the answer if you don't just tell him."

"That sounds exposing."

"Relationships are."

"How exhausting."

Xe shrugged. "For that beautiful face, I would…" xe said then laughed, standing up straight looking behind me.

"Luca?"

I turned then I stalled as I let my eyes take in the tall, beautiful black man with curly grey hair, a *lot* like my own who was stood on the other side of the till.

"Hello?" I offered as he smiled at me. "Avory?" I added.

"Bingo," he confirmed, nodding. "Jackson told me you worked here."

"Jackson," I repeated, Mateo sounding gleeful behind me, I wondered if Avory would notice if kicked xem.

"Pot of tea," he said. "I'll sit over there, come over when your brain reconnects," he teased.

I bit my lip. "No cake?"

"Oh no, it's my husband with the sweet tooth," he smiled as I looked away.

"I'll bring your tea over."

"Thank you, sweetheart."

I turned to reach for a teapot.

"He's talking about me at home," I whispered to Mateo.

"You're such a chaotic Queer," Xe said laughing. I turned to look at xem. "Just tell Jackson you like him, for the sake of us *all.*"

"I should talk to Avory first."

"What'll that do?"

"Might tell me if Jackson spoke positively about me or not."

"I swear to God, Luca."

"I'm going," I said as I put the teapot on the tray alongside two mismatched teacups and a little pot of sugar.

I walked warily towards Avory, holding the tray with two hands against my stomach and then I hovered.

"Sit down, baby," Avory purred.

"I'm working."

"This place hasn't been busy since it opened."

"Jackson said you used to work here," I said as I slid the tray onto the table.

He nodded. "I loved working here. It was so nice and simple, and I assume you know the Queen wage is cushy, so..." he paused, I figured it was because I was frowning. "Check your bank, baby."

"I..." I paused as I reached into my pocket for my phone. I glanced at him as my bank app loaded then I choked. "*What.*"

Avory laughed as he drank from his tea. "Exactly. The first time I was paid I thought it was wrong. I genuinely believed they'd made a mistake." He lifted his hand, "I know now Jesse never makes mistakes. He's like a machine but I genuinely believed it was wrong.

"Anyway, I stayed working here because I loved it, it didn't matter to me I got a fifth of my salary at the Rose Quartet from working here. It's all about the community."

"I've never had this much money in my life," I said.

"It's a life saver," he laughed. "We went from not making our rent to buying a flat, and Milo starting his own makeup business. It changed our life. It's helped our Jackson out..."

Our eyes met when I finally looked away from my phone. "What do you mean?"

"Well, you know he makes dresses?"

"I didn't," I said in a gasp.

He smiled at me. "He runs his own dressmaking business, he makes them for Queenie a lot, mostly but he's made them for Daisy and Jasmine, too. He makes prom and bridesmaid dresses, but he wouldn't be able to do it if he wasn't earning what he does at the club."

"I didn't know that."

"I figured there's still a lot you guys don't know about each other."

I looked down.

"That isn't a bad thing. Milo and I met, he left his phone in my flat, a handful of weeks later he'd moved in. We didn't really know each other at all and it was definitely make or break."

"I..."

"It was one of the best decisions we spontaneously made, he just kept staying over until he didn't leave."

"Are you here to advocate Jackson and I getting to know each other?" I asked.

"No, I came to give you something," he said pointing at my apron so I looked down. "I love that this caught on. Carter and I just did it for fun but it really became a thing," he said as I examined my own badges.

A gay pride flag, a yellow badge that read SHINE BRIGHT, two cute avocadoes with the words 'Let's avocuddle,' and a smiley face with round glasses on.

"Here," he said. I looked back up then smiled at the badge he had in the palm of his hand. "George gave me this after he came in for a coffee and discovered I worked here and we wore badges on our aprons. He told me I had to fly my flag with pride, and I did. I wore it every day after that."

"I didn't know Drag Queens had a flag," I said lightly as I looked at the badge, it was a very simple purple, white, and dark blue stripes with a pink crown central in the white one.

"No, nor did I when George gave me it."

"Why aren't you giving it to Jackson?" I asked.

He smiled. "It's meant to be worn on an apron, I guess. Just wouldn't feel right. Which I know sounds *so* stupid but when Jacks told me you worked here and you were the new Queen and everything. I figured I should pass it on to you."

"Thank you," I whispered. "I wore one of your dresses on Saturday," I said as I pinned the badge to my apron.

"Which one? Was it one of my favourites?" he asked.

I grinned as he lifted his teacup again, drinking from it as I opened my photos to show him.

Text Message 22:46

Luca: Met your grandfather today. I think I'm his new favourite grandchild, ngl.

Jackson ♡: Avory?

Luca: Very same.

Jackson ♡: Ha-ha! I wouldn't be surprised; did you show him you wearing his dress? You're right you probably *are* his favourite grandchild now.

Luca: He's really nice. Told me loads of things about the club back in the day.

Jackson ♡: He'd be delighted being able to tell his stories given I was raised in the club.

Luca: It was great, honestly, I really enjoyed it.

> Jackson   is typing…
> Jackson   is typing…

Jackson ♡: Can we video call? My hands are full!
Jackson ♡: We don't have to of course, don't worry if not, just hard to text…

Video Calling **Jackson**   …

Jackson

I glanced down at my phone as Luca watched me from the other end. I laughed softly taking the pins from between my teeth, one by one before raising my eyebrow at him.

"What?" I whispered; it came out far more self-conscious than I was expecting.

"I'm just watching," he told me before looking away. He didn't look away long before he glanced back at me again, the barest slither of silver showing in his smile from his brace. "Anyway, you were saying... you were practically raised in the club?"

"I was," I confirmed, nodding to him as I put the final pin in. "But so were my parents, that was how they met."

"Really?"

"Really. They're both adopted, of course."

"Of course? Why of course?"

"Well, I mean Jamie and Dylan didn't have much of a choice but to adopt my dad, and Avory and Milo didn't either, so adopted my mum. Why? Aren't you...?"

"Did you just ask me if I'm adopted?" he laughed.

My cheeks felt hot.

"No, all natural here, but I'm interested in your

parents right now… I'll tell you about mine after."

"Okay…" I said softly. "Well, obviously Jamie was Queen Blossom, and Avory was Queen Robin."

"Alongside Jesse and Jason?"

"Daisy and Jasmine, right. My dad was adopted at birth, like Jamie, and Dylan took him home from the hospital kind of adoption and he was practically raised amongst Drag Queens.

"My mum, I think, was three or four when she was adopted and since Robin and Blossom still worked there, they brought them to the club during rehearsals. They had no one else to play with, I guess."

"And they fell in love?"

"Years and years later. When I talk to my Mum about it, she says she never saw him as anything more than a brother for so long. They were twenty-one and twenty-two when they actually went on a date." I paused as he grinned happily at me. "They married at twenty-five. Had Rosie and I two years later."

"Wow," he murmured. "How were you raised in the club then?"

"Well Jamie was somewhat livid his son didn't grow up to do drag."

"Valid," he said.

"So, when I practically walked out in heels he was made up. Sure, he'd retired by then, well retired but Jesse and Jason were both named my Godfathers and he took me to see them at the club a lot. Jesse taught me the piano and signing."

He frowned.

"What?"

"I just didn't know about the signing, that's cool."

"Jesse's partially deaf. Apparently always has been. It was a big USP for Daisy because Jesse signed and sang. He taught me to sign from quite small.

"So, I was always there, just hanging around. I was there so often that if I got into trouble, my punishment was I couldn't go to the club."

He laughed happily, I grinned as I picked up my phone and took him over to my bed.

"Tell me about your family."

"Oh..." he said as if he was settling in for a story. I grinned as I rested my phone against my pillow. "Well, I mean, Riley, my grandpa, did grow up in Foster care."

"Oh," I repeated.

"And, actually, my dad is adopted."

"Ha," I stated.

He laughed. "But my Dad was adopted by Kaiden and Imogen. Adoption was in fact the only option as Kaiden is trans.

"But my Grandpa Riley and Grandad Kieran had all their kids naturally. Kieran's also trans. Riley is nonbinary. Riley carried my Pa and Oakley."

"For real?" I breathed. "That's amazing."

He grinned then cleared his throat.

"My Dads then proceeded to have Connor and I naturally, but I was an accident."

"What?" I laughed.

He nodded. "My Dads weren't even together when they got pregnant with me. They had been sure, they met when they were fourteen, when Dad was adopted, they fell in love instantly, or so the story goes.

"They were together for the entirety of school, then broke up before university, for multiple reasons. They didn't see each other again until Kieran's fiftieth. When they were twenty-four-ish, and well... I was conceived."

"No way," I breathed.

He nodded as he picked up his own phone, I watched, intrigued, as he moved me across his bedroom.

"I was a big accident, apparently they weren't even

95

planning on getting back together. Pa says he made Dad date him again, so they didn't go straight back to Alistair and Rory like they were before.

"I think they said they were about five months pregnant when they got back together. They moved in together at seven months, then got engaged."

"Just like that?" I asked.

He nodded as he sat on his bed, balancing me on something. I fell down. He picked me back up again. "They didn't get married until I was eight. They were engaged for a long time and obviously had Connor in that time."

"Was *he* an accident?" I laughed.

"Yep," he smiled. "He was a shock to us all."

We laughed together.

"I don't know if this question is rude and, please tell me if it is…" I said slowly, warily, because the last thing I wanted to do was offend him. He nodded back to me curiously, so I bit my lip. "Which of your Dads carried you?"

His grin told me I hadn't offended him, or his family. *I guess.* "My Dad. Alistair… he's…"

"Also trans?" I asked.

He nodded, laughing. "You know how you were raised in the club; I too was raised in a club."

"Oh?"

"Rainbow Connection. It's an LGBTQ+ support group and youth club, my Grandad Kaiden owns it, well *owned* it. Everyone in the hierarchy of my family is trans or nonbinary because they all met there and just fell in love. I guess.

"It's amazing because gender just doesn't exist in my family, not really, we're all so fluid so, when I stated that I wanted to do Drag it wasn't a big deal at all."

"Another intrusive question."

"Oh, I'm counting three so far, I will get to ask these back when I see fit."

"Three, I thought it was only two," I squeaked, my voice in a frequency that I was not at all pleased with.

"You asked me if I was adopted."

"Oh... yeah," I bit my lip.

"What's your question?"

"Were you... I can't remember the word for it, when you don't gender your baby?"

"Theybie," he said easily, I nodded. "Nope I've always been raised a boy. My dads didn't know what I was going to come out as, not until I was out but I was always a boy. His twin, my dad's twin, Enzo, is raising zir children as theybies though."

"Your family genuinely fascinates me."

"And yours me," he said quietly.

I laughed shaking my head. "I thought my family was unusual and interesting, but I think you straight-up win."

"I hear that a lot. I'll give you a pronoun cheat sheet, believe me. You'll need it."

I grinned as I lay back, resting my hands under my pillow so I could still look at my phone. "That implies I'm going to meet your family."

"Someday," he whispered back as he mirrored my position.

"I'm going to do the dangerous thing that is taking my glasses off," I told him as I pulled them off by the nose, folding the arms over each other.

"Don't worry I'll wake you back up if you fall asleep," he said. I laughed as I reached over my phone putting my glasses on my beside. "What can you see now?"

"I can still see you," I said, his eyes examining me. "It's distance I can't see..." I looked over my phone towards my fuzzy door. "Hence why I wear contacts on stage, otherwise I'd probably fall off it."

His laugh sounded sleepy.

I didn't remember setting an alarm. I *don't* understand why I would've, in fact. I had no-where to be, so why had I set an alarm. I turned towards my clock, ready to hit it so I could turn over and go back to sleep. It *wasn't* beeping.

But something definitely was. I sat up, rubbing my eyes before reaching for my glasses. I looked around my room, before lifting my cover.

I laughed as I picked up my phone watching as Luca rubbed his eyes before reaching for *his* alarm that was beeping. I let it be quiet for a moment.

"Good morning," I said.

He jumped, turning towards the screen then smiling at me as he picked his own phone up. "*Good* morning?" he replied, although he sounded unsure. "I don't remember falling asleep."

"No," I whispered. "I don't remember at all. Why do you need to be up at seven?"

He groaned as he got out of his bed. "Work," he told me as he carried me somewhere. "Early shift. Wait, did my alarm wake you?"

I nodded then quickly shook my head at him. "It's okay. I've got loads to do so it's probably a good thing I'm up this early."

I went to the bathroom as he settled me on his mirror, so he could brush his teeth. He was delighted when I walked back towards my room.

"Can I see your rats?" he said around his brushing. I stopped walking. "Please. I'm dying to see them," he said holding his hands together, his toothbrush still in his mouth. I tried not to show him how cute I thought he was as I changed direction towards the rat cage that sat on our landing.

It was three stories high and had come from Jamie and Dylan's first ever flat. Dylan had always had rats since he was a teenager, his first pair being Bubble and Squeak. After them, they were never without a pair of rats.

Now we had Sugar and Spice and with Dylan's health deteriorating they had become solely my responsibility after I had volunteered my services to Jamie at least.

I'd told Luca all of this last night, and he'd begged to see them when I finished telling him, but I told him *no* because I didn't want them to wake up the entire house.

"Okay I never thought I'd say this but they're *adorable*," he said as I held the camera to the cage.

Sugar climbed up the bars sniffing at my phone so I rested it on top of the cage, flipping the camera back around and lifting Sugar out.

"*Yep*. I love them," he said.

I laughed grinning at him as Sugar sniffed at me and nibbled the end of my finger. "You'll have to come and meet them in person," I said quietly.

"I agree," he whispered back so I looked up at him, then I jumped.

"You're up early Jacks."

We both turned looking towards the voice as Jamie closed the door to the attic behind him.

"Good morning," I offered, then looked back at Luca as he attempted to see *around* my phone.

"Rats wake you?"

"No," I said slowly then pointed at the screen, "*his* alarm did."

Luca waved guilty when Jamie came to stand next to me. Jamie laughed and waved back.

"Luca, I assume."

"Queen Blossom," Luca replied, curtsying appropriately.

I laughed as Jamie grinned at him.

"I like Luca," Jamie told me, "he knows his place."

Luca laughed happily then cleared his throat. "I best get ready to work. I'll see you Saturday, yeah?"

"Yeah," I said shyly because Jamie was *right* there.

He squeezed my shoulder. "I'll make you some tea," he told me stroking the back of my neck.

I nodded watching as he went downstairs. I turned back to Luca. "This was nice. Unexpected."

"But nice," he agreed.

"See you Saturday, okay?" I whispered.

He nodded and I blew him a kiss. He blew one back his cheeks flushed as he reached for the phone ending the call.

I smiled, biting the end of my thumbnail before going downstairs. It was easier than going back to bed. I wouldn't have been able to sleep given the butterflies.

I went down to Jamie as he stood dipping a teabag into his cup, he looked a bit glazed over.

"Rough night?" I asked.

He jumped lightly touching his chest as he turned to me. "Jackson," he gasped.

"Sorry," I whispered, biting my lip.

"Don't worry, baby," he said reaching his arm to me, so I walked towards him. "Just a restless night, *nothing* to worry about. Luca looks nice."

"He is," I said. "*Really* nice, far too nice to be a Drag Queen," I teased.

Jamie laughed knocking against me. "Don't ruin him," he teased back so I pulled my tongue at him. "You like him, don't you?"

"Yep," I whispered, then sighed. "I haven't admitted that yet. That's *terrifying*."

"First step is acceptance."

"I'm not an alcoholic."

100

"*No*, you're apart of RA," he said as he took the cup he was dipping the bag into and went to leave the room.

"RA?" I asked.

"Romantics Anonymous," he smirked. "I'll take this to Dylan," he added laughing at me as I gaped back at him.

"That's not even a good joke."

I blew into the glittery horn whilst trying to simultaneously pull the cord of the party popper. Reed practically cackled at me as he was covered in colourful strips of confetti.

"Happy Birthday," I said as he caught the confetti then he hugged me.

"Thank you, gorgeous."

"I made you another dress, but I know that isn't much of a present as I make you one every week."

"Hey! I don't have to pay for this one so that is a present."

"I got you something else as well," I told him, "but that's for later."

"First, we have a show to do," he shook my shoulders, "and I brought doughnuts." Jesse turned to look at us intrigued as Luca laughed from the stage. "And Quinn's coming to the show tonight."

"Oh, I've missed Quinn Giovanni's face."

"You've been getting your own fill of a face," he said turning us towards the stage.

I bit my lip as I watched Luca rehearse. "I told Jamie I liked him," I whispered.

Reed squeezed me a little tighter.

We'd sat for hours that morning, both with a cup of tea and talking, *just* talking. He didn't push or ask. He just waited and soon enough I word vomited all about Luca. He just smiled and that's when he started asking me questions.

Our conversation stopped when Dylan got out of bed, *again,* apparently according to Jamie as he'd been up and down all night. My dad had soon woken up as well and relieved Jamie so he could have a nap. I'd then proceeded to watch a weeks' worth of Four in a Bed and Come Dine with Me *with* Dylan.

"So, it's official now, the Queen knows," he said.

"Yeah, I'm not denying it," I said. "I definitely *like* him." He shook my shoulder happily, I laughed then turned towards him. "You said something about doughnuts," I added.

He nodded as he looked towards the stage. I figured he also saw Charlie. "Jackson."

"I don't want to deal with it," I told him. "I want a doughnut."

"After rehearsal," he stated. I pulled a face at him. He did it straight back.

"Come on birthday Queen, it's your turn," Jason called.

Reed laughed taking my hand and walking me to the stage. He spun me into a seat as Luca jumped from the stage and sat on the seat next to me.

He nudged his knee against mine, I grinned at him. He blushed as he grinned back.

Luca was stood by the doughnut box after rehearsal had ended and we'd had our sandwiches – curtsey of Jesse. I'd left to go the bathroom *before* choosing from the wide selection of doughnuts.

I stood beside him, bumping our shoulders together. He laughed as he swayed with me.

"Can't decide?" I asked.

He shook his head. "I'm not having one."

"Go on," I whispered. He looked at me as we

continued to sway. "Just one, it won't kill you."

"It might," he whispered back laughing, then shook his head. "No no, I can't. It wouldn't be wise." He cleared his throat, "which one are you going to have?"

"Strawberry, I think," I said softly as I watched him. "I *like* strawberry doughnuts."

He nodded as I reached for the one that was iced pink with little pink and white balls on top.

"I'll do your makeup as well, if you want?"

"Thank you," he whispered his eyes not leaving the box in front of us.

"Go on," I whispered straight into his ear.

"*No,* Jackson I can't."

"You've barely eaten today," I said, weakly, because *this* was becoming a habit I didn't quite know how to approach. Maybe I should talk to Jamie about that, too. Well, when he had time.

"What?" he whispered.

I shrugged. "I think we're ordering something later, but you've only had your salad and… energy." His eyes met mine. "And you like chocolate," I added. "You told me you liked chocolate over our call."

He rolled his eyes but was definitely amused. "*Go on,*" he laughed. "You're too good at persuading."

I pulled my tongue at him, I don't know why I *considered* licking his cheek.

I'm glad he made a move to pick up a doughnut so that I *didn't* lick him – because that'd have been bad. He glanced at me as he picked it up, then bit his lip. I nudged against him before taking his hand and leading him towards the dressing rooms.

Luca

I attempted to ignore the knock on my bedroom door, opting to cuddle my pillow closer and regret *all* my life decisions.

My choice ultimately didn't matter, the door still opened.

"Grandpa?" I said, frowning at him as he smiled back at me. "What are you doing here?"

"What did you eat?" he asked, his voice soft and warm. I buried my face into my pillow again. He laughed as he came to sit on my bed. "I called your Pa," he told me as he found my leg through the duvet and squeezed gently. "Just to talk. Nothing out of the ordinary. He mentioned you were really sick, and he didn't know why, couldn't figure it out at all. He told me how sick and well, I know those side effects well."

I turned my head so I could look at him. I frowned. "You never..."

"Are you about to say I never broke the rules, because Luca, honey, you're going to get a shock."

"You've known since you were small."

"So have you and although primarily my fault you also had me. I was five when I was diagnosed. I also went to a lot of birthday parties between the ages of five and twelve. They had cake."

I groaned, because how I had longed to eat the cake at so many parties. "You?"

"Ate the cake. Yep. I was young." He squeezed my leg again. "Other times, well sometimes, wheat just sneaks in. Kevin and Ellie almost brought down my school because they were coating the potatoes in the hot dinners in flour and hadn't told anyone."

"That's shit," I commented.

"Wait until you hear about beer," he said, smiling.

I laughed. "It was a doughnut. Reed brought doughnuts to the club. It was his birthday. It'd have been…" I sighed, "rude to decline."

"Huh," he said. "You must really like him."

"Reed?" I asked, trying to keep my voice level, he rose his eyebrow at me. "No. I mean, sure, Reed's great, but no."

"Weird. Not like you not to be careful. You're renowned for being careful."

"Sometimes wheat just slips in," I repeated, burying my head into my pillow again.

"Into a doughnut."

I rose my eyes to look at him.

"Maybe not Reed then, another of the Queens?"

"Princess," I whispered then looked up at him. "I'm sick, stop teasing me."

"I'm not teasing, I'm figuring out your motive."

"Please don't tell Dad I ate a doughnut. Willingly."

"No, no I won't, and I definitely won't tell him it was because of a boy, either."

"You're the worst," I informed him.

"Do you regret the doughnut?"

"No," I winced. "It was really good."

He laughed happily, squeezing my leg again before kissing my forehead.

"It'll pass. You'll be fine."

"I know," I said quietly then rose my eyes as my phone buzzed against my bedside cabinet.

"And you're lucky it's just your stomach," he added as he reached for my phone. He passed it to me without looking at it. "I used to get rashes on my hands, and they burnt."

I winced. "Just from food?"

"Beer, mostly. It was, I think, my second date with your grandad, we had some pints. I had regrets the next day."

"But *beer*…"

"*But* I liked him."

I met his eyes, then looked down at my phone.

Text Message

Jackson ♡: hey x

He smiled at me when I looked back up.

"Just tell him. It's really not that bad."

I sighed, looking back down at my phone.

Luca: hey

Jackson ♡: how are you baby doll? Free at all this afternoon? X

Luca: not feeling all too good tbh. Been up all-night sick.

Jackson ♡; oh no! Do you know why?

Luca: 🫠

Jackson ♡: I'm sorry 🥺

106

Jackson ♡: guess I owe you some TLC

I looked up toward Grandpa. He almost looked smug.

"Are you staying?" I asked.

He scoffed, "No. Kieran is taking Connor to the match. I'm going out for lunch with your Pa. We were going to invite you but you're definitely not up for it."

I shook my head because I was not up for it at all.

"Try to rest," he said then looked towards my door, so I also did as Pa came through it.

"Figured it out yet?" he asked as he looked me over, his expression was far too sympathetic.

"Contamination. We think," Grandpa replied. "Accident. No way it could've been prevented." He glanced back at me as I thanked him.

"Definitely from eating something?" Pa asked.

"Eating or drinking," Grandpa nodded. "Either could have done it, but it's definitely wheat related."

"Good," Pa said softly then shook his head. "I mean good it isn't more serious. Good that we know…"

"It's okay," I interrupted him. "I got it," I said as he came further into my room. He stroked his fingers through my hair then kissed my forehead.

"Take it easy. Okay?"

I nodded.

"Enjoy the fact the house will be quiet for a few hours," he added.

Minutes. Minutes before the doorbell rang through the house. I ignored it.

It rang again.

And again.

And again. I groaned, pushing myself out of bed and

towards the front door.

It rang again as I reached for the door. I went to fume at the person at the other side expressing my bitterness at being dragged out of bed, until I saw who was stood on the other side.

"Jackson?"

"Hey," he said quietly then he cleared his throat. "Hey, Luca."

"What are you doing here?"

"You're sick, so, I brought…" he said twisting his backpack around to show me.

"Come in," I offered, before I rolled my eyes. "I'll try that again, just a bit less manic. Come in, no one's here and it's… cold."

Jackson nodded, chewing on his lip as he stepped over the threshold. I closed the door behind him leading him up the stairs and into my room.

I sat back on my bed, cuddling my pillow to my chest and watching as he took in my room.

A quiet smile on his face as his eyes roamed over the posters, over the fairy lights. They settled on a picture frame sitting on my dressing table. A picture of Grandpa, Pa, Oakley, and me at a Pride a few years back.

"You look exactly like them…" Jackson said tilting his head. "Didn't get the ginger hair though?"

"No," I laughed. "All three of them did. I just got my dad's curls instead."

"That isn't a bad thing." he assured me then pointed at the picture. "Isn't that your dad?"

"That's my Pa, with his Pa and his little brother. My Dad…" I glanced around my room. "There."

He walked towards the string of photos on the wall. His eyes jumping over all of them until they settled.

"You are a poster child for genetics," he cooed. "How do you look so much like both of them?"

I shrugged, as I rested my chin on my pillow. "Most people don't believe I'm related to my Pas side of the family. Like, they see ginger and white and suddenly they're not related to me."

"I get that. My entire family is white except my Mum, Grandad Avory, and my sister," he shrugged. "I don't see why it should matter at all."

"No," I said quietly.

Jackson turned fully to me. "Feeling rough?"

"Very," I admitted.

Jackson examined me then went to sit on my bed. I nodded to him, watching as he took off his shoes before crossing his legs underneath himself. "Because of the doughnut?"

"Almost definitely," I said nodding. He looked concerned, and I watched as he seemed to think something over.

"Is it... was it..." He paused. "do you want to talk about it?"

"Do I? What? Why?"

"Well, eating..."

"Oh, no. No. I no..." I sighed. "Wait, is that why you thought I didn't want to eat it, you thought I was suffering with ED?"

"I mean... I don't know but I thought, if it *was* that. I could help I guess and..."

"No, Jackson," I said reaching for his hand. "No, I'm coeliac," I said. "I've got a gluten intolerance."

"Oh... *oh*," he hit my shoulder with his other hand. "Why did you let me persuade you to eat a doughnut?"

I shrugged, muttering quietly. "You said you'd brought things with you."

He frowned, until it dawned on him what I meant. "Oh, yes. I brought you..." he reached for his backpack again. He pulled out a fluffy cow. I laughed as he grinned and held it against me. "Hot water bottle," he said softly as I took it from him, cuddling it close. "I felt bad. Still do but a little less because, why didn't you just tell me?"

I shrugged as I stroked my nose against the cow. "I just, wanted a doughnut."

"Luca."

"I've always been really careful. I don't get sick like this often because I'm so careful. For once I just wanted to… taste the forbidden fruit." I sighed as I cuddled the cow closer again.

"You've never had a doughnut before yesterday?"

I shook my head. "Dad, well everyone, says when I was really small, like still in a highchair small, I just straight up refused to eat anything. They were so worried about me because I didn't eat a thing. Until my grandpa, he's also coeliac kind of figured it out.

"It turns out when they started weening me, cereal, bread, crackers, I kept getting really sick and even though I was a baby I just associated getting sick with eating." I sighed, "Grandpa started giving me his food, then he was the only one I trusted to feed me. That's when they got me diagnosed."

"You've never had a doughnut."

"No, or others birthday cake."

"I mean, that might be a good thing. Think of all the spit."

I laughed before burying my nose into the cow.

"When you say sick, are you actually like…" he mimed vomiting.

"I had stomach cramps most the night. Its more so painful than a sick feeling if that makes sense… I think our relationship is too fresh for me to tell you how the cramps eased."

He scrunched his nose at me.

"Exactly, why though?"

110

"I can't deal with vomit, but I was just going to suggest... offer... I was going to cuddle you whilst watching Disney musicals."

"I haven't produced any kind of bodily fluids in the last three hours." I laughed then groaned rubbing my face. "This is far too candid."

"Is that a yes?"

"*Yes,*" I gasped. "Wait, wasn't that clear?" I mocked.

"I think the real question is..." he began then he frowned at me. "Can I take my pants off?"

I squawked. He covered his mouth to stifle his laughter almost immediately. "For comfy reasons," he ensured I was aware.

I nodded. "Yes... was that the real question?"

"No, oh no. No, the real question was which film are we going to watch?"

"That's a good question."

He watched me curiously as I buried my face back into the cow. "It's your choice, you're sick," he said.

I held three fingers up to him. "Cinderella..." I said then pursued my lips, "Beauty and the Beast, then Mary Poppins."

"Live action, or?"

"Live action."

"Perfect."

"I'd love a Belle dress..." I whispered as we watched Belle and the Beast dance. I had put my pillow on Jackson's legs when he'd sat back down after changing the film. The cow against my somewhat settled stomach, my arms wrapped around my pillow. His fingers were threading through my hair.

There'd been a *few* incidents of his fingers getting caught in a particularly tight curl of mine and him yanking my head back up, but we'd started giggling at it

111

rather than being overly apologetic.

"I could definitely make that," he whispered.

I rolled over so I was looking straight up at him. "Excuse me?"

"Oh, definitely." He reached for his phone, scrolling though it before turning it to me. "I made Rapunzel for Reed."

"I'm in love."

"I love making costumes. They're harder usually but so much more fun."

"What do I have to do to get you to make me a dress?" I asked.

"Ask," he grinned. "And pay me."

"What are your rates?" I whispered.

He laughed looking back towards the screen. "Now that depends."

"Jackson?" I asked, he looked back down at me. "How did you know where I lived?"

"Oh," he said. "I sent you a text when I was leaving my piano lesson with Jesse. When you said you didn't feel well, I asked Jesse where you lived. It took so long for me to get here because he kept refusing to tell me."

I laughed and he smiled back knocking his head back against my headboard.

"He gave in, in the end because Jason told him to. He kind of figured I didn't have bad intentions."

"You didn't?" I teased.

"I felt bad. I still kind of do, but I *mean* you could've said no to me."

"I…" I paused, "wanted a doughnut."

He frowned at me, I wanted to reach up and stroke his head so he'd relax. I managed to resist that temptation.

"Luca, you can always say no to me, you know?"

My eyes met his.

"Really," he whispered. I smiled at him then sat up turning towards my door as it opened.

"Oh," my dad said as he came in. "*Sorry*," he added amused. "I was just coming to check on you, given you're not well."

"I feel better now," I said quietly then looked at Jackson as he covered his face. "Jackson, this is my dad... Dad, this is Jackson he works with me in the club."

"Oh, you're a Queen too?"

"I am... Sir."

"I'm glad you're feeling better."

I nodded lightly.

"Nice to meet you," he added.

Jackson smiled back at him. "I *had* better go, actually. My parents are probably wondering where I am."

"I can make you some food if you're feeling up to it?"

"I don't know," I admitted. "I'll come down..."

Dad nodded tapping against my door before leaving my room. I looked back at Jackson; he widened his eyes at me.

"Did I just invoke a potentially awkward conversation?"

"Nah," I said grinning. "It won't be awkward." I laughed as I reached down the side of my bed. "Here's your pants," I added.

Jackson sniggered as he took his jeans from me.
He followed me down the stairs once Beauty and the Beast had finished. I wrapped my blanket closer around my shoulders as I opened the door for him.

"Oh, I forgot to tell you," he said turning to me before stepping out. "We're going on a trip."

"We?" I repeated. "Is this spontaneous? Are you kidnapping me?"

"No," he laughed. "The Queens, the club. We're going to Winter Pride down in London."

"There's a *winter* Pride?"

"I know, I didn't think such thing existed but apparently Jason and Jesse find a way."

"When are we going on this *trip*?"

"Next week." I felt my eyes widen at him. "Sorry, I completely forgot to tell you. I don't think you *have* to come but we're leaving Saturday morning, back Sunday evening, so…"

"It'll be the show that week?"

"Yeah," he cleared his throat. "And we get paid for it."

"Why didn't Jesse mention it? Or Jason?"

"You *can* ask them," he said. "I'm just… giving you a heads up I guess."

"We need to talk more in depth about this, because what on *earth* do I wear to a Winter Pride?"

"Buzz me," he said then he lifted my chin with his finger, "and feel better, yeah?"

I nodded. He winked at me before stepping out of my house. I leant my head on the door as I closed it, letting out a deep breath before turning.

My Dad stood in the kitchen doorway, a coffee in his hands.

"So…"

"I told him I felt bad, he came over…"

"Nice of him," he said. I nodded as I walked towards him. "How do you feel now?"

"Better, my stomach doesn't feel as bad."

"Up for some food?"

I moaned at him.

"You don't have to eat, Peanut. *If* you feel like shit Your Pa sent me a text, contamination?"

"Couldn't be helped," I agreed.

He rose his eyebrow at me. "Going back to bed?"

"No," I answered. "I'll join you in the living room, after I've put some socks on."

He nodded as I started towards the stairs.

"And you can tell me all about your new friend."

I stopped on the stairs, looking down at him as he smirked. "What?"

"I've never met Jackson before; I'm just intrigued in my child's life."

I continued up the stairs. "Well stop that," I joked.

He laughed happily as he went into the living room. I continued to my room.

I stopped when I saw the cow sat on my bed, I retrieved my phone from my pocket, opening my Snapchat sending a picture of him to Jackson.

Jackson Bennett

Luca: Looks like you left someone behind…

Jackson: He was enjoying your company far more than mine. I guess you'll be looking after him from now on xx

I grinned stroking the nose of the cow before retrieving a pair of socks.

Jackson

I attempted to ignore the knock on my bedroom door as I had started to pack again. Jamie had come by a *number* of times ushering me along because I needed to catch the train, but I'd packed and repacked *both* mine and Madison's parts of my bag.

"Okay, let's talk."

I turned from my bed rubbing my arm behind my back as I chewed on my lip.

Jamie sighed. "You're putting this off for *some* reason or another, so what's wrong?"

"Nothing's wrong," I said.

"Jackson," he frowned. "It's not that you don't want to go, you *love* this trip. Every single year. You *love* it so what's wrong."

I shook my head.

"It's not Luca, is it?"

I laughed because *no*, definitely not. If anything, that friends to *more* trope was thriving. We'd been messaging late into the night, through text and Snapchat at the same time. We video called regularly, if there was an opportunity to be talking, *we* were talking.

I'd made his Winter Pride dress after he'd stressed

about what he might wear. Which, of course, meant *more* visits for measuring and fittings and *every*thing else that came with making a dress – although granted a few unnecessary visits, too.

"No, it isn't Luca."

"Then what, Jackson?"

"I don't want to talk about it."

He frowned at me. "Jackson you…"

We both looked towards my door when my dad knocked on it.

"Dad *needs* you," he said to Jamie.

Jamie bit his lip and nodded. "This isn't over," he told me as he left my room. I watched him go before looking back at my dad. He closed the door.

"What's wrong?"

"There *isn't* anything wrong, why do you all keep asking me that?"

"Because something *is* wrong and you're *not* telling Jamie, so, talk to me."

"Dad I…"

"I know we don't talk that much anymore, but we used to… do you want to talk to your Mum?"

I bit my lip. "I'm worried."

"What about, Jacks?"

"Dylan," I said far too quietly, but I knew he heard.

He sighed nodding to my bed, so I sat. He sat beside me. "Jackson, it's not…"

"I can't mention it to Jamie, can I, he's his husband, and you're his son. It's so not my place to talk to you guys about it, you've got enough going on but he's *not* getting better, is he?"

"No," he said softly. "The last few weeks have been really tough on me, on Dad. On you, I know they have. I don't know how to fix it, Jackson." He paused as he squeezed my knee. "I don't know what to say to you either. It's killing me to see Dad like this, both of them in fact.

"Dylan was always the strong one of us. I mean, Jamie's tough as nails but Dylan, Dylan was the one who could rationalise, who could talk us down. He was always there for *me*, he was who I went to when I'd fallen and scrapped my knee, or I had…" he laughed, "girl trouble. He was my rock, always. These last few years have been… hard.

"Jamie needs *me* to be his rock now. Jamie is struggling more than I've ever seen him struggle before. I'm sorry we're neglecting you."

"What?" I said. "What? I didn't mean that, I'm so sorry I didn't mean to…"

"No, we have been, because as hard as it'd been for us, it's been as hard, if not harder, for you. He's your Grandad as much as he's my dad and Jamie's husband and we've been so fixated on what we're doing to think about how it's been affecting you. You can tell us if you're worried."

"No, I can't." I whispered. "I can't because Jamie needs me to be strong too, and you're always working, or busy with Dylan or…"

"Come here, kid," he whispered as he wrapped his arms around me. "You are strong. So strong, I envy you in fact. I wasn't anywhere near as strong as you are at eighteen, you're incredible, Jackson, and I'm so proud of you, but we're also *idiots* because, yes you are strong, you're brave, but…"

"Only on the outside."

"I'm going to be truthful with you."

He looked like Rosie, or I suppose she looked more like him than I did, *but* I had his eyes.

"Dylan doesn't *have* long left with us. He's getting very weak, and remembering less, simple things. He's getting frustrated and tired…" he shook his head. "We *know* we don't have much time. We *also* were told that he could have moments of remembering, he could recite things, memories or facts clearly, without issue."

"That's good," I said, he sighed lightly. "It's not?"

"It means we should prepare to say goodbye."

"Oh."

"You need to go on this weekend, Jackson."

"I can't… what if you need me? Or he… he isn't here when I come back?"

"I think he will be," he said nodding so I nodded with him. "It's *one-night*, Jacks, just *one* and you need it. You need to be eighteen, you need to do the things you love, you need to have so much fun that you have things to tell us for at least a week. You need to go and spend time with the boy you like…"

I frowned at him, "How do you know *that*?"

"You're not discreet, kid," he said then wiped my cheek. I swallowed raising my hand to my face and wiping the tears I didn't even *know* were falling. "Go and be eighteen, Jackson, the most helpful thing you can do for us all right now is *have* fun, make memories.

"If you need some support, or you want to make sure everything's okay, you can call. You can call *me* or your Mum," he sighed. "And if anything happens, if *anything* changes, I will make sure I call you and I'll let Jason know as well. I figure he'd be happy to give you a hug if you need one."

"Okay."

"Okay?" he whispered.

I nodded. "Did you tell Jamie that Dylan needed him just to talk to me?"

"Oh no," he said. "Dylan wanted go the toilet. *Whilst* Jamie can still deal with that, Jamie's dealing with it." I smiled, as he nudged against my shoulder. "I'll drive you to the train station, okay? But you need to zip up your suitcase and get moving. Jesse can do *many* things but he can't hold up a train."

"Are you sure? Because that seems like something Jesse could do," I said as I stood.

"Actually, I *wouldn't* put it past him."

We weren't late. *Somehow* miraculously my dad got me to the station early after I'd said goodbye to Dylan and Jamie for a little longer than I normally would've.

I came into the station behind the group, walking towards Luca who was stood on the outside of them, watching them as he played with the handle of his suitcase. I touched his arm. He barely jumped turning to look at me.

"Hey, come on," I said nodding towards the group. He swallowed nodding as he followed me. I hugged Reed the moment I spotted him.

"Was starting to worry you wouldn't turn up, Princess," He started, then a bit closer to my ear, "everything okay?"

"No," I answered. "But I'd never miss this."

He nodded raising my hand to kiss the back of it. "If you need to talk, yeah?"

"Course," I whispered then looked behind him. "Oh, *Luca*…" I said turning to him, his expression surprised when I found him. "Meet Quinn."

"You're the new Queen, huh?" Quinn said, Luca nodding as he came to stand beside me. "I'm sad I haven't gotten to see you yet."

Luca laughed, "I was just getting started, don't worry, you haven't missed anything yet."

I grinned knocking against him, he knocked me right back.

"Tickets," Jason said, passing a little envelope to

120

Reed, "I'm sure you four are planning on *behaving,* right?" he said amused as he passed me a second envelope.

"No," I told him, "of course not."

"How could you even suggest such a thing," Reed stated in a gasp. "I've heard the stories of *your* trips."

Jason laughed as he passed the last envelope to Luca. "Don't listen to them, they're a pair of lying Queens." he told Luca. "I was as innocent as a snowflake. Never stepped a *toe* out of line."

"That's not even a little bit believable," Luca told him.

Jason scoffed. "You *were* my favourite."

"Not as if I'm his godson or anything," I said to Luca.

"Get your butts on that train," he pushed. "Jesse's waiting on the platform," he added as he turned to get his own suitcase.

Jesse was on the platform outside the right carriage, his husband, Isaac, at his side holding onto their suitcase with a *big* happy smile on his face. Jonathan was stood with them as this trip was Queens *plus* consorts but if you wanted to bring your King Consort you had to pay the difference.

I didn't know if that *quite* applied to Jason and Jesse but I knew it applied to Reed and the technicians that travelled with us. We'd caused *much* confusion in Jesse's office on this trip when I was sixteen.

I wanted Charlie to accompany me as my consort *but* he was an apprentice technician and they didn't tend to go on trips *with* us, except in rare circumstances – Jesse couldn't decide whether to pay Charlie for the weekend or have me pay for him to accompany me.

In the end Jason had covered it and told Charlie he was *first reserve* if any of the technicians had an emergency.

They didn't.

Now, Charlie came on this trip *as* one of the core technicians. I stuttered in the aisle when I saw him because I didn't want to have to deal with his face today.

Luca pushed me from behind, I turned to look at him as he rested his hand on my back, a soft push that simply asked me to move on, so I did. Passing the table seat of technicians and sitting on a two seat, next to the window.

Luca sat beside me when he was done battling with his suitcase.

Reed and Quinn sat on the two seats across from us.

"I don't think it's fair," Luca said, "that Quinn is even more gorgeous in real life."

I laughed. "True. It is a travesty," I said dramatically then smirked at Jason as he passed us. Jonathan followed.

"Who is he?" Luca whispered.

"Jonathan?" I asked, Luca turned back to me, "he's Chandler's grandfather..." I said slowly, "he's also George's widower."

"Oh," he breathed as he looked around the seat to Jonathan.

"And *now* Jason's bit on the side."

He squawked as he laughed clapping his hand over his mouth as he turned back to me.

"For real?"

I nodded as Jesse stopped at our seats. He passed something to Reed and Quinn before turning to us. He gave me a sandwich.

"Are you mothering us?" I teased.

"It's my turn to do the sandwich run," he said as he passed me a bottle of Diet Coke. "But no chocolate until you've eaten your dinner," he teased back, as he passed Luca another bottle, then a sandwich.

"I can't..." Luca began, Jesse shushed him touching the packet so we both looked. **GLUTEN FREE** was written in bold above the words Chicken, Bacon and

Lettuce. "How did you know? I didn't tell you."

"I figured it out," Jesse said lightly as Luca looked at me. "He didn't breathe a word, if you're worried about that but I figured you were getting tired of that potato salad so, I've got three more sandwiches for you *and* the restaurant our reservation is at tonight already knows, too."

"Thank you, Jesse."

"You're most welcome," he replied as he squeezed Luca's shoulder. "I've got you kid."

"I…" he began then shook his head, "I don't get it."

"You're family…" I told him, "there's no escaping now."

We took Ubers to the chain hotel from the train station. Jason getting there before the rest of us and checking in. He was coupling up the technicians as we walked through the door.

"Reed and Quinn, of course," he said passing over a room key to them. "Next door to Jesse and Isaac."

"Great," Jesse mused as he took the key from Jason.

"And next door to you, Jackson and Luca," Jason said softly, I took the key.

"You've put us between *them*?" Jesse said.

Jason laughed as he nodded and showed the last card to Jonathan. "I figured you could take your hearing aid out. *I'd* have to listen to it."

Jesse laughed before saying something quietly to Jason, that for some reason made me suspicious. Especially when they both glanced our way.

"Do we have a call time?" Reed asked as he also watched them both sniggering like children.

"We're due for a debrief at three o'clock. Freshen yourselves up. We'll meet here at two thirty." Jesse said.

"Drag or?" I asked.

"No need. We'll be going to eat after it as well."

"And will baby faced Jackson need his ID?" Reed cooed at me; I rose my middle finger back at him.

"Possibly," Jason laughed. "We'll see where the night takes us. Now move, Queens, I want to shower."

We were on the third floor, the technicians down the corridor from us. Reed and Quinn led the way, finding their room and letting themselves in. I passed them, tapping the card to the room next door but one to them and opening the door. I stepped in far enough that my suitcase held the door open.

I turned back to them. I caught Luca first, he frowned at me.

"There's just one bed," I said.

Jesse smirked as Luca looked down at his feet. "That was all they had."

I scowled at him and he laughed as I walked further into the room. Luca followed.

We both stood at the end of the double bed. Jesse followed us in.

"There were only double rooms left."

"Bullshit." I laughed

"I'm sure you two will figure it out," he shrugged. "Two thirty," he reminded me before turning to leave. He stopped at the door, winking at me before he closed it over.

I almost laughed, rubbing my forehead as I turned to Luca.

"I can sleep on the floor, if you want."

"No," he said then cleared his throat as he looked straight at me. "I mean, it's okay." He scrunched his nose at me, "you got in my bed when I wasn't *well*, I'm sure we can handle sleeping next to each other for one night."

"Yeah?" I whispered.

"I think we can make this one bed business work," he smiled.

Our debrief was at a Drag Club in Soho called Shirley Temple's. Jason had filled us in on the club's history as we crossed London *then* Jonathan had informed us it had been owned by one of George's ex-boyfriends.

We'd spent the remaining length of the journey mocking him because he was *totally* bitter about that even though he'd been married to George for about fifty years.

The club stood out even in the quirkiness that was Soho, a big neon sign read *Shirley Temple's* with a martini glass and an olive that kept raising and falling from the glass. The sign was on, even though it was the middle of the afternoon but I guess it was somewhat like a beacon calling all the Drag Queens to the mothership.

"I want to ensure you know; I didn't know *anything* about the one bed deal," Reed said as we walked into the club.

I leant my head back before looking at him. "They're scheming and I want to be so mad at them."

"But?" he asked.

"But I can't be, because…" we both turned towards Luca as he stood and took in the club, "of *him*."

"Tell him," he whispered. I looked back at him, "there's few better times than being in bed with him."

I hummed. "He doesn't know I'm demisexual. That could be a deal breaker," I said.

Reed sighed as he looked back towards Luca. "I don't think it will be."

"That's just the tip of the iceberg," I muttered.

"Hey," he said, I looked back at him. "Are you okay?"

I shook my head. "Dylan's…" I began then choked; he pulled me into a hug. Shushing me lightly as he squeezed me tight. I swallowed deeply in an attempt not to cry. I didn't want to do *that* again.

"We can get some air if you want?"

"No, no I'm here, fully here. I'm having fun," I said.

He lifted my chin. "You're having fun."

"I am. Can't you tell?" I laughed.

"You need a break," he said kissing my forehead. "Tell me, okay? I'll take one with you."

"Thank you," I whispered. We turned together when we were called.

I was seriously contemplating bopping Luca's nose.

I think he could see it in my eyes as he lay opposite me. His hands resting under his head as he searched out the cover and attempted to wiggle underneath it. I helped him out, lifting it to his chest.

"What are you thinking about?" he asked. I bit my lip and bopped his nose. He instantly laughed, burying his head into the pillow.

"I enjoyed today," he told me, his grin growing almost instantly. "A lot. Jesse and Jason *are* fascinating." He laughed as he played with the duvet. "And I am *totally* in love with London's Drag Clubs. Like, I've always known I've loved Drag. No doubt in my mind but I don't know. Today just encouraged it, I guess." He paused watching me as I watched him right back. "You didn't have to not drink because I didn't," he whispered. I frowned at him lightly because we hadn't even discussed the fact neither of us were drinking when we found a bar in Soho after our meal. We'd just enjoyed multiple mocktails with colourful names.

"I don't drink," I said then I shrugged. "I just don't like alcohol, as simple as that. Well… I've been known to like wine, but I'm not attached to it."

He laughed. "No, nor do I…" he paused. "Well, I

mean, when I'm out I don't. I've heard plenty of horror stories from my grandpa about unwashed glasses making him sick."

"Okay but when you do, what do you drink?"

"Vodka," he laughed lightly. "Smirnoff. But I only drink at my grandparent's parties."

"Noted," I said quietly. He smirked a little looking down before whining lightly and rolling onto his back. "What?"

"Braces digging into my cheek," he muttered. "They're *great*, really."

I laughed letting my eyes roam him as he looked up at the ceiling. "There's something I need to tell you." He frowned tilting his head towards me, "I..."

"Jackson?"

"I'm demisexual," I said quickly.

He turned onto his side again looking back at me, although his expression was definitely confused. "What does that mean?" he asked. I rose my eyebrows at him. "What?"

"I would've thought the LGBTQ encyclopaedia would know," I teased.

He laughed lowering his head before humming. "No, I've got trans, nonbinary, theybies, Oakley's genderqueer. Gay, Pa's bisexual, Grandpa and Enzo are pansexual. Connor's straight."

We gasped dramatically at the same time.

"I know one of my Dad and Pa's friends are asexual but I don't know much about that."

"That," I whispered.

His eyes examined me even through the dark. "You're asexual?"

"I'm demisexual," I whispered then cleared my throat, "so, it basically means I don't really have feel sexually attracted to someone unless I have a *strong* emotional bond with that person."

"Oh," he whispered. "*That* makes sense," he added thoughtfully. I went to interrupt him, because I'd *heard* time and time again the old gem of, *isn't that just normal attraction.* "I mean, it makes sense because *I* can look at someone and instantly think about sleeping with them – and I've known that since I was *what* fourteen?"

I smiled before burying my face into the pillow.

"Thank you for telling me…" he said, "but why did you *need* to tell me? Wait, do I need to tell you that I'm gay?"

I laughed. "Oh, I'm also gay. Jesse told me all about that, he's asexual, homoromantic. We went around and around when I was figuring myself out. Turns out I'm homosexual and demisexual."

"Jackson."

"I needed to tell you because you needed to know."

"Oh," he whispered, moving closer to me so he could lean his forehead against mine. "I thought it might be a different reason."

"What reason?"

"Well, I'd feel the need to tell someone that if I maybe… liked them."

I rose my head, his didn't move but I heard his breathing stagger. "Oh." I whispered.

"Because I think that I'm… I think that I'm starting to *really* like, you."

I tried to get him to look at me. He wouldn't. I sighed pushing my forehead against his, he pushed back. "That's good," I whispered as he looked up ever so slightly, "because I know that I *really* quite like you, too."

Luca

This was the second time the alarm had beeped. The first we'd both mutually agreed to ignore it without uttering a word between us. The second not so much, as he sat up groaning. I turned my head to look at him, *still* refusing to actually commit to waking up.

"Seven," he whispered then looked back at me. "Hey."

I smiled before covering my face. "What time do we have to be *functioning?*"

"Ten," he whispered. "Sorry for the early alarm, but Madison needs…" he smirked at me, "preparing." He got out of the bed. I sat up, tucking the duvet under my legs.

"How is this going to work?" I asked.

He turned back to me from his suitcase. "Oh, I erm, I haven't thought about it *just* yet. I guess we could go on a date…"

"Jackson," I said, he met my eyes. "I meant Winter Pride."

"Shit," he sighed as he knelt next to his suitcase.

"I'd very much like to go on a date with you though…" I added. "But for now. Winter Pride?"

"Yes, so we'll have to go down to breakfast

practically ready to go."

"In drag?"

"No," Jackson said as he stood and rested his washbag on the end of the bed. "Ready as in shaven, tucked, in shapewear, *ready* so that when we arrive it's just makeup and outfit."

"Right."

"The parade is at twelve. Then I believe we have some sort of cabaret this afternoon."

"Suitcases?"

"They come with us to the club. We store them there. We'll have a chance to get out of drag before the train home."

"Full day then?"

"So much fun, though. *So,* get out of bed we've got to get ready," he said. I laughed pushing back the cover and getting out of the bed. "I'm going to get a shower. *If* you need to come in don't worry."

He walked past me, turning back given I was *just* staring at him. "What?"

"Don't worry about the bathroom."

"I'm not ashamed of my body." I coughed as I laughed.

"If it's embarrassing to you, don't worry. I'm not going to force you," he said as he opened the bathroom door winking at me as he stepped in, flipping the light switch so the bathroom came to life. The fans loud even *after* he closed the door behind him.

I emptied my bag out onto the bed, running my hand over my makeup then down the dress Jackson had made for me. It was a long Christmas Tree green gown, made from a material Jackson had told me was called Velour. It had long sleeves and fur around the hem and the neck.

I'd let Jackson take the lead on it as he advised me to wear something warm *but* glamorous. He'd sent me a design merely an hour later and it had been *perfect*.

"Do you like it?"

I turned as Jackson stepped out of the bathroom nodding as I did. "It's gorgeous," I said then bit my lip, he tilted his head at me his expression confused as I let my eyes run down his chest. "You have a tattoo," I added.

Jackson laughed stroking his fingers over his rib cage as he nodded. "When I told Jason I wanted a tattoo he said I either had to get good enough foundation to cover it on stage or get it somewhere no-one would see."

"Really?" I asked.

He laughed as he looked at the tattoo. "Nah, he was taking the piss, *apparently*. I didn't know this until after, otherwise I'd have gotten it..." he stroked down his inner bicep, "but I kind of love it so it's okay."

"What is it?" I whispered.

He walked closer to me. He was so close I could smell his soap. I swallowed before looking *purposely* at his chest. It was a rose, a simple bloomed rose that lay on its side. I wanted to run my fingers over it, *and* I think he might've let me if we hadn't both jumped out of our skin at a knock on the door.

"You answer it," he said, "you're wearing more clothes than I am."

I laughed, nervously, then went to open the door.

"Jason?" I said, he smiled at me then looked over my head and nodded to Jackson. I turned to look at him as he hid behind the wall of the bathroom.

"I realised I didn't give you your clothes."

"My clothes?" I repeated.

Jason nodded. "I don't expect you to come to breakfast in your shapewear," he said amused as he held out a brown paper package to me. I took it with a frown. "It's okay, I promise."

I took the package as I walked back into the room, Jason following me in.

"How did you know we'd be up?" Jackson asked as I unwrapped the package.

"Come off it, Jackson," he laughed. "You're like Jamie in so many ways. *This* is one of them," he said. I glanced at Jackson as he chewed on his lip. "Put some pants on, I want to speak to you."

"Is everything okay?" he asked.

"I promise, I just want to ask you something…" he said then looked at me as I unfolded the grey zip-up hoodie that had been wrapped in the bag. I stroked my fingers over the embroidered *Rose Quartet* on the chest. "Turn it around," Jason whispered. I looked at him then turned the hoodie. I laughed as I gasped at the word *Queen* on the back. "It's official," Jason added as I grinned. "There's joggers too, might as well stay comfortable."

"Thank you," I whispered.

He nodded squeezing my shoulder before nodding Jackson in the direction of the hall. They went together, standing close to each other as I gathered my soap bag. I stopped on my way to the shower watching as Jason gave Jackson a tight hug, whispering something to the top of his head before kissing it. I stepped into the bathroom for my shower.

Jackson was in his shapewear when I stepped back out. I tripped over the step up to the ensuite. He laughed lightly, rising his eyebrow at me.

"Is everything okay?" I asked, clearing my throat. "You know, with Jason and all?"

"Yeah," he said as he continued through his bag. "Course, he was just asking me about a few things for today, *nothing* important."

"You hugged," I said.

"We *do* that," he said laughing. "Are *you* okay?"

I nodded. "Nervous. Hungry."

"Hungry definitely," he agreed. "Let me just change your life first."

I frowned at him, he grinned as he reached into his bag and held out a pair of tights to me.

"They're *so* thick, you won't even feel the cold, but they also don't look thick, in fact they don't even look like tights."

"Skin coloured?"

"Well... mine are red, there wasn't many skin tones at *all*, and I didn't feel like much of a caramel."

I laughed lightly as I took the tights from him.

"Yours are slate, apparently. Grey, I figured your dress was so long it wouldn't matter."

"You bought me tights?"

"I made your dress," he reminded me. I laughed as he stepped into his own tights *then* his joggers. I sat with my back to him to take off my joggers and put the tights on like he had. "I just need to shave then, breakfast?"

I glanced at him.

"My *face*," he laughed. "Shave my face. I am *not* bothering with my legs. May I remind you about the tights," he said as he went back into the bathroom. I followed him when I'd put my joggers back on.

"I have this fear I guess that if I ever grew a beard... it'd be ginger," I said as I leant on the doorway. He smirked at me in the mirror. "It makes *no* rational sense though because..."

"Your dad has a beautiful beard," he said. "Like for *real*. I'll never grow one, but that man's beard is..." he mimed a chef's kiss.

"And the same colour as his hair."

"*Ah*, so yours will be purple," he said with a glint in his eye.

133

"Let's be honest, though. I'd rock a purple beard."

He pointed his razor at me through the mirror. "True."

We were ushered into one of Shirley Temple's *large* dressing rooms to get ready for the parade. Jackson, Reed and I all together – much to Reed's dismay.

Our technicians were stationed outside the door *if* we needed them but we weren't moving anywhere anytime soon because Jackson had told Reed to show me *his* tattoos and I was *so close* to calling off the parade all together to go and get my own.

Reed had four. One in the same place as Jackson, a mini galaxy with *Dreaming with my eyes wide open* written in cursive. Rainbow filled comedy and tragedy masks on his ankle, Saturn and a shooting star on his wrist, and a crown on the back of his neck, all loopy and circular.

We were complimenting *that* one when the door to our dressing room opened.

"Why aren't my Queens anywhere *near* ready."

We turned together and dissolved into a group of shrieking queens when we saw HRH Queen Jasmine stood in the doorway, in a to-the-floor silver evening gown, the bodice was embroidered lace and beads, all the way down the three-quarter length sleeves, the skirt tulle. Her black hair was pinned up small curls held in place with gems. A small tiara resting on the top of her head.

As expected, her makeup was *immaculate*.

"I didn't know you were walking in drag, too," Jackson squeaked at her.

"I'm not too old yet sweetheart," she said laughing, then turned and grinned at Queen Daisy as she stood alongside her in a chiffon evening gown, the neck a low V, the sleeves flowing. Her blonde hair cut into a gradual bob and a crown of *what* I think were periwinkles.

"All my dreams are coming true right now, I'm *not* going to lie to you," Jackson told me as I squeezed his hand.

"Makeup, Queens. Makeup," Jasmine barked at us, clapping her hands so we *moved*, all of us standing in front of the same mirror to do our makeup as Jasmine and Daisy unwrapped our dresses.

"So have you been fooling me all along?" Jackson whispered to me as I painted my lips.

I paused to laugh turning to him as he winked. "You're such a good teacher," I whispered back, he rose his eyebrow so I scrunched my nose back at him. "I kind of liked you doing my makeup. The first time I was genuinely nervous, after that... I just enjoyed it."

"We've got a lot to talk about, Mr Madison-May," he said pointing between us, "but first, *we've* got a show to put on." He spun away from me, reaching for his dress and stepping into it.

His dress was white, with long sleeves and it stopped around his mid-thigh the entire dress was covered in sequins, there wasn't a stitch on the dress missing a sequin. I wondered whether he sewed them on individually or not. I smiled as I watched Jasmine zip up his dress, talking softly to him as she helped.

"Come on."

I turned then smiled lightly as Daisy picked my dress from the hanger.

"I assume it'd be a stupid question to ask if you've ever been to a Pride?" she asked as I stepped out of my joggers.

"Yes," I laughed. "Pride is like a holiday in my house, Christmas, New Years, Birthdays, Pride."

"How do I join your family?" I laughed then paused as I held the zip of my hoodie. "Hey, you're good," she whispered.

I swallowed deeply. "I don't... it's nothing."

"It's *not* nothing, I know it isn't, I mean look at me I'm not exactly thin myself, am I?"

"I..." I said quickly, pausing because I didn't *know* what the right thing was to say.

She laughed fondly. "Don't worry, I won't be offended, I've always been more on the heavier side. *Always.* I asked George when I'd barely been a Queen a month if I was too big because... well, I assume you've seen Avory and Jamie?"

"Where did they store food?" I whispered.

"Exactly. It was me the spud, and them two long glasses of water *and* Jasmine." She nodded behind me. "Now we're a bit more diverse."

We both turned to Reed. My initial thought had been *right*, Queenie did have a killer hourglass, which I now knew was made through cinching her waist with a corset until it was breathlessly tight, it created quite a startling illusion of breasts also. I'd been in awe when I'd sat backstage watching Reed get ready for her show. Reed himself was big, tall, and so damn confident I somewhat envied him.

I figured I should've been thinner given the whole not eating bread thing. I felt pretty cheated out of that. Even more so because it was all in my stomach.

"What did George say?"

"He said I was beautiful," she smiled. "And never to forget it. He also said he'd rather his Queens be healthy and happy than sickly thin, and Luca, I fully agree. I'd rather you be healthy and happy than anything else.

"No one here is going to judge you, *no one*. But if you want to, you can stand facing that wall and I'll put your dress on from the back?"

"Yes please," I whispered.

She nodded, turning on the spot so I stepped around

her shrugging off my jacket, then stepping into my dress.

Daisy zipped up my back and brushed off my shoulders.

"This dress is *gorgeous*."

I turned to her, covering my mouth when the skirt bellowed out around me.

"Jackson," I said.

"He's a keeper."

"I know."

"Wig."

"Wig," I agreed.

I walked hand in hand with Madison and Queenie through the streets of London. The Christmas lights bright against the early sunset.

The parade itself was *alive*. I'd been to Pride parades since I was born. My first I was barely a month old, attached to my Pa's front in a carrier, big ear defenders on and donning a rainbow vest. I'd been every year after that, Prides and Trans Prides, and People's Prides and *every* other event over my nineteen years of life. I'd also walked in the parades for every one of those nineteen years with Rainbow Connection and my family.

In fact, I had a brightly coloured vivid memory of a Pride when I was thirteen, *the* Pride Enzo told us zie was pregnant with the twins in fact. I'd left the tent and walked the stalls, until I found the main stage.

I had sat down before it just watching and waiting and then three Queens came onto the stage. Robin, Cherry Blossom, and Daisy and I was captivated.

I told this story when we sat together drinking hot chocolate and mulled wine in the Christmas Market-esque Pride stalls before the cabaret.

"Did you just say *thirteen*?" Daisy asked. I nodded meekly before drinking from my hot chocolate. "*Wow*

137

old."

s at that Pride," Madison said. I turned to her as

ped the marshmallows into the cream on top of

hot chocolate. "They dressed like the flags, right?

ossom was the trans flag. I *adored* that outfit."

"Yes," I confirmed. "oh my god yes, you…" I turned to Daisy, "you were the bigender flag."

"Oh, I remember that dress," Daisy said fondly.

"I was twelve," Madison commented.

"Oh, I remember, I had to babysit you backstage," Jasmine sighed.

"You bought me an ice cream," Madison said.

"I did," she replied happily then turned. "Oh, hello," She said kissing both of the cheeks of the man who'd tapped her shoulder. "I'll be right back, *behave,* Queens."

"Never," Queenie whispered raising her mulled wine and winking at us then laughing loudly when Quinn wrapped his arms around her waist, kissing her neck gently.

"Aren't you cold, gorgeous?" he whispered. Queenie tutted lightly, running her fingers through Quinn's hair.

"I think you've forgotten baby that I'm Scottish," she said.

Quinn laughed as he ran his hands down the three-quarter length sleeves on Queenie's tartan Hepburn dress. She'd told me just before we left the club the tartan of her dress was her families tartan of the McDonald house after I'd complimented the green and dark blue with red stripes.

"Well, you're making me feel cold," Quinn told her. She laughed turning to him and wrapping her arms around his shoulders to kiss him.

I whined then covered my mouth, Madison turned to look at me.

"What?" she whispered. I shook my head. She

examined me then held her hand out to me. "Take my hand." She squeezed our hands together and for a moment I thought she was *just* offering to hold my hand and then she pulled.

"Be back by five," Daisy called after us.

Madison laughed before twirling me closer to her. "This dress looks gorgeous on you. I'm *so* looking forward to working with you."

"Is this a business meeting?" I asked.

"Of course not, but we do need to talk," she said, "and I kind of want some chocolate covered strawberries," she mused. "*But* I'm wearing white and I'll cry if I drop it."

"Did you sew the sequins on one by one?" I asked.

"I bought this one..." she paused lifting her finger to her lips. "Don't tell anyone."

"I wouldn't dare."

"Date," Madison said. "We're going to go on a date, and then we'll figure out the finer details, okay?"

"Okay."

"I'm suggesting this date with the intention we will become boyfriends," she laughed. "*girlfriends*?" She rose her eyebrow at me. "I, want to make sure you know exactly what you're getting into with me. I've got *so* much... baggage."

"I doubt that," I whispered, "but I am happy to take it as slowly as you want to."

She squeezed my hand again. "Thank you," she whispered. "Can you eat *anything* from here?" she asked waving around the stalls.

I looked around. "With some risk. Everything," I said. "Probably not. Don't worry I won't risk it. I'd rather not have to deal with *that* on a train."

She laughed.

"Nothing's stopping you from getting chocolate

strawberries though."

"White dress, Beau! White dress."

The cabaret was almost like an open mic Madison, Queenie, and I had been signed up for without prior agreement. There were drag performers, ukulele players, comedians, and readings of slam poetry.

The act before me was twin Drag Queens. They'd been introduced as Lemon and Lime, yet we didn't *really* know which was which. They wore long-legged jumpsuits, with as long chiffon skirts over the top. One wore an ice blue suit and a white glittery skirt, the other a white glittery suit and ice blue skirt. Both wore white block heels.

"So, what do you think?" Jasmine whispered.

"Of?"

"Lemon and Lime," she waved in their direction; Daisy nodded.

"They're incredible, beautiful, *funny*. I like them, why?"

"Thinking about hiring them." Jasmine said flippantly, Madison turned to look at her a laugh playing on her expression.

"What?" Daisy whispered.

Jasmine smiled amused as she sipped from her cocktail. "They're moving up our way to complete their Masters. They've been working here for three years or so, their boss reached out to me because they didn't want them to stop drag, so their boss signed them up and well, they're auditioning."

Daisy laughed. "We've never had twin performers. I feel like we really missed the chance of getting your twin into drag."

Jasmine laughed before moving closer to Daisy to talk directly to her.

I turned back looking at Madison as she smirked at me.

"You weren't the newbie long, huh?"

I touched my chest. "I'm hurt."

The train home was quiet. We'd been given an hour to get out of drag before we had to make our way to the station. We'd had a *big* group picture before we stripped ourselves then a second one in our hoodies and joggers. With our arms wrapped around each other and laughter on our faces.

I felt a part of them, a part of their little corner of the universe and I loved it.

Quinn and Reed sat across from us like they had on the way here, their heads together as they shared earphones barely a word between them. The technicians sat the carriage over, with Jason and Jesse as they talked through their notes and other details. Jonathan and Isaac sat behind us, also quiet, enjoying the solitude of a late Sunday train.

Jackson sat next to me, his legs crossed on the seat, a drawing pad on his legs although so far it only had the drawing of a body on it. He hadn't gotten much further as he was looking out of the window.

He had taken his contacts out when he'd taken Madison off, opting for putting on his glasses although he'd blushed deeply as he did. He seemed far more relaxed now. In fact, he seemed like he might fall asleep at any given moment.

I smiled at Jesse and Jason as they passed me in the aisle, them both nodding back. Jason squeezing my shoulder fondly as he did.

"Do you want any food?" Jesse asked. I shook my head slowly. "Well you're taking some home with you. I have a *lot* of food."

I laughed as he winked at me then continued back to his husband. I watched him sit down before turning because I felt Jackson's head rest on my shoulder.

I looked down at him, smiling at him when I saw his eyes were closed and pulled his glasses off by the nose, folding the arms over each other before sliding them into the net on the back of the chair in front of us.

I thought about kissing the top of his head, a light thing *but* ultimately decided not to, instead opting for sliding down in my seat and resting my head on the top of his.

I let a breath out, slow and steady, watching as the sun set out the window.

Jackson

This was the second time the alarm had beeped, and I really gave consideration to ignoring it again, telling my speaker to snooze and rolling over to go back to sleep.

It didn't happen, but mostly because I could hear the rat wheel squeaking over and over and I didn't *want* to listen to them any longer, so I forced myself out of bed and into a hoodie.

Stopping at the rat cage and picking Sugar off the wheel and onto my shoulder. She climbed into my hood nesting happily so I put my hand out for Spice. She sniffed at my fingers before huffing at me.

"Suit yourself," I whispered before turning away, she began to squeak so I turned back, smiling as she stuck her nose out of the cage. I held my hand to her, she stepped onto my palm nosing at my sleeve before climbing inside. I took them both downstairs and into the living room.

I frowned at Jamie when I walked into the living room, he smiled back at me.

"Good afternoon," he said. I lifted my arm to him, he watched me intrigued until Spice's nose poked out my sleeve.

"Is it really the afternoon?" I asked as Spice left my sleeve to sit on Jamie's hand.

"Tired?"

"Very," I told him then looked at the TV.

"Did you only bring one down?"

I shook my head. "Sugar is asleep in my hood."

Dylan gasped, we both turned to him, and I smiled as he was watching Spice clean herself on Jamie's hand.

"Do you want to hold her?" Jamie asked. Dylan nodded, so Jamie stood to pass her over. "Still loves rats. Regardless," Jamie said to me as Sugar went to sit on his hand.

"Rat therapy," I said.

Jamie nodded as he stroked his finger down Sugar's back. "I'm glad, I was worried he'd be afraid of them or something," he said smiling at Dylan as he lifted Spice to his face. Spice took the opportunity to sniff at his nose and climb up his cheek. "How did the weekend go?" Jamie asked as he sat beside Dylan on the couch. "Did you have fun?"

"I loved it," I replied. "So much, as always. Jesse totally set me up though?"

"How so?"

"There weren't any other twin rooms, *apparently*."

"He put you and Luca in the same bed?" Jamie asked, the laugh obvious. "I love him. He's obviously shipping this relationship. How did it go?"

"With Luca?" I asked.

"Luca," Dylan whispered. We both glanced at him as he let Spice climb up his chest.

"Well, he found out I have a tattoo."

"He saw you naked?" he replied.

Even Dylan looked at me in shock. I laughed as I held my hand up.

"I got out the shower, he saw it. Calm yourselves."

144

"I feel like you're teasing me," Jamie said.

"I found out his braces hurt his cheek when he's lying on his side."

"Oh yes," Jamie said.

"You never had braces."

"I didn't," Jamie agreed as he stroked his fingers down Dylan's cheek. "I remember frequently things *stalling* because the inside of his cheek was basically bleeding. It was totally romantic."

"We talked *late* into the night, so late we shouldn't have even been functioning the next day."

"Did anything come of it?"

"He turns twenty in April," I offered.

"Jackson."

"He *now* knows I'm demisexual. I'm not sure if he fully knows what that means but he knows it." I shrugged, "he's gay."

Jamie laughed.

"He told me he liked me."

"Oh."

"I told him I liked him too."

Jamie beamed at me, so I grinned sitting up straighter as Sugar began to climb down my sleeve. "Are you boyfriends now?" Jamie asked.

Dylan smiled happily at me. "Boyfriend," he repeated then turned to Jamie, "you're my boyfriend."

"I'm your husband sweetheart, *you* proposed."

"Wow," Dylan sighed turning back to me, "how lucky am I?"

"The luckiest," I assured him.

"What happened with Luca?" he asked me.

I stared back at him because it *was* him, he was right there as clear as day.

"Well?" Jamie pushed.

"I asked him on a date. We're not boyfriends, not yet

we're going to go on the date and decide what we want to do after that. No strings, no commitment, nothing, just a date."

"Very mature of you," Jamie said.

I looked down as Sugar popped her head out of my sleeve.

"Where are you going on your date?" Dylan asked.

I shook my head. "I don't quite know yet. I was wondering if you had any suggestions? I've never been on a date. I've never planned one."

Charlie and I had gotten together in school, we were the classic friends to lovers when we *finally* admitted to our feelings being more than friends when we were fifteen.

He was my *friend*, so we didn't date. We never did that. *Sure,* we went the cinema, we went for food, we did all kinds, but we were kids, a grand meal out was McDonalds. I wanted to do it properly with Luca.

In fact, I wanted to do *it* with Luca.

"There are things like the museum, or the beach. They're always good cheap days out, but money isn't an issue for you. Right?"

"Right," I laughed. "And I can drive so it's not like travel is an issue either."

"You're a catch," Dylan said.

I laughed loudly in shock.

"How formal do you want it to be? Do you want to dress up and eat at a restaurant, or go the cinema, or something?"

"I don't know," I admitted. "I just want to spend time with him and to be able to call him my boyfriend by the end of it."

"Then not the cinema, you don't want to go somewhere where you have to sit quietly for two hours. You said he was coeliac?"

"He is."

"Then don't go somewhere to eat that'll be stressful for him, because I can only *imagine* how hard it must be, if you're choosing a restaurant make sure they've got a gluten free menu." He shrugged, "you want the least amount of stress and the most amount of time together." He reached for Dylan's hand, retrieving Spice from him before Spice fell off his legs. I glanced at Dylan, frowning lightly as he was watching the TV, his eyes almost glazed over.

I swallowed deeply before meeting Jamie's eyes.

"We can never tell how long he'll be with us," he sighed. "It's okay, it's okay. What other things could you do?"

"We could avoid food," I suggested. "Ice skating, or the games on the dock. Something like that."

"I think that sounds like a lovely date."

"I think I agree."

Luca

My Dad was waiting for me when I walked down the stairs, dressed and ready to leave to meet with Grandpa. I frowned at him, shaking my head.

"Has Grandpa cancelled on me?"

"No," Dad laughed. "Of course not. I'm offering you a lift. Riley's at the club helping Sky out. *Unfortunately*, I need to see my father." I pulled a face at him. "I know, but you don't," he said jingling his keys at me. "Come on, can't keep Riley waiting – and I think the baby might be at the club."

"You should've led with that," I informed him as I jumped the bottom few steps and left the house. I could hear him laughing behind me as he followed me out the door.

"Where's Pa?" I asked as I got into the car.

Dad looked back at me. "The café."

I frowned.

"Mateo called in sick and he knew you were going out with your grandpa, so he took the shift."

"Is Mateo okay?"

"I don't know," he said shaking his head. "I assume

he's hungover. Rory didn't say anything he just got up and went to work."

"Remind me to thank him later," I said. Dad nodded as I reached for my phone.

Text Message

Luca: Are you okay?   Let me know if you need anything, can provide some ❀nice❀ gluten free food for you, that likely won't make you feel better!

Luca: Let me know if you need anything!

There were people everywhere all over painting walls and cleaning chairs for the clubs reopening under new management.

Sky was in the office talking to my *other* Grandad, Kaiden. I was truly surprised that it was talking and not shouting given they'd been having shouting matches since Sky was fourteen.

Dad squeezed my shoulder as I stood watching them. I jumped turning with him as he pointed towards the kitchen.

"I recommend you head in that direction," he said, stepping around me. "I'm going to have a chat with my father." I laughed nodding to him and walking towards the kitchen.

Oakley was in there with Grandpa and his friend, Frankie. They'd been friends for almost as long as Sky had been shouting at Kaiden. They were best friends Sky, Oakley, Frankie, and his partner Sam, all of them nonbinary. I'd totally idolised them growing up. I, *of course*, already completely idolised Oakley, I wanted to grow up to be like him, be as proud, as unapologetic and happy as he was.

And I wanted a group of friends like his, too. Friends who loved each other and cheered each other on, friends who could be completely their authentic self with, just like the self-named Butterfly Boys.

Frankie and Sam recently had a baby, who they had agreed to raise neutrally, the last thing I'd heard was they'd arrived and were just called Baby.

Now, in the kitchen, Grandpa was holding them smiling as he spoke to them softly. They were tiny, little arms and legs wiggling about in the air.

Frankie was sat on the countertop next to Grandpa smiling at their baby as Oakley watched them both amused. He wrapped his arm around me when I walked into the kitchen.

"Hello, darling. I *need* you to tell me all about this weekend," he said laughing.

I grinned at him reaching into my pocket so I could show him some of the pictures.

"I was about to come and pick you up," Grandpa cooed at me.

I laughed looking back at him as he stroked Baby's hair. "Dad brought me, he wanted to speak to Kaiden." Grandpa looked up at me surprised. I shook my head. "He wouldn't tell me anything. I didn't ask, I try to stay out of Kaiden matters."

Grandpa hummed as Oakley did then he squeezed my arm.

"You look gorgeous," he gasped. "Look…" he added then turned my phone to Frankie.

"Wow," Frankie gasped. "Luca you are *stunning*."

"Come meet baby," Grandpa whispered, so I did, standing alongside him and stroking my finger down baby's hand.

"Have you given them a name yet?" I asked as baby wrapped their hand around my finger.

"We have," Frankie said softly. "Tell me your Queen name and I'll tell you my babies name."

I laughed softly stroking my thumb over the back of baby's hand.

"Beau," I whispered. "Beau May."

All three of them cooed back at me completely harmonised. Baby gurgled at me.

"Sydney, Sydney Addison."

"You went with Sam's name?"

"Yeah," Frankie whispered as Sydney began to whine. "Much prefer them to be an Addison," he continued then took Sydney back from Grandpa, soothing them as they began to grizzle.

"Come on, let's go before baby starts to scream," Grandpa whispered as he picked up his coat. "Let me know your plans," he said to Oakley who nodded back.

"I'll give you all the wedding details, don't worry. Luca you *do* have a plus one."

I narrowed my eyes at him. "What do you know?"

"Oh, more than you could ever imagine." He blew a kiss, "enjoy lunch."

I turned to Grandpa.

"Ignore him," he laughed. "Come on." He ushered me out of the kitchen. I stepped back into the gym as Sydney began to cry.

It had been a long-standing arrangement that Grandpa and I went for a gluten free afternoon tea at least once every few months. It had been something Grandpa's foster mother had started with him. She'd take him to get his hair redyed then for a gluten free afternoon tea. Something that was few and far between when he was a teenager. Now, we went to a different café, or restaurant or tea room every time we went out.

"You do look beautiful, Peanut," he said as he sat

across the table from me, looking at my phone. "That dress is something else."

"Jackson made it," I said.

"Do you want to talk about Jackson?"

I let out a long breath. "I really do," I said then winced. "But I don't want to jinx anything."

"Oh, tell me only what you want to," he said softly, so I nodded raising my hands from the table as our waitress placed a three-tier cake stand between us. We both took a moment to fully appreciate the sandwiches, upon scones upon cakes and chocolate covered strawberries.

"We're going on a date tomorrow," I said as I took a sandwich. "He said we were going ice skating."

"Excited or apprehensive?"

"Both," I whispered. "The nerves are unnecessary. It's just so easy with him, so simple. I know we won't run out of things to talk about. I know we're... I guess, compatible."

"It's likely he'll be your boyfriend?"

I nodded once, crinkling my nose at him so he reached across the table.

"I'm happy for you, Peanut."

I nodded. "He said he's got baggage though. He said he didn't want to call me his boyfriend because of baggage and I don't know what that means."

"That could mean anything, Luca. Literally *anything*. When I started dating, *just* dating, not your Grandad. My baggage was me being trans, me being coeliac, me being a foster kid. He could have any kind of baggage. If you're uncomfortable with it though..."

"Get out, I know. I'm just trying to figure out what he could possibly mean."

"Don't. If I can give you any piece of advice you *might* take is don't try and figure him out, let him tell you when he is comfortable to. Don't *ruin* the relationship because of your own imagination."

I nodded.

"And try a scone, they are *definitely* placing the top three."

"Fluffy?"

"The fluffiest," he said grinning at me, so I picked it up, soothing the jam and cream over it then raising it to Grandpa. He smiled, knocking his scone against mine.

"Hello, darling." Jamie said fondly when he opened the front door. I smiled at him before looking down at my shoes, his laugh was soft. "Come on in, Jacks is upstairs, I'll hurry him along," he added as I stepped over the threshold. "Dylan's in the kitchen." He pointed vaguely in the direction of the kitchen. I looked towards it. "You don't have to go and speak to him, don't feel like you have to by any means. Just to save you standing awkwardly."

He'd barely gotten up the first step before I made my way into the kitchen. Dylan was sat at the breakfast counter, a cup of something that looked warmed next to him, a wordsearch in front of him, some of the words circled. I sat on the nearest free seat.

He glanced at me, as if not taking much notice of me. I still ensured I smiled at him, even if he didn't catch it.

"Leaves," I said. He frowned at the wordsearch so I touched my finger to it, running it across the word.

"Ah! Thank you," he said pleased, circling it with his pen before looking up at me again tapping his pen against his chin. "You're not mine, are you?" He asked. I shook my head slowly, warily. "You're Jackson's boyfriend."

I figured I was blushing, especially when he smirked at me.

"Not said that yet, huh?"

"Not quite," I replied quietly. "Not quite."

"Jackson's a lot like Jamie was when we met," he continued thoughtfully. "Well, Jackson's far more confident than Jamie."

"Really?" I asked.

He looked back at me again then nodded. "He never spoke a word when we met. We were seventeen, just started college, *no,* sixteen. We always laughed saying it was a miracle we got together because he literally wouldn't speak a word to anyone. When we went out as a group with the other boys in our class, he'd hang back, but stayed close to me mostly. When we were together, he'd hold onto my backpack strap so I always knew he was there but he just…"

"Didn't speak?" I laughed. "I don't believe it. He's Cherry Blossom, *she's* not shy."

"No, Cherry Blossom was what gave him confidence. He was nineteen when he started in RQ, and I got to see him grow. I got to see him become who he is now.

" It was incredible. I've loved him since we met, since we were small and still in the awkward stage of puberty, and I was so, so pleased people began to see the Jamie I knew when he grew in confidence." He let out a short breath. "Beautiful man, that Jamie. And as I say Jackson is a lot like him, always has been. I'm so pleased Jackson has always had the confidence to go after his dreams, though."

"So, you guys got together, pre-Blossom?" I asked.

He nodded as he grinned. "I didn't sign up for a Drag Queen, now look at me."

"You wouldn't have it any other way."

"Exactly," he said nodding.

I grinned then turned. I sat up a little better when I saw Jamie in the doorway, his hand over his mouth, he looked like he was about to start crying.

"I'm sorry," I said quickly, he shook his head. "I, he just started telling me and…"

"Don't be sorry, Luca." Jamie said as he came towards me, his hand resting on my back as he smiled at me.

"Luca," Dylan repeated nodding. "I knew it was something like that." He muttered to himself then looked up at Jamie and smiled like it was the first time he'd ever lay eyes on him. It made my heart stutter over a few beats. "I told you he was beautiful," he stated.

Jamie scoffed shaking his head. "I don't know what you're after but you're not getting it," he told Dylan, who smirked right back at him.

"I'm not after anything," Dylan whispered loudly to me; I covered my mouth so I wouldn't laugh out loud. "I mean, I already married him."

"You remember that, huh?" Jamie said.

"Like it was yesterday. You were worried because it was raining when we woke up." He glanced at me, "we broke tradition the night before you see…" he told me before looking back at Jamie. "We had matching suits, and we both had cherry blossoms on our waistcoats and ties. We walked down the aisle together, because that was the only logical thing for us to do, and it stopped raining just before the reception."

"Yes, yes it did." Jamie said.

"We should do that again sometime."

"What? Get married?" Jamie laughed but it almost sounded sad.

"Yes," Dylan stated. "It's been… fifty years." He shook his head, "fifty-two. Wow."

"Wow is right." I said amused. We all turned towards the door when Jackson came through it.

"Sorry. I was deep in pins for Reed's dress this week, I couldn't walk away from it. It'd literally all fall apart."

"Don't worry," I told him, "I've been having a very interesting conversation with Dylan." I said.

He frowned at me, the confusion clear before he turned to look at Dylan. "What?"

"Jackson," Dylan said fondly. "Your Grandad and I are getting remarried."

"You're what?" Jackson laughed. "Does that mean I get to be there this time, I feel like I missed out on quite the party last time."

"You did, Jackson," Dylan informed him. "Oh sorry you guys are off on a date aren't you. I don't mean to interrupt. Don't want to eat into time with your boyfriend," he added.

Jackson blushed almost instantly, I assume as much I had been when Dylan had called me out for it.

"That was a mean Grandfather move," Jamie told him. "But I am also curious of when you two are going to get on with admitting this?"

"I... I'm not... well we're not putting it off," Jackson said quietly. "We've just..."

"Not used that word yet," I offered. "Not because I don't want to use it... like."

"No, no not for that reason, no I just... I don't know we..."

"He's definitely our Grandson," Dylan said.

Jamie laughed. "We've just made it really awkward for the two of you, haven't we?"

"Yep," Jackson said. "Thanks guys."

The dock was all ready for Christmas. I don't quite know when they found time to put all the decorations and the markets up, *nor* the giant central Christmas tree that was yet to be turned on, but town had been transformed into a winter wonderland and I *loved* it.

"What?" I whispered when I turned and caught

Jackson's eye. He grinned at me lifting our hands together and squeezing gently.

"You just look so happy."

"I am. I love Christmas. Well, I love Winter and all the lights." I cleared my throat, "sorry."

"Do not apologise."

"I've never been ice skating, " I told him. "I don't even know if it'll stay upright."

"Honey. I have no doubt you will," he said. "I've seen the heels you can walk in. Ice skating? Pfft."

I laughed happily. "I bet you a hot chocolate, I'll fall on the ice within seconds of stepping onto it."

"Bet's on," he said. "I like cream and marshmallows for the record."

"I bet you do," I laughed.

We paid for half an hour. We were given perfectly white ice skates, the blades sharp and then we were just let onto the ice. No guide, no tips, just *off you go*.

Jackson owed me a hot chocolate the *moment* I stepped into the rink. I turned to look at him as I sat on the ice, smiling as he laughed bending over himself with the giggles.

"Marshmallows, cream, the whole lot. For *that*, you can have the hot chocolate, marshmallows, cream *and* a cake if you want."

I managed to stand myself up with the help of the side. Holding on tight as he stepped on after me, his arms flailing so I grabbed for him. Linking our arms together and somehow keeping him upright.

He squeezed me a little tighter, holding my arm with both of his and then we began to move.

157

Jackson

My Dad was waiting for me when I pushed open the front door. I stopped as he stood from the stairs, he didn't say a word as he walked towards me. I pulled my key from the door.

"We..." he cleared his throat. "We didn't want to interrupt your date. We thought it'd be best to let you enjoy that."

"When?" I whispered.

"Three," he swallowed. "He... he told Jamie he was tired. So, they went up to bed. Jamie stayed with him, just *because*. He was there."

I nodded taking a step closer to him. "Dad." I saw him break a little, his posture stuttering so I hugged him. He wrapped his arms around my head, hugging me back, kissing the top of my head and then he let go.

"Go to him," he said as I looked up at him. "Go."

So, I did. I ran up the two flights of stairs, into the attic. I took a step in then stopped as Avory looked towards me.

"Come in, baby," he said gently, so I did closing the door behind me and walking around the bed. I stopped at the end, kneeling at Jamie and Avory's feet. I reached out, stroking my hand down Jamie's leg.

He looked up at me, from where he had his head buried in Avory's chest. His eyes red rimmed, his face tear stained. I swallowed.

"Jackson," Jamie said, his voice rough.

"I'm sorry," I whispered.

He reached for me taking my hand then pulled me between them. "Oh, baby, don't be." I sat between him and Avory. His head against mine, as Avory took my hand, stroking his thumb over the back of my hand as we weaved our fingers around each other's. "He was *all* here today. Dead set on us renewing our vows. We talked about things we hadn't recounted in years. It was nice, *bittersweet.*"

"Dad said he felt tired," I whispered.

Jamie nodded as he stroked down my cheeks with his thumb. "He did, but that wasn't uncommon, I didn't think anything of him wanting to sleep for an hour or so but I don't normally come up here with him.

"For some reason I did, I don't know why. He fell asleep, and I just stayed."

"He was asleep?"

Jamie nodded a single tear rolling down his cheek. He sighed wiping it. "He wasn't in pain. If anything, I'd say he was the most content he's been in a long time."

I nodded then looked at Avory. "He sent me a text." Avery told me nodding towards Jamie. "I came over as soon as I received it. By the time I got here, Evan knew, and the ambulance was on its way."

"I'm sorry I wasn't here." I said.

"I'm not," Jamie said so I looked at him. "I'm not at all. I'm glad you weren't here in fact. Your last memory will always be him embarrassing you and Luca." His smile was wary. I looked down at my hands.

"What did he do?" Avory whispered nudging my

arm, I shook my head lightly.

"He basically said that Luca was my boyfriend, and we hadn't really got around to saying that, *quite* yet."

"Oh," Avory sighed. "Why *aren't* you boyfriends yet?"

"We should be talking about this, we…"

"I want to know too," Jamie said. "I don't understand why you two aren't boyfriends either."

"I…" I said then looked back at Avory and frowned. "I…"

"Milo and I went from not really knowing each other, to boyfriends," Avory said.

"So did Dylan and I. I mean we *knew* each other, we were in the same class, but we hardly knew each other we just had a few conversations and then we were boyfriends."

"Thirty-six years later…"

"Forty-three, we were together for seven years before we got married," he said softly, his hand stroking through my hair.

"We've only got forty-two years under our belt," Avory said. "But it was still the best spontaneous decision we made. I'm sure Jamie will agree."

"Oh, Dylan was the best decision I ever made. He took great delight in telling everyone who'd listen that I was shy when we started dating, and I was.

"I mean, my Mum didn't want anything to do with me. I lived with my Auntie, and she was *good*, I mean she was great. She made sure I was well looked after but I *always* knew my Mum didn't want me, didn't love me, she was clear about *that*.

"I went quiet because of that. I hid and kept out of trouble because I didn't want to give her any further reason to not want me and then I met Dylan, and Dylan was…" he let out of breath. "We were sixteen. I hadn't quite finished puberty yet, I looked like a *baby* and he, he had braces and *so* many freckles and was letting his hair grow because we were just out of school and he didn't have to have a buzzcut anymore.

"But he was beautiful, he was one of the first boys I really looked at and thought 'you're beautiful'. I figured I liked freckles, too." He crinkled his nose at me, I did it back. "I thought about him so often it was *embarrassing,* really. I kept trying to find ways to talk to him, but I was so scared, so shy."

"How did you two end up talking then?" I asked.

"Jonathan," he answered. "He was mine and Dylan's acting tutor. He tried so hard to get me to talk, to perform. He tried *everything* and then, one lesson I was paired with Dylan for an exercise and well apparently, he felt like he'd cracked it.

"He manipulated his lessons so we kept working together. He set us as partners for an assignment and Dylan gave me his number. We talked and talked and talked and well, a week later he asked me out on a date. We were boyfriends by the end of the date."

"Really?" I breathed, he nodded amused. "I also didn't know Jonathan was your teacher, too."

"Oh, yes," he said a soft laugh in his voice. "He was who made me audition for the Rose Quartet."

"You've never told me that," I said.

"Dylan and I did a degree year after our two years in college. Jonathan taught us on that, too. That year we had to do an original show Jonathan wrote.

"The character he wrote for me a kind of fairy godmother role. I was the narrator, and the advice giver and the observer." He looked at me. "I was a Drag Queen."

"He was that blatant?"

"Yep," he said nodding, "He worked with me individually until I got to a point of being confident enough with performing on my own, *then* he told George about me."

"So, it was Jonathan. *This* was all Jonathan?" I asked waving my hand in the air around us.

Jamie nodded. "My career, my family, the love of my life. Yeah, that was all Jonathan."

"Jonathan got me into the Rose Quartet, too." Avory stated. "George was ready to not give me another chance."

"What do you mean?"

"Well, I'd just left a club and found another, but it was particularly bad, paid me in alcohol encouraged me to take drugs. Then, well, you *know* the story. I was drugged. George took me to his home, made sure I was okay. Jonathan fought for him to give me another chance. So, I'm going to be your Jonathan."

"I'm already a Queen," I said.

"I know, an incredible one by the way."

"Definitely," Jamie whispered as he kissed the back of my head.

"You're a Queen without... I was going to say King but they're both Queens," Avory said to Jamie.

"Two Queens can rule."

"You think I should ask Luca to be my boyfriend? You both do?"

"Yes," Avory sighed.

"Was Dylan one of your reasons?" Jamie asked. My face must've given me away. "Baby," he sighed hugging me a little closer.

"It was just so hard, and I didn't want to bring someone else into it. I didn't want Luca to start dating me then get *oh I'm asexual*, and *my Grandad's really sick*. I didn't want him to run away."

"I don't think he would've," Avory whispered. "I spoke to him, remember. I don't think he'd have ever ran."

"I'm sorry," I told Jamie, "It was selfish and *stupid* and childish, but I was so scared and then he started to get worse and I just… it went from not wanting to bring Luca into all of it, to feeling bad because it wasn't the time for me to get a boyfriend when I was losing my Grandad."

"Oh, sweetheart," Jamie sighed as he hugged me closer. "Oh, darling, no. Dylan loved Luca *and* he hardly knew him but he was so invested in your relationship, he wanted to know details. He wanted to know how things went. You made him so happy. You and Rosie, anything you did made him so happy, so proud. He'd have been elated if you'd told us you were with Luca. He would've loved that, I would've. I'd go as far to say even your parents would've. None of us would've been upset with you. None."

I nodded letting out a long breath. "Tell me more stories about Dylan."

"Where should I begin?" Jamie asked.

I smiled at him as I pushed back more comfortably against Avory. "The beginning, please. With baby faced Jamie and the boy with freckles and braces and too-long-hair."

Luca

I stopped as I stepped through the door. Frowning deeply at Mateo as xe sat on the tabletop, the brush between xer knees, xer head buried deep in xer hands as xer shoulders shuck.

I didn't even think, I walked towards xem, wrapping my arms around xem and hugging them tight. Xe jumped looking up at me then gasping and wrapping xer arms back around me.

"Coffee or tea?" I asked. Xe shook xer head, swallowing deeply as xer continued to sob. "Hey hey, Mateo talk to me. Talk to me." I whispered.

Xe composed xemself, wiping xer cheeks and breathing in and out a few times. "I…" xe breathed again. "I got a text last week from a guy I slept with a few months back," Xe buried xer head in xer hands again. "He said I needed to go the doctors."

"What?" I whispered then shook my head. "What is it? Chlamydia? Gonorrhoea?"

"HIV," Xe breathed. I met xer eyes as they swallowed roughly. "It's HIV, I've got HIV."

"Mateo," I whispered.

I… I assumed like you its Chlamydia or Gonorrhoea. I've had both before, antibiotics cleared up. All his message said was you need to go to the doctors, so I asked him what I was looking for."

"And you're sure? Sure you're positive?"

Xe reached into xer pocket, pulling out a booklet. It read, *Information on HIV and AIDS*.

"I got called back in and they told me, they sat there and just said you're positive Mateo your test results came back positive. They did another test just to make sure, and it came back positive, too."

"I…" I said.

"It's okay, darling, I know you don't know what to say. If I helps, I'm okay, in the sense that I don't feel sick. I don't have any symptoms. I'm not quite okay in the sense of mentally. Honestly."

"Mateo," I breathed.

"He didn't know, at all. Like I called him just to talk, not to shout. We talked for hours. He was distraught so apologetic and I felt so bad for him. I really did. I don't blame him. I blame myself."

"Why?" I whispered.

"I…" xe rubbed xer forehead. "I don't use condoms." Xe cut me off before I could shout. "I know it's stupid. I know okay, I don't need a lecture I just… yeah. He was happy to go without. We both agreed, consented. It's happened now. I don't know what to do. Well, I do, I know I've got to go to see a specialist who'll give me pills."

"You'll be okay," I whispered. Xe looked at me so I nodded. "You will, you'll be fine. People with HIV live long, healthy lives now. It isn't… it isn't like it used to be."

"I know, I know," Xe said. "I know. I just… you don't think do you? My grandparents told me stories about their friends, their friends dying from this cancer-like-disease that there was no cure for, so many boys died."

"It's been so long. So much has changed. You're going to live, Mateo."

Xe hugged me, burying xer head into my shoulder.

"What do you want to do?" I asked.

Xe shook xer head running xer fingers through xer hair. "I don't know, Luca. I don't want to cry anymore. I've been crying since I left the doctors."

"Come see the show," I suggested. "On Saturday, come to the Rose Quartet. You deserve a night out to just chill and I *figure* you don't want to go out on the pull so to speak.

"You also haven't seen me do drag yet, and I think you'll enjoy it, and it's Lemon and Lime's first show. They're moving down here this week, so…"

"Luca," xe sighed.

I shrugged. "One night, at *least* come see Beau, if you want to leave after that do so, but you need to be… distracted."

"Luca I…"

"Please. *Come* on you need to meet Jackson, right?"

Xe smiled. "Okay," xe breathed. "Okay, okay. Fine, I'll come see you do drag."

"You don't have to finish the shift."

"You can't say I need to be distracted then insinuate I shouldn't work."

"That's true," I said thoughtfully.

"It's okay. I'm okay." Xe stood from the table. "I'm not okay but fuck it. I'm going to eat some cake don't tell your Pa."

"Course not," I whispered as I took my apron off the hook.

"I love you, Luca."

"I love you, too," I said. "I really do."

"Tell me about your date."

"No, I…"

"Luca. Please."

"We went ice skating…"

I took a few steps back after I'd knocked on the door, ready to run away if it was called upon. I wasn't sure if I was *invited* but if there was anyone I could talk to right now it was Jackson.

I frowned at the man who answered the door because I hadn't seen him before.

"Hello?" I offered.

"Luca?" he asked, his voice uncertain. I nodded and he smiled at me. "Hello, Luca. I'm Evan."

"Jackson's Dad," I said. He nodded his smile soft but his eyebrows furrowed.

"What are you doing here?"

"I wanted to talk to Jackson."

"Did he call you?"

I shook my head slowly. "I can leave."

"No, no. I just…" he looked into the house then back to me. "He'll probably want to see you."

"What's happened?" I asked. "He hasn't said anything."

Well *technically* we hadn't really talked. Now that I thought about it there had been a somewhat radio silence from Jackson, but I hadn't really noticed because my phone had been full of Mateo and Oakley with wedding plans.

"Dylan passed," Evan said quietly.

"I'm so sorry."

He nodded. "Thank you. He's in his room, have you ever been to his room?"

"No."

"Well, I don't know, you might've visited other times *and* been in his room."

"I... no... we've..."

"Luca?"

I turned towards Jamie as he passed through the hallway a teacup in his hand. I let out a thankful breath because I was so close to telling Jackson's Dad that we hadn't had sex.

"Came to see Jackson, I *think* I just made him nervous."

"I'm sure," Jamie said. "You know how I like it." he added passing Evan the cup. "Come on, chick, I'll show you to Jackson's room."

I stepped past Evan, trying to hide my blush as I followed Jamie up to the stairs.

"I'm sorry about your husband," I said.

He squeezed my shoulder. "Jackson didn't explain about Dylan, did he?" he said softly as we reached the top of the stairs.

I shook my head. "Well, no, but he did say he was your King Consort and that you guys were like meant to be."

"I'll let Jackson tell you," he said then stopped so I stopped alongside him and turned and gasped at the rat cage. I touched my fingers to the wiring grinning when the white rat sniffed at my fingers. I glanced up at Jamie as he watched me, his expression *almost* pleased.

"Do you have rats?"

"Cats," I replied. "My grandparents love cats."

"Do you want to hold them?"

"Please."

He smiled as he opened the cage. "Cup your hands, Sugar will step into them when she decides whether she likes you."

I cupped my hands.

"We'll take them into Jacks, give him some rat therapy," he said as the white rat sniffed at my fingers, before reaching for me. Her nose lifted towards the sky before she seemed to decide that she liked me and stepped into my palm.

"Hello," I whispered.

"Sugar... and Spice," he said as he offered his hand to the black rat. The rat climbed onto his hand and began up his arm without thought.

"Sugar and Spice," I repeated happily before following him to one of the bedroom doors. Jamie knocked gently.

Jackson welcomed him in from the inside.

"Visitors," Jamie said as he stepped into the room. I followed watching as Jamie took Spice from his shoulder and put her on Jackson's bed.

Jackson sighed happily so I looked up. He was lying on his bed, his back to the door in a gorgeous canopy bed with little pink fairy lights wound around each of the posts. They were all turned on.

"You okay, baby?" Jamie asked softly stroking his hand down Jackson's arm. He sighed but turned to look at Jamie.

"I'm okay," he answered, his eyes meeting mine. He sat up. "Luca?"

"Hi," I said awkwardly.

"Hi," he repeated, then looked down towards Spice as she ran around his bed.

"Aw young love," Jamie commented. "I'm going to leave you two be." He squeezed my shoulder again as he went to leave.

"I'm sorry I didn't text you back," he whispered.

"I'm sorry about your Grandad."

He nodded as he sat himself up better on his bed. "Come sit," he offered before directing Spice with his hands. I walked around the bed, sitting next to him, kicking my shoes off then crossing my legs. Sugar ran up my arm then down my chest before going around my crossed legs.

I turned to Jackson when he leant his head on my arm.

"Dylan had Alzheimer's," he told me. "He developed it when I was fifteen. This last year he started getting worse. He started forgetting who I was, or who Jamie was."

I leant my head on his, he sighed.

"When you spoke to him, when he remembered everything, Jamie told me it was something called terminal lucidity. He'd been told he could remember but that'd mean it was close to the end."

"That's why he looked so sad when he came into me talking to him?" I whispered, Jackson nodded against my shoulder. "I'm sorry that should've been your conversation."

"No," he said. "No, that's okay and he was peaceful. I just... I miss him."

I wrapped my arm around him, stroking my fingers over his arm. "Was he your baggage?" I asked, then cursed myself, looking up towards the top of his canopy.

Jackson nodded against me. "I didn't want you to have to deal with this. I didn't think that was fair *to* you."

"Jackson, he isn't baggage," I said. "He's family. I understand, don't worry. I just... this isn't a burden."

He looked up at me, I offered him a wary smile before wiping his cheek with my thumb.

"Tell me about Dylan," I suggested. "Tell me things about him. I only met him once."

He gave me a wobbly smile back before looking up at the top of the canopy. "These are his rats. Rats were kind of his thing. And he made my bed."

We lay quietly facing each other in his bed. Sugar and Spice running around between our legs, as we took turns stroking over each other's palms.

He'd recounted all kinds to me, childhood memories, and holidays. Things Dylan had done for him like his bed, or a playhouse he'd built when him and his sister were small. He spoke and cried, and I listened until he fell silent.

I wasn't all too sure how long we'd actually been lying like this before he frowned.

"What?" I whispered.

He looked up at me. "Why did you come here? It wasn't because I wasn't replying."

"No," I said quietly. "I got some... news." I cleared my throat. "I just wanted someone to talk to."

"What news?" he asked. I shook my head. "Don't be daft. *You* wanted someone to talk to, so, talk to me."

"But..."

"Luca," he said, so I looked down at our hands. His finger was currently drawing circles on the palm of my hand.

"My best friend, Mateo," I said then cleared my throat. "He told me he's positive."

"Positive," he repeated, "like HIV positive?"

I nodded.

"Shit."

"I invited him to the club this week to watch the show, but I didn't really know what else to do, or say. Anything. I just..."

"It's good you invited him to the club," he said as he weaved our fingers around each other's. I shook my head. "The clubs got a lot of experience with HIV."

"Why?"

"The owner, like, the man who started it all was

171

positive. He was a really early case, in the eighties when no-one knew anything about it. He died in nineteen eighty-five, a few weeks after George was hired as a Queen.

"Since then, the Rose Quartet has been a *big* pioneer for the AIDS movement, they've held fundraisers and benefits and rallies. All kinds and they still are.

"I've grown up hearing about his legacy always, but it's always kind of partnered with a safe sex lecture." He rose his eyebrow at me.

"What was his name?"

He laughed. "Jack."

"Like Jackson?"

"Yep. His drag persona was Rose."

"Wait, *wait*, Jack and Rose, like Titanic?"

"The club opened in the late sixties so *no*," he said shaking our hands together. "But I *was* named after him and my sister, her."

"Rosie," I whispered. "Oh my god, Jackson and Rosie, Jack and Rose."

"It was George, he influenced my parents, *but* he'd also managed to persuade his son to name his child Chandler."

I frowned. "I don't get it."

"George's drag persona was Crystal Chandelier."

"He named his grandson after his Queens last name?" He nodded. "I'm really scared for Mateo."

"HIV is scary." he whispered. "But it's come so far, it's not the death sentence it used to be."

"I know, but it's still not *good*."

"No," he agreed. "We'll help you though. I will, and Jesse and Jason will."

I nodded.

"We'll look after you *and* Mateo."

"Thank you," I whispered, he lifted our hands,

kissing the back of mine.

"Luca? Will you be my boyfriend?"

I smiled looking down at our hands before raising them to my lips. I kissed the back of his hand.

"Yes, Jackson. I would *love* to be your boyfriend."

He smiled, big and wide then laughed covering his mouth so I grinned back at him before doing it myself.

He touched my wrist. "I like your braces. *And* have only just realised your caps are purple."

I nodded. "I like your glasses."

He blushed lightly as I pushed his glasses up his nose.

Jackson

I stopped as I stepped through the door. Smiling beside myself before running towards my sister. I knocked her backwards when I wrapped my arms around her. Us both bouncing on my bed as she cuddled me back.

"I have missed you," I told her. "Tell me *everything* about university. Right now."

She shook her head tapping my chest as she laughed. "Not right now. Tell me, how everyone's been? How's Jamie doing?"

I sighed. "He's walking around like he's okay," I told her as we moved to sit properly on my bed. "But I *know* he's excusing himself to his bedroom to cry a lot. I accidently walked in on him two nights ago."

"Oh no, did he play it off?"

"No. He welcomed me into his bed. We hugged, cried, and spoke some more. I didn't tell Dad though, I figured that'd make it worse."

"Course."

"I invited Jamie to the club tomorrow, to watch me because I figured he needed a distraction."

"And the club is the ultimate distraction," she agreed.

"Did he remember? Towards the end? Did he remember anything?"

"Some. He was really clear the days leading to *it*, but it was… fleeting."

"I'm sorry I wasn't here."

"Don't be," I whispered. "I wasn't here either."

"Where were you?"

I bit my lip.

"Spill Jackson."

"I was on a date," I said. "But we'll talk about that another time, too. Have you seen Jamie?"

"No, only Mum, then I came up here. Did you bring Avory back with you?"

"And Milo," I said in a sigh. "They've been around a lot this week."

"Hard to believe they once hated each other," she said amused as she took my hand and stood pulling me behind her. We stood outside my room, looking towards the attic then the stairs.

"I think they're downstairs. Well, Avory and Milo are. Jamie might not be." I spun her around so I could lead her upstairs. Jamie *was* in his room. He turned surprised to me when I stepped through the door.

"Hello, gorgeous," he said before turning back to his wardrobe. I wasn't all too sure what he was doing.

"Avory and Milo are here."

"I believe they're responsible for tea tonight," he said then turned completely to me. He smiled at me *then* his entire expression lit up. "Rosie, darling."

Rosie let go of my hand, stepping past me to go to Jamie and hug him. They began talking quietly to each other. I took a seat on the end of Jamie's bed. A position I'd been in a *lot* especially before I got a room of my own as I stored many of my body dummies in his bedroom *and* his lair.

175

In fact, his room looked pretty bare without all *my* stuff. It was all clean and straight lines. The walls cream with wooden borders, large built-in wardrobes, with a mirror on the furthest door. A big multi frame on the wall, with pictures of my Dad when he was little, and Rosie and I when we were as small. Memories of Jamie and Dylan from when they were teenagers to holidays when I was a teenager and of course so many different Queen memories.

"How long are you home lovely?"

"Just the weekend, I've got a lecture on Monday but I had to come home."

"Thank you," Jamie whispered. "Are you *also* coming to the club tomorrow? To see Jackson *and* his new boyfriend perform."

"You didn't just do that." I laughed. Jamie winked at me as Rosie turned to me, she hit my arm.

"You said a date, you didn't say a date with your *boyfriend*."

"Later," I stated. "I'll talk to you as I prepare for the show, okay." I gasped, looking towards Jamie, "and I'll get you back for *that*."

Jamie laughed it *actually* sounded joyful. "So worth it."

Dinner was loud given my entire family was in attendance, *most* of our conversations centred around Rosie and her University experience, so no one focused for all too long on how sad we all were.

It was a bottle of wine later when Rosie and I excused ourselves to go upstairs. Wishing our family a good night as Jamie began to open a second bottle.

"I want to hear *everything* about your boyfriend," Rosie said as I picked up my wash bag.

"Come on then," I replied quietly raising my eyebrow at her then leading her to the bathroom. "His name is

Luca," I started as I sat on the edge of the bath, unzipping my wash bag and holding up a packet of blackhead strips to her.

She laughed reaching out her hand to me, so I gave her a strip.

"How did you guys meet?"

"The Club. He's a new Queen." She gasped as I flattened the strip over my nose. I grinned as she did the same.

"That's so right," she said, I rose my eyebrow at her. "Well the only person who'd be a good match for you would also be a Queen."

"Really?"

"Well yeah."

"You also thought Charlie was perfect for me."

"Does he still work?"

"Yes. Jason said he can't fire him for cheating on me," I shrugged.

"He wasn't right for you, I mean come on, you were together in school, I'm not with *any* of the boys I was with in school."

"It still hurts sometimes."

"Why?" she whispered. I frowned at her. "It's been over a year, Jackson; I assume he's gotten over you."

"I don't know, he didn't get with Zach. At least as far as I know."

"Well, you've gotten over him then, *because* Luca."

"Yeah, but he still cheated and what if that's because I'm demisexual, what if he cheated because of who I am?"

"He cheated because he *cheated*. It wasn't anything you did. You're *not* to blame for Charlie cheating on *you*. You gave him everything. I remember you giving him everything. You gave so much of yourself and a lot of the time you did so unwillingly.

"Jackson you're not the reason he cheated, *he* is, and *he* shouldn't be the reason you're *what*? Hesitant with Luca?"

"I really do like Luca," I whispered. She grinned as I got my razor out of my bag. "Queen Beau."

"Oh, I think I like Luca," she offered, then waved at me as if to say *give* me more. "I want to hear solely about Luca from now on. Okay, deal?"

"Deal." I laughed then pointed at my nose. She nodded squeezing her eyes shut.

"Three," she whispered.

"Two."

"One," we said together and then we pulled.

I was in Jason's arms the moment I stepped through the door. His hug loving and tight, almost as if I'd had a weighted blanket wrapped around me that smelt like home.

I wanted to stay wrapped up in him forever.

"How are you doing, Princess?" he whispered.

I nodded. "It's been… hard. Really hard, but Rosie's come home for the weekend and Milo and Avory have been around every day."

"Good, good. Jesse and I said we were going to drop by tomorrow. Take some flowers for Jamie have some tea." He hummed, "or whisky." I laughed quietly as he kissed my forehead. "You didn't have to come today."

"I did," I said nodding. "For Jamie. *He's* coming to see the show. I thought it'd distract him for a little while."

"Good idea," he said. "Very good."

"Jason."

We turned together, I smiled when I saw Luca crouched at the end of the stage, talking to Jesse. Although now they were both looking at us. Luca

178

grinned at me; I winked back at him.

"I better return to the rehearsal. If you need *anything*, Jackson."

"You'll be the first person I ask."

He nodded squeezing my arm gently before saying, "Yes Jesse, what do you require of me?"

I smiled then turned to walk to the dressing rooms. I was stopped immediately.

I went to snap; Charlie rose his hand, a sigh in his shoulders so I bit my tongue.

"I'm sorry. I heard about Dylan."

I looked down at my feet.

"I wanted to give you my condolences. That was all."

I nodded. "Thank you."

"I loved Dylan. Really, he was always interesting and so funny."

I hummed then looked up. "Thank you, Charlie."

He sighed. "I'm sorry you know, I've said it over and over, I'm sorry."

"And I don't forgive you. I've said *that* over and over."

"I know you got me moved. You were who got me moved from Beau."

"And if I was?"

Charlie shook his head. "This is my job, Jackson; you can't just demote me. I got a pay rise going from an ASM to a Queen's ASM and then what? Xavier decided to go in a different direction."

"Once a liar always a liar," I said. "I know for a *fact* that when I, yes, I asked Jesse to move you from Beau that he planned to allocate you to the fourth Queen that they were hiring.

"In fact, have hired and start tonight. Don't try and guilt trip me. Don't try and make me feel like shit."

"*This* is my job."

"And *this* is my family so leave me alone."

"You're impossible, Jackson. You've always been impossible, and it won't work out with him," he said pointing behind me. I didn't need to turn to know he was pointing at Luca.

"Oh yeah, whys that?"

"Because of you, because of who you are. He says he can handle it now, but he can't, and he won't want to. I wouldn't be surprised if he slept with someone else."

"Shut up," I shouted at him. "You don't know anything about us. You don't know a thing."

"I know you; I know you better than most people and I know you don't deserve love. The way you treated me, the way you lied to me, and made me feel bad about wanting sex."

"Shut up, Charlie, *shut* up and fuck off."

I was grabbed. An arm wrapping around my chest and pulling me back. "Don't you have some tech notes to get." I looked up at Jesse as he scowled at Charlie. "Go."

Charlie rolled his eyes turning and walking away from us. Jesse held me a little closer.

"Don't cry," he whispered. "You'll ruin your makeup."

"I'm not wearing any yet." My voice was weak.

"Be strong." We both watched as Charlie stepped through the door. "Come on," he added turning us and taking my hand. "Nothing to see here," he said to Jason and Luca. "Continue, Queen," he added as he took me up to his office.

He sat me on the chaise lounge that looked out over the club, I turned on it watching Luca through the large window as he ran through his rehearsal.

Jesse soon came and sat beside me, passing me a teacup. His hand rubbing over my back.

"You can cry now if you want." I buried my head

into my hands. "What did he say, Jacks?"

"It doesn't matter."

"It does." I turned to look at him. "It really does, and I would like to know what he said that upset you so much."

"I don't deserve love."

He turned to me. "You know that isn't true."

I shook my head. "What if it is? What if I don't deserve it. He said he wouldn't be surprised if Luca cheated. He'd go and sleep with someone else." I began to cry. "He said I made him feel bad about wanting sex and what if I did? All this time I thought of him as the one who pressured me, but what if it was me?"

"Jackson, no."

"No?"

"No," he repeated so I looked at him. "No. You *do* deserve love, you do, and Luca will *not* cheat on you."

"You don't know that for sure."

"No, I don't know that for sure, but you know what I *do* know?"

I shook my head.

"I know that Luca arrived here at eleven this morning – as requested. He asked after you right away, when I said you weren't coming in until twelve, he was disappointed *and* even then he didn't stop talking about you.

"Everything we said he'd find a way back round to you and he spoke with such, I don't want to say love, I don't want to say that for you but such admiration, such joy.

"We could all feel it. He's a good kid and he'll be good to you as I'm sure you'll be good to him. Ignore Charlie okay, he's bitter and vindictive and most of all he is wrong.

"You do deserve love, you in fact are so loved and you do deserve Luca."

I knocked my head against his chest.

"I know it's hard. Believe me, I know. I'm going to be sixty *far* sooner than I'd like to admit. I realised I was asexual when I was sixteen and I put that domination on myself. I told myself that love was about sex *so* I didn't deserve love.

"I didn't let myself love anyone. I didn't allow myself to do that. Even the beginning with Isaac. I refused to believe he could even entertain the idea of loving me and you know *what?*"

"What?" I whispered.

He smiled at me stroking my hand. "At this point I hadn't even *spoken* to him, never mind told him I was asexual."

"And he doesn't care?"

"No, baby. He loves me and *honestly,* he has to remind me of this a lot. Sometimes, even now, I will be lying opposite him in bed and *have* to ask him if he still loves me, even though I don't give him sex. He always does."

"Has he ever cheated?"

"No," he said quietly then cleared his throat. "No, when we were in our thirties, I offered it to him. I said, he could go and sleep with a random guy if he wanted to, if he needed to. He said no, he didn't want to. He is just gay, *straight* up homosexual and he has never, *never* resented me for being asexual. *Never.*

"Charlie is not a nice person, Jackson. Simple as. He's being horrible for the sake of being horrible so don't listen to him. *Don't* enable him."

I nodded taking a deep breath.

"Talk to Luca," he continued. "The only people who get a say in your relationship is you and him, so talk to Luca, and ignore Charlie.

"He's been allocated to Lemon and Lime so he won't be anywhere near you but if he pulls something like this again…" he sighed.

"Who's Beau's new ASM?" I asked quietly as I watched the end of Luca's rehearsal through the window.

"Chandler."

I glanced at Jesse.

"Well, we figured *now* you're together you're more likely to keep getting ready in the same dressing room, you might as well have the same technician *and* Chandler will keep you two in line."

I laughed wiping my cheeks with my hand as I did. He smiled brightly at me.

"Be honest with him, okay. Be *transparent* and truly honest with Luca. Your feelings might change and that's okay, so long as he always knows where you're at and you know where he is."

"He's gay," I whispered.

Jesse nodded looking out the window himself. "There's other reasons someone might not be comfortable with sex. They're not always to do with their sexuality, it can be any reason like not being ready, having body issues, or confidence issues. Just talk to each other, yeah."

"Yeah," I sighed.

"Now come downstairs and meet our new Queens," he said so I stood, looking down at the club as Luca and Jason waved towards the door.

Out of drag, Lemon and Lime were a presence. They looked completely identical in their face but other than that I was *sure* once I knew their names, I would be able to tell them apart. I followed Jesse from the office down the stage. Stepping up onto it as Jesse reintroduced himself to Lemon and Lime.

"Jackson…" he said. I waved, they both waved back. "Or as you saw her, Queen Madison."

I bowed my head as Luca laughed beside me nudging

against me so we rocked together.

"You okay?" he whispered into my ear. I swallowed nodding lightly before turning to him, his eyes examined me until he seemed to decide that I *was* in fact okay.

"This is Felix and Phil," Jason said. I ensured I took note *completely* of who he'd pointed to when he'd said their names.

"He, him?" Luca asked.

"They, them," Felix said then cleared his throat. "*He's* he, him. I'm genderfluid."

"Awesome," Luca said quietly.

Felix smiled back at us. They had their black hair tightly braided and pulled up into a bun, their eyes a deep brown and snakebite piercings. They wore dark green dungarees with a mustard long sleeved top underneath, and white high-top converse.

Phil had his hair shaven. His eyes as deep of a brown and wore a simple grey hoodie and ripped skinny jeans with classic Vans. He appeared far shier than Felix.

"Your accent, isn't London?" I said.

Felix shook their head. "South Africa," they said then glanced at Phil. "Originally anyway, we've lived in London since we were twelve."

"And which of you is which Queen?" Jason asked.

"I'm Lemon, he's Lime," Felix answered.

Jason nodded then waved behind them, so I looked, grinning at Reed as he stepped through the door.

"Ah, just in time our Queen." Jason said.

Reed laughed cheerfully. "Were you waiting for me?"

"Aren't we always." I teased.

Luca

"I'm not going to lie to you," I said as I fastened my jeans. "I fancy them a bit." He scowled; I tried my best not to laugh *but* I did grin at him. His scowl softened as I pulled my hoodie over my head. "I'm not going to do anything... I just thought you should know."

"They're your type?" he asked.

I shrugged as I thought about it *because* I'd never really had a type, at least not that I was aware of. "I guess so... maybe I've just got a thing for drag queens." I widened my eyes at him, he smiled back although it wasn't all there. "Jackson?"

"I just *wasn't* expecting you to tell me you liked someone else. Less than a week..."

"Oh no, I..." I sighed. "I don't know, my dads have always done it."

"What?"

"They have, they'll frequently talk about this cute barista or someone they work with who they have a crush on or whatever. *Sorry*. Did I just completely mess this up *one* week in?"

"No," he said quickly. "No, I'm just... I've never been in a relationship like that *but*..."

"My Dad's trust each other a lot," I said. "I mean my Uncle and his partner also do it, I'm sure my Grandparents do. They all trust the other because they know they love them." I swallowed deeply. "I didn't..."

He touched my leg. I stroked my finger down the back of his hand.

"I know," he whispered. "I know, I know I'm just. This is very new."

I rose my eyebrow at him. "I've messed it up."

"No," he sighed. "No, no. I still have baggage. I've just got to shake it off."

"I won't do anything," I clarified. "At all. He's just pretty, and I quite enjoy looking at him, *but* I enjoy looking at you far more."

"Bet you didn't expect me to be so insecure."

I laughed. "Just you wait."

"Felix is *very* pretty, I do agree. I just didn't want to admit it."

"Oh, don't do *that*," I whispered. "I want to look at the cute people too, if you see someone tell me."

"Deal." He laughed then kissed my knuckles. We both turned towards the knock on the door.

"I've got someone here claiming to know you," Chandler said.

I frowned at him as Jackson laughed. "Me?"

"Luca," Chandler said softly then stepped back.

I stood. "Mateo." I squeaked as I ran towards xem, xe caught me hugging me tight. "You came, I'm so glad you came."

"Luca you were incredible," Xe gasped. "Sorry, sorry, *Queen Beau* was incredible, thank you for inviting me," xe said then kissed my cheek. I hugged xer again then turned.

"Jackson," I said putting my hand out to him, so he walked towards me, he took my hand when he was close enough, squeezing gently. "This is Mateo, my best friend."

Jackson smiled. "Luca told me your pronouns, but I just want to make sure I'm pronouncing them right."

"X-e, x-e-m," Mateo said. "Pronounced zee, zem." Xe said, then "thank you."

Jackson smiled. "I've not had too much experience with neopronouns, I just wanted to make sure I got them right."

"Queen Madison?" Mateo asked. "I'm not worthy."

"I like your best friend," Jackson told me.

I laughed as I squeezed his hand. "We need to get out front, I want to see Lemon and Lime's debut show," I told Jackson.

"And I think you'll enjoy the Queen," he told Mateo.

Xe held his hands up. "I'm willing to experience *everything*. I so wish I'd come earlier," xe said as xe followed me down the corridor and through the door into the club. We lined the back wall as, like always, the club was full, not a table to sit at.

Jesse and Jason sat near the front, *just* off to the side so that there was never a point when on stage we'd be looking at them directly. There they took notes and quietly critiqued us.

The rainbow of lights began to run around the stage before flashing brightly twice and then, the stage lit up and *one* of them was stood on the stage.

The Queen on stage stood with her hands on her hips, a multi-coloured sequin covered bra tied around her neck and hung low on her back paired with high-waisted black shorts that were turned up at the leg and a lemon sew on patch on the right leg.

I guess that made the Queen onstage, Lemon.

She wore high block heels silver and covered in glitter, and her wig was long, to her hips and crimped. It was gorgeous.

"Wow," Jackson and I breathed at the same time.

Lemon waved at the audience, grinning happily before walking down the stage and turning on her heel, she pointed towards the wings as Lime stepped out from them. Dressed identically but with a lime sewn onto her shorts.

The audience screamed in response, Lemon and Lime both laughing joyfully as the music grew around them and they began to sing.

Queenie followed Lemon and Lime's *highly* energetic set with an equally as energetic Hamilton set, that Jackson had made an impressive gown for.

We'd all congratulated him on the feat as we sat on the stage awaiting our notes from Jason and Jesse, us all a little rowdier than we'd normally be.

Mateo stayed behind with us, somehow finding himself in a conversation with Jamie and a girl who looked around my age as we waited for Reed to join us on the stage.

"Okay, okay quieten down you gaggle of Queens," Jason laughed as walked towards us with Reed. "The sooner you receive your notes, the sooner you can all go. First and foremost, I'd like to congratulate Lemon and Lime on a spectacular first show."

We all applauded together, whistling and stamping our feet as they both laughed. Waving their hands in the air and bowing dramatically at us.

"Queen Beau," Jason said searching me out, I waved at him to help him along. "Beautiful. Simple as, beautiful. Your voice, and you're growing in confidence you can tell. Your sets as always are immaculate. I would still like you to come in early next week, though, only for one more week just so we can iron out some of the things related to your stage presence and talking to the audience."

"So, Jesse is bad cop this week," Jackson whispered in my ear. I giggled then turned as Felix gasped.

"Sorry, sorry," they said reaching for their phone. "It's our meds reminder," they said as Phil passed them a pill.

"Anything we should be aware of?" Jesse asked.

Felix waved his hand. "Nothing to worry about. We've got HIV, but it's well managed."

I glanced towards Mateo as xe looked our way. Xe appeared to be thinking something over as Felix repeatedly told us to stop worrying.

"I *will* need to make note of that," Jesse said a little warily.

"Course, yes. Sorry, we should've said. It's just, a part of us now. Don't even think about it sometimes. I take two pills a day, once with breakfast then now, and Phil takes one *now*. Sorry for interrupting. I didn't mean to. Please continue with your good-cop-bad-cop routine."

Jackson and I snorted at the same time as Jason smiled at them.

"We'll talk tomorrow when we sort out your pay," Jesse said.

Felix nodded again holding their hands up whilst mouthing 'sorry' over and over. I met Mateo's eyes, xe frowned at me *so* I frowned back.

"Did you know?"

"No," I gasped. "No, I swear. I only met Felix and Phil today, I've never spoken to them before."

Xe sighed looking over my head towards the club as they locked up.

"I didn't set you up, Mateo. I wouldn't, ever, and I hope you know that," I added then turned myself, watching as Felix and Jackson laughed together. "They *could* help though, Felix is genderfluid by the way."

"I feel like you're my overbearing mother trying to get us to play with each other."

I scoffed. "I'm your concerned friend who thinks you should speak to the exceptionally cute genderfluid drag Queen who is *also* HIV positive."

"Don't say *also*," Xe whispered. "Not quite yet. I'm still trying to *figure* all that out."

"They could help you. Figure it out, I mean."

"And how are you and Jackson?" xe said. "Have you kissed yet?"

"No," I muttered.

"Had sex?"

"What do you think if we haven't even kissed."

"Well, maybe *you* should kiss him, and I'll talk to *them*," xe said.

"Deal."

"Wait, what?"

"Deal. I'll kiss Jackson, *you* talk to Felix."

"Shit," xe sighed.

I was whining, I knew that for sure. There was no way what was coming out of my mouth could be interpreted any other way than a whine, but I also didn't want to stop whining.

Oakley had impressively not hit me yet.

"Okay. I give," he stated as he passed me a bowl of popcorn. "I can't listen to it any longer use your words, Luca."

I rolled my eyes. "You sound like Grandpa," I muttered. "There, I used my words."

He scoffed hitting my knees to the side before sitting next to me. He reached out for my legs before they hit the floor, resting them over his thighs.

"From your whines I got that you're in unrequited love," he said raising his eyebrow at me as he reached for the bowl himself. I shook my head. "No? I'm wrong, which part?"

"It's very much requited," I said as I played with a particular kernel of popcorn. "In fact, we're boyfriends." I shook my head, "or partners."

"He can be your boyfriend." Oakley whispered. "We're still allowed to use the word boyfriends."

"I just didn't want to offend."

"Who, *me*?" he asked, a smirk threatening at his lips. I sighed. "It doesn't offend me that you, a cis male, have a cis male boyfriend, that's fine. It's only that both Sky and I are nonbinary that we use the word partner. It's only that Pa..." he laughed softly. "Your Grandpa is nonbinary they also use partners. You don't have to use the gender-neutral term if it's literally not applicable."

"Oh."

"He is cis male, yeah?"

"Yes," I said. "He has a trans Grandad, too, but nowhere near the level of gender nonconformity in his family. Give or take the odd Drag Queen."

"We're a very special family," Oakley said, grinning at me. "So what's the problem exactly? You like a boy who likes you back? I'm pretty sure that's a good thing."

"It's awkward."

"The beginnings of most relationships are." He stroked over my legs. "Even my relationship with Sky was awkward and we'd been best friends for two years before we finally admitted to liking each other."

"Why is it like that?"

"Honestly...?" he asked. I nodded once. "I think sometimes the prospect of sex makes it that way, which is stupid, right? Usually when you like someone, nine times out of ten you want to have sex with them."

"Even Sky?"

"What? Do I even want to have sex with Sky?"

"No, I mean was that bit awkward with them?"

"Yes, even though we were so close beforehand. We kissed and we were very open with each other but going from talking about sex to *doing* it is a big change, you have to get over the embarrassment of being naked with someone, being vulnerable, making noises you can't control."

I laughed like a child. "But you can't control them, what if they're horrendous?"

"Exactly," he sighed. "The first time we discovered I liked my piercing being played with was an experience… but, spoiler alert, usually the other person likes those noises because it means they're doing something right. Wait, is this what you're worried about, sex?"

I shrugged meekly burying my hand into my popcorn bowl again.

"You don't have to worry about sex, you've had it…" he began, before pausing and meeting my eyes. "Oh."

"Yeah," I whispered then cleared my throat, "and Jackson's asexual."

"Oh," he laughed then covered his mouth. "Sorry, sorry. I didn't mean…"

"It's okay…"

"Have you two spoken about this? Is he comfortable with sex?"

"No…" I said quietly. "He's had a boyfriend before, though."

"That doesn't necessarily mean he's comfortable."

"I know, I know that but he told me he could be, he told me the name for what he was but I can't remember it…"

"Explain it…"

"He said once he develops strong feelings, he'll feel

192

inclined to have sex, but before that there's no chance."

"Oh, he's demisexual," he said. I nodded. "Did he bring it up?"

"He did. He said he thought he was developing strong feelings for me and maybe we should talk about the whole boyfriend thing, then a bit later we were just talking and that's when he mentioned sex."

"There's nothing to be ashamed of, you know," he whispered. "It's not a bad thing to be a virgin."

"I'm nineteen."

"So?" he said.

"Even Connor's…"

"Do you *truly* believe that?" he asked. "All things considered, your little brother is all mouth and no trousers, but he's also not the point. People are ready for sex at different times."

"It seems like everyone's done it," I muttered. "When did you?"

"I…" he sighed. "I was sixteen, but my situation was complicated and I should've waited."

"For Sky?"

"For Sky," he agreed.

"Everyone I know is having sex."

"And have you been ready to?" he asked. "Well? Over the last, let's say three years, have you been ready to have sex?"

"No," I whispered.

"Then you're *exactly* where you need to be." He squeezed my knee. "You're ready now, though aren't you?"

"Why?"

"You're talking to me about it."

"I can't talk to Pa…" I said then shook my head. "Let me rephrase that. I could definitely talk to Pa about it…"

"You just don't want to," he laughed. I nodded. "Hey, count yourself lucky, we had your Grandpa who is very vocal about how conversations about sex should be normalised. I almost sliced my finger off with a potato peeler because he just started talking to me about my sex life with Sky when I was sixteen. I get it, it doesn't matter how open you are, how open minded, how confident you are, talking to your parents about sex is awkward."

"You're as open as them..." I accused.

"Now. Yeah sure, I'll sit with my dad and talk to him about that or with my Pa. I mean they've been through it; they've got a wealth of knowledge that it's worth listening to sometimes."

"Only sometimes," I laughed. He nodded knocking his head against mine. "I don't want to tell him I'm a virgin."

"Why?" he whispered.

"What if it puts him off because he thinks I have no experience or, that I'm a prude or something..."

"He was a virgin before he had sex, too," he said. "Everyone has their first time, and it's usually messy and awkward and over in a matter of minutes. Even if he's had sex, I doubt he's some sort of expert, he's only what? Nineteen?"

"Eighteen."

"He'll still be learning, too; I can guarantee that. I mean, Sky and I have been together for six years Luca, and we're still learning."

"How?"

"You've got to keep it interesting," he said dramatically. "Sometimes you might just throw something new in and see the reaction. Sometimes you might discover that, huh actually, I like that."

I laughed.

"Bring Jackson to my wedding," he suggested,

tapping my hand. "Please. Bring Jackson as your plus one."

I nodded once because I was *already* planning on it.

"And I'm sure he'll be invited to…"

I groaned. "I forgot about Christmas Tree lunch," I said lowering my head to his hand. "That's like a baptism of fire."

Jackson

"I'm not going to lie to you," Rosie said as we washed up after dinner. "Your boyfriend is the cutest person I think I've ever seen."

I laughed as I dried the *same* plate again.

"Don't you think?" she nudged against me; we swayed a few times before I sighed.

"He..." I said, then I shook my head. "It was Charlie's fault, actually. Completely Charlie's fault, if he hadn't put Luca cheating in my head I wouldn't have been bothered." I looked at Rosie as she rose her eyebrow at me.

"What?" she asked.

"Charlie said Luca will likely cheat on me, you know with the *whole* demisexual thing." I swallowed as her expression shifted to angry. "Then Luca told me he *liked* one of the new Queens and I just..."

"Wow," she said. "He sounds like he wants a healthy relationship."

I narrowed my eyes. "Are you being sarcastic?"

"No," she laughed. "He didn't feel threatened by his feelings, he didn't *think* you would either. He straight up told you that he *liked* someone without expecting repercussions for it."

"Oh," I said quietly.

"Honey, he is mature. I am envious."

"I'm so paranoid," I said. "All the time, always thinking *what if.*"

"You need to relax, Jacks. Not everyone is Charlie, *not* everyone is going to do what Charlie did. I think you need to talk to Luca about it."

I met her eyes.

"I think you're going to need to talk to Luca about sex."

"We've only been dating a week."

"So? I've usually fucked the guy by then."

I laughed in a squawky sound, she smiled at me.

"I love you, Jackson but you need to let go a bit, just talk to him, figure out where you both stand in all of this. If you don't do that, you'll forever be paranoid that you're not on the same page."

"Ugh," I moaned, she frowned at me. "*Why* do you have to start making sense?"

She laughed happily. We both turned when there was a knock on the kitchen door.

"We'll take you back to Uni," Milo said as he came into the kitchen putting his coat on. "Save you getting the train."

"That's a long drive, I couldn't possibly, Grandad."

"I'm offering," he said, then wrapped his arm around me and kissed my head. "You're not off the hook either, by the way," he added. "Avory and I would like to meet your boyfriend. Properly."

I nodded smiling at him. "Next week. How's next week?"

"Perfect," he answered before nodding to Rosie. "Come on lovely."

"Talk to your boyfriend," Rosie whispered before

kissing my cheek. "I'll see you for Christmas, I expect regular updates."

"You're *not* going to get them."

"You bore." She laughed before following Milo. "You'll have to persuade him for me," she told him, he chuckled deeply following her out of the house.

I watched them go, focusing on Milo's reverse lights through the front door window before putting the rest of the dishes away.

I boiled the kettle, poured a cup of tea and took it upstairs. Pausing in my bedroom, resting the teacup on my bedside table as I changed into my pyjamas then continuing up to the attic.

I knocked gently, opening the door as I did. Jamie barely jumped but he did wipe his eyes quickly to disguise the fact he'd been crying. It didn't work.

"Are you okay?" he asked. I nodded walking towards him and sitting beside him on the bed, I passed him the tea cup.

"Are *you* okay?"

"Yeah," he breathed then drank the tea. "Just, *first* Sunday lunch without Dylan," he nodded. "A lot has happened this weekend. I just needed to be strong."

"What?" I whispered. He looked at me, shaking his head gently. "What do you mean?"

"Something George taught us all," he sighed. "Don't cry…"

"You'll ruin your makeup," I finished. "Jesse said that to me last night."

"Why?" he asked, sounding alarmed.

"We were talking about you."

"Shut up," he laughed. "Why?"

"Charlie."

"Oh baby," he sighed. "I've got to put on a strong face. Even if I'm hurting because I've got to, haven't I.

Milo and Avory have been here every day since and I'm so grateful for them but I don't want them to see me falling apart.

"I don't want to fall apart around your Dad, or you, *or* Rosie, so I put on a brave face and stand strong. And I don't cry until I'm alone."

"Grandad," I said. "You're allowed to cry, you lost your husband."

"I know," he swallowed. "I…" He shook his head. "I miss him so much, kid. I've literally been sleeping next to him since we were seventeen because I ran away from my Aunties and moved in with him. I've never spent this long away from him and it's about to get longer and I don't quite know if I can do it."

"You can," I said softly. "Because you're one of the strongest men I know and I mean you've had some tough competition, I've literally grown up surrounded by strong men, surrounded by Queens in fact, but you are definitely the strongest Queen."

His scratched his fingers through my hair.

"I miss him, too," I told him. "I hate that life just needs to go on. I think about him all the time, when I get in bed, or when I feed Sugar and Spice. Whenever I look at Luca"

He frowned at me.

"It's stupid but I keep looking at Luca and thinking Dylan will miss everything with him. He won't be here to see me cause our first fight or help me with the relationship with a level head."

"Even though he's not here, he's still a part of your relationship, huh?"

"It's like in films when you have a guardian angel and devil on your shoulder." I looked at him. "Just so you're aware, you're the devil."

He laughed. "Good. I'm going to go to bed," he told

me. I looked down at my hands.

"I was kind of hoping I could stay with you tonight."

"You haven't stayed in my bed since you were nine. You were sick. Dylan came home from work to find you wrapped in our bed, with me where we'd been all day."

"I remember," I whispered. "You read me a book for most of the afternoon, I think it was…"

"Charlotte's Web," we said together.

"We didn't get to the end because you feel asleep. It took me almost a week to get you back out of our bed."

"Your bed was the most comfortable. Now, mine is a big competitor."

"Yes, you can stay here tonight."

"Thank you," I whispered. "How did you get me out of your bed?" I asked as he stood.

"It was Dylan," he said nodding. "I was too soft with you, always was with you but Dylan wasn't swayed by your puppy dog eyes."

I laughed as I walked around his bed and got in.

"He got you ready for bed *in* here then played with you for a bit until he could piggy back you downstairs. Amazingly, it worked."

"I can't believe that worked."

"I can," he whispered. "Dylan always had his ways," he said cheerfully before going into the bathroom. He came back out in pyjamas.

He got in his side of the bed, so I lay down. Looking back at him.

"Do you have any experience with HIV?" I asked.

He moved his head back in shock. "You?"

"No," I breathed. "No, no. Luca's best friend has just been diagnosed and the two new Queens are positive. I just… don't really know all that much about it."

"Me personally, no, but George did. George was around Jack and Bill…"

200

"Bill… Oh, Queen Evelyn. Wait, Bill was positive?"

"Yep."

"He got meds though; I remember George telling us one night. Jack kind of refused to take the medication, it was *new,* it wasn't trusted. Jack died in eighty-five, they found out he'd developed lymphoma. Evelyn lived until the early noughties."

"Wait, wait, what is lymphoma?"

"Cancer," he sighed. "Cancer brought on through the virus. It's *horrible,* really, but they didn't know Jack had developed it."

"But Bill had the medication?"

"He did. George said he was vigilant with it. He got a different illness and that was ultimately what killed him."

"Oh," I whispered. "But it's not like that now? Right? People with HIV live now?"

"Long and happy lives," he confirmed. "The new Queens?"

"Felix and Phil."

"Did they seem ill?"

"No way," I said. "Not at all, the only reason we know is because their medication alarm went off during our notes. Felix was very open about it."

"I like the sound of Felix."

"Felix is kind of awesome," I said. "Luca fancies Felix."

"Does that bother you?" he whispered. I shook my head. "Jackson?"

"Why *does* it bother me so much?" I muttered.

He laughed gently stroking my hair back from my face. "Memories, mostly. I remember the first time I let it slip that I liked another boy in our class. Dylan pouted for *most* of the night."

I laughed softly.

"I was the worst to him, not going to lie. Then, he

dropped that he liked someone in another class, and I flipped."

I laughed. "You're kidding?"

"Nope. A day later we were both laughing beside ourselves because of *how* stupid we were both being. We knew we wanted to be with each other, we knew how deep that ran. It was so stupid to be, I guess, jealous over something like that. We might have smiled at a particularly pretty boy that day, but it wasn't them we were having sex with that night."

I scrunched my nose at him.

"Did Luca panic?"

"Yep," I said quietly.

"I personally admire Luca felt *that* secure with you after what, a week?"

"How does Luca always end up the hero in this story?"

He laughed lifting my chin, so I was looking straight at him. "Don't worry about the small stuff, otherwise you'll never get to the big stuff."

"Profound."

It was *extremely* cold, so cold in fact Luca and I sat facing each other, my legs between his, his knees practically at my chest because he was taller than I was.

We both had a hot chocolate and were waiting the fifteen minutes until the film we wanted to see allowed us into the screen. My hot chocolate was resting on his knee. Whilst he ran his free hand up and down my shin to generate some kind of heat.

"Jesse sent me a text," he told me. "Christmas night out?"

"Oh. Yes," I said nodding. "We do it the first week of December because Reed goes home for Christmas."

He hummed thoughtfully as he drank from his hot

chocolate.

"It's a lot of fun, we all go in Drag, too, which makes it *ten times* more fun."

He grinned.

"Now you bring up this weekend, I was wondering if you were free on Sunday?"

He frowned at me. "That depends on what the offer is," he said. "I believe so, I work most Sunday mornings then go to my Grandparents for Sunday lunch, but I can probably miss that, *this* week. Why?"

"Milo and Avory want to meet you properly."

"Oh."

"Milo mentioned it and then followed it up. Told me they wanted me for tea on Sunday and they didn't want me if my boyfriend wasn't in tow."

He laughed raising his feet as he leant backwards. I caught his foot just before he inflicted a world of pain on me. He blushed when he looked back at me covering his mouth.

"So, will you come?"

"I think that can be arranged."

"And, of course, I'll make the correct arrangements to meet your family, too," I said.

"Oh."

"Oh?"

"Well…"

Luca

Tradition was really big in my family as our family history was pretty new, given my grandpa was raised in Foster Care and my Grandad's parents disowned him when he came out as trans. They, of course, took the opportunity of creating their own family to make their own traditions.

It had started with my Pa. When he was small, Grandpa and Grandad wanted to make sure he never wanted for anything and that he always felt loved, something neither of them had growing up. It started such traditions like Vent It Sunday and Friday Movie Night and soon became Bank Holiday Beach Day and First Day of Summer Dye Day – although that one came about with Oakley more so than my Pa.

We partook in most of their traditions as my dad's adoptive family didn't have very many of their own either and sure we had some of our own as our little family of four, Dad, Pa, Connor, and I, but Christmas Tree Dinner was a whole family affair and I mean *whole*.

There was Grandad and Grandpa, Pa, Dad, Connor and I, Oakley and Skylar, Dad's twin Enzo and zir family Caleb, zir husband and their three kids Emma, Marley, and Quinn.

It was chaotic and Grandpa had suggested I invite Jackson along for the ride.

I hadn't fully decided if I wanted him to enter into the alternative universe of the Madison-May clan even as I walked with him to my grandparents' house.

"You don't have to do this," I reminded him.

He laughed happily. "Luca." He stopped us walking, touching my chest lightly to ensure I stopped with him. "I put on a Christmas jumper for this."

"It's a very nice jumper," I told him stroking my fingers over the reversable sequins that turned on the fairy lights on his jumper.

"If you don't want me here, tell me."

"I want you here," I told him. "I do. I just… they're a lot."

"I grew up with two drag queens. I think I'll be fine."

"That is a valid point."

"If it gets too much and it isn't fun anymore tell me and we'll get out of there."

"Okay," I said quietly.

He smiled before tapping me back. "Quickly, just to make sure…" He closed his eyes, "your Grandparents are both he, him, as are your parents and your uncle, right?"

"Right," I confirmed.

"Your Uncle's partner, is they, them?"

"Yes," I said through my grin.

"Your…" he paused.

"Enzo, my Enzo…" I laughed.

"Is zie, zir – which made me research neopronouns further which was fascinating. Their partner is also they, them. Their eldest, she, her, then…"

"The twins. They're still quite little, their pronouns change regularly. Last time I saw them Quinn was he, him. Marley was still they, them."

He nodded.

"That was impressive, Jackson. I... yeah... I'm impressed."

"You told me; it was the least I could do to remember it."

"You're the best," I said. "Let's do this," I added taking his hand and squeezing.

"Let's do this."

He kissed my knuckles then winked at me. I twirled him around under my hand, before walking ahead of him. I didn't need to knock on the door, I simply just pushed it open then let go of Jackson's hand so I could pick up my Grandparents cat Sonic as they attempted to escape.

"Hello," Jackson whispered near to my ear; I turned my head to him as he lightly fingered Sonic's paws.

"Oh yeah we have lots of cats," I said then winced, "is that okay?"

"Yes," he told me. "But Sugar and Spice might not agree with that." He crinkled his nose at me.

"Are you trying to escape again?"

We turned together as Grandpa came towards us taking Sonic from my arms then moving his head away as Sonic pawed at him.

He smirked then cleared his throat. "Sorry, hello." He offered his other hand to Jackson who grinned as he shook it back. "You must be Jackson, right?"

"I am."

"Good luck," Grandpa said amused as he turned and placed Sonic on the floor. "Now what team do you want to be on?"

"There's teams?" Jackson asked.

Grandpa nodded as I did, we followed him as he walked into the living room. The smell of pine was all encompassing because my grandparents always had a real tree.

"There's the tree team and the dinner team," Grandpa explained to us before stopping by Grandad and whispering into his ear under the guise of a kiss on the cheek.

Grandad turned to look at us. "Hello," he said warmly.

"Kieran heads the tree team," Grandpa continued, amused. "Alistair, Luca's Dad is on that team, Connor, Caleb, Sky."

"The masc among us," I whispered to Jackson.

"They put up the tree and the lights and the other decoration things…" Grandpa explained. "They do the labour-intensive jobs. Rory, his Pa, heads the dinner team."

"Pa likes to cook," I said.

Jackson smiled at me. "Are you on that team?"

"Oh no," I laughed. "Grandpa and I stay as far away from the cooking as we can."

"Why?"

"It's like torture," Grandpa gasped. "All the cakes and treats and…" we groaned together.

Jackson laughed covering his mouth. "So, what do you two do?"

"Mostly make tea," Grandpa answered.

I hummed. "I usually play with Marley and Quinn."

"I think I'm better at cooking than labour," Jackson told Grandpa. "Even though that's also debatable."

"Oakley," Grandpa called, who then appeared. "New victim for you," he cleared his throat. "I mean, wiling volunteer."

Jackson grinned *apparently* going willingly as he followed Oakley into the kitchen.

"Boyfriend?" Sky asked. I jumped turning to look at them as they fed Christmas lights to Caleb.

"Boyfriend," I agreed. "Officially and everything."

"That's your boyfriend?"

I glanced at Connor as he frowned back at me, I nodded once.

"Nice one," he said.

Grandpa laughed. "Do you want to make the tea? So, you can keep an eye on them in the kitchen?"

"No, I trust them."

"Your Pa, Oakley, *and* Enzo," he said.

"Yeah, I'd *totally* trust them," Dad muttered behind me. "Did you want Jackson cross-examined?"

"I'll go make the tea," I said.

I could hear them all laughing after me as I went into the kitchen.

I stopped when I saw Pa place an apron over Jackson's head before directing him to a clear bowl. Pa glanced at me.

"Don't worry. We're not being mean," he said amused.

"Grandpa sent me to make the tea."

Pa nodded raising his hands. "Sure, sure," he laughed.

Jackson turned to find me. "I'm making gingerbread," he told me. "I'm very excited by this, *I'm* not going to lie."

"Have you never made gingerbread?"

"We're not a baking family," he told me. "Not really but I do have a gingerbread eye shadow palette."

"Like, gingerbread colours?" Enzo asked.

"Kind of, I mostly bought it because it smells like gingerbread."

"That sounds incredible," Enzo said. "Did you know about that?" Zie asked Oakley.

"No, but now I want it."

"See we're all getting along," Pa said. "Don't worry, Peanut."

"Wait…" Jackson said. "*Peanut?*"

208

"Peanut," Enzo repeated as Oakley laughed.

"Luca *is* Peanut," he said.

Jackson's expression was definitely amused as Pa wrapped his arm around my shoulders.

"Sorry," he whispered although he was laughing, *so* I also laughed. "A baby is the size of the Peanut at nine weeks," he explained.

"The foetus," Enzo added. "The foetus at nine weeks, not a *baby*."

"Oh."

"We found out we were pregnant with Luca at nine weeks. *Alistair*, his dad, didn't wish to find out his gender so I called him Peanut because I'd been googling pregnancy late into the night and found the food analogy."

"It stuck," I informed Jackson.

"I'm changing your name in my phone."

I scoffed.

"Connor, his brother, is Spud," Oakley informed him.

"We found out about Connor far later," Pa said nodding.

"What are you changing my name to?" I asked.

Jackson rose an eyebrow at me, "Peanut, of course."

"We can watch one film, right," I whispered to Jackson as I watched my family get comfortable in the living room. Jackson nodded, looking at his watch before sighing.

"Yes, I definitely think so," he smiled. "I want to, if we're late for the Christmas night out I don't think anyone will really care."

"We still need to get ready."

"How long does that really take?"

"You want me to answer that honestly?"

I laughed as he knocked against me then turned to hide into my shoulder as Oakley passed us a blanket. Oakley winked at me as I lifted the blanket to cover my mouth and nose then walked away from us, sitting beside Sky on the floor in front of the couch Enzo and Caleb had sat on. Marley asleep on Caleb's thighs whilst Quinn opted for jumping on Sky the moment they sat down.

I sat on the floor in front of where my Grandad had sat, throwing the blanket over my knees then holding the side open for Jackson. He sat next to me without a word between us.

"What are we starting with this year?" Pa asked as he followed Grandpa into the room who smiled as he passed me a wrapped box.

"Are we finally all old enough for Love Actually?" Grandpa asked as I frowned at the box. "Sweets," he explained. "As everyone else gets endless snacks, I thought you deserved it, too."

"Thank you," I said.

"I don't think Connor's quite ready for Love Actually."

We all glanced at Connor as he looked up from his phone. "What?"

"There's sex in it," Dad told Connor who shook his head.

"No," he stated.

"Elf?" Enzo suggested.

"Elf," Pa agreed taking the remote and sitting beside Dad. I held the box to Jackson who grinned at me while taking a sugar dummy from the box.

Jackson

Tradition was really big in my family which meant that getting ready for *any* Queen event happened at Jason's as it had done since he moved in when he was nineteen.

His flat was always a hive of activity regardless of the event, and I was *usually* the first person to arrive.

This evening, however, I was the last to arrive *with* Luca in tow.

"Ah, Queen Madison, thought we'd have to leave without you," Queenie said as I stepped through the door.

I shook my head opening my arms to hug her tight. "Of course not, Peanut and I had a prior arrangement."

Luca shook my arm telling me to shut up, I laughed happily turning back to smile at him. He grinned straight back.

"Well come get ready, I fear *they'll* be starting pre-drinks if you don't hurry."

"I hear you," I laughed then tugged on Luca's hand taking him into Reed's bedroom.

"How long are you going to dine out on Peanut?" he asked as we put our dress bags onto the bed.

"As long as I can," I informed him. "It's so cute,

Luca," I added. "And I think I made a good impression."

"You definitely made a good impression," he whispered before unzipping his bag. "Now I have to make one on your grandparents."

"They're easy. Milo is makeup, Avory just drag," I told him as I unzipped my own bag. I watched him as he attempted to see in mine. I lifted it out grinning as he gasped.

"That is *gorgeous*."

"I know," I sighed touching my chest lightly. I twirled the hanger side to side so the light caught all the glitter that covered the black playsuit which was all long sleeves and short legs. The neckline low. Low enough that I had to wear a particularly frilly bra over my shapewear in case of a slip.

"But also, *so* simple."

"What are you wearing?" I asked.

"I bought one."

I waved my hand at him laughing as he lifted the dress from the bag. "Oh my God," I gasped. "I kind of want it."

He moved it away from me, smirking at me *just* short of saying neh neh as I took in the high-low dress that was a midnight blue, with stars scattered around the skirt.

"We can totally share dresses, right?"

"This'll hang off you," he said shaking his head.

I tutted lightly so he met my eyes. "I *know* your measurements; I respectfully disagree with you."

"We're *not* the same size," he said quietly.

I shook my head as I walked back around the bed to begin to change. "No, we're not but there's really not much in it."

Our eyes met over the bed; I frowned lightly but shook it off quickly.

"We need to get dressed otherwise they'll all be drunk

on pre-drinks before we even leave the flat."

He laughed nodding to me as he began to take off his hoodie.

He had kissed me.

Just like that, he had reached over for me and kissed me as we'd stood outside of the third club of the evening, *everyone* inside in the really loud and giddy stage of drunkness, whilst we were still cold sober.

Well, except for a singular vodka coke Beau had ordered in the club before this one. We'd stepped outside for air, both taking in the cold night as we whispered about how we'd make our exit. Our bodies close, our heads closer given how cold it *actually* was. We had decided to come back to my house both agreeing to say goodbye when we went back in.

We didn't move straight away. Neither of us made an effort to, we stood shivering *and* then he had kissed me.

As simple as that and given the look on his face when he came into my bedroom stripped of Beau except her makeup, he was obviously ruminating over it, too. I tapped my bed in front of me, moving back ever so slightly so he could see that I had makeup removal on my bed as I hadn't taken off Madison's makeup either. He warily came and sat in front of me. I pulled a wipe out of its packet.

"It was okay, you know," I said as he met my eyes. "The kiss I mean, it was okay."

"Really? It wasn't the best timed and I..." he paused.

I lifted his chin wiping the lipstick that remained off his lips. I figured he appreciated the distraction from talking.

"I agree it wasn't the best timed," I said, "but there's no such thing as perfectly timed first kisses."

"How did you know that it was my first kiss?" he

asked.

I paused. "I meant *our* first kiss." I cleared my throat, "was it your first kiss ever?"

He looked away again.

"Luca?" I whispered as he pulled some wipes out.

"I have three intrusive questions," he said quietly. I nodded folding the wipes over on each other as I checked his face. When I lowered my hands, he began to wipe off my makeup. His thumbs stroking my cheeks as he worked on my lips.

"You're asexual," he said. "I overstepped the line."

"That isn't a question." He rolled his eyes at me, so I smiled. "You didn't overstep the line; I like you, Luca. I like you in a romantic way, I've wanted to kiss you for weeks, but I don't know, I kept putting obstacles up."

"How does asexuality work?" he asked. "This is my first intrusive question."

"How does asexuality work in general? Or with me?"

"With you specifically."

"I'm demisexual," I told him. "Which means my feelings can develop into romantic, then sexual over the time. I like you, Luca. I've liked you since I lay eyes on you, then I started to get to know you and my attraction went from thinking you were pretty to actually having full blown feelings for you."

"Oh," he breathed. I down casted my eyes as he stroked over my cheeks. "Have you done this before?" he asked. I frowned without looking up at him. "Like a boyfriend, kisses..."

"Sex?" I said for him. He hummed so I looked up as he nodded. "Yes. I... I had a boyfriend, we broke up the summer just gone."

"What happened?"

"Is that your third intrusive question?"

"I've only asked one."

"You just asked me if I was virgin," I reminded him. "I was with Charlie."

"As in technician Charlie?"

"Yep." I cleared my throat, "he cheated on me." I looked up as he frowned back at me. "I found out during Pride because he got caught backstage with... with another of the technicians. It hurt because obviously I did had sex with him and I had a relationship with him. He'd been my best friend and well, I lost a lot when I lost that relationship."

"I'm so sorry," he whispered.

I nodded slowly. "For a long time I thought he did it because I was asexual. I thought he wanted more, wanted what I couldn't give him but I was wrong, I *am* wrong because I was making myself uncomfortable for him. I was having sex with him when I didn't want to and forcing myself into those kinds of situations when I didn't feel in anyway ready or happy to." I cleared my throat. "He just cheated because he chose to."

"Is that why you were shouting at him?" he asked.

I shook my head. "He was being a dick."

"Oh. So, you're not on speaking terms now?"

"No," I sighed. "No I can't. I can't even look at him sometimes, but I don't need him because that night, when I found out, I went home with Reed and since then Reed and I have been so close, so, so close then you came along and well... hi." I waved. He waved back so I smiled at him.

"So... I didn't overstep the line?"

"No," I assured him. "No, I wanted to kiss you, I was putting it off because I was scared the same thing would happen again. Then you kissed me."

"Then I kissed you."

"I liked it."

"It was crap," he moaned covering his face, so I

laughed. "I've never kissed anyone; I've never done that before…"

"Well…" I said softly as I collected all the wipes on my bed. "I mean, the only way to improve is to practice."

His head sprung up so quickly I'm surprised he didn't headbutt me. "What?"

"Let's practice," I shrugged dramatically. "I like kissing. Kissing's a lot of fun to me."

"Oh, that's good," he said nodding. "How do you kind of, start kissing?"

"You did it before…"

"That was spontaneous, and I don't know what came over me," he said his voice an octave above normal, so I pulled him towards me. Our lips clashing together before either of us made any attempt to actually kiss. He got quicker and quicker, his tongue licking against my lips eagerly. I pushed him back by his chest.

"Okay, baby you don't need to eat me I'm not going anywhere."

He blushed brightly covering his face. "Oh my god I'm a terrible kisser."

"No. no, no," I assured him. "No. You just… well… we can take it slow," I whispered moving towards him again. I hovered over his lips, my eyes tracking his as he watched me intrigued, he went to move towards me connecting the kiss. I rose my lips. Kissing the tip of his nose lightly. "Slow and steady," I reminded him then kissed his cheeks, his left then his right. He smiled so I kissed the corner of his smile. "It doesn't have to be heated every time," I whispered almost into his mouth, before kissing his chin.

He naturally rose his head, watching me intently as I stroked my nose over his chin before placing the softest of kisses on his lips. I moved away before he could deepen it then I pulled my tongue at him. He almost frowned but pulled his tongue back, smiling when I moved towards him again. The tips of our tongues touching before I deepened the kiss.

My hand sliding up from his chest to his neck, holding him as he returned the kiss, his eyes falling shut, so I grinned. He grinned right back, and I could feel it.

"Something like that?" he asked.

I nodded without moving my head too much. "Something like that."

"You guys kissed," Reed whispered as we watched Luca rehearse.

"A lot."

"That's where you disappeared to?" he asked.

I nodded scrunching my nose as I did. "You were all *very* drunk."

"I was *not*," he gasped. "Actually neither was Jason. I don't think I've ever seen Jason drunk. We noticed you guys leaving assumed you were getting air."

"We *were*," I said. "Then he kissed me, so I took him back to mine because he seemed to freak out. We kissed a whole lot more."

"He's adorable, he kind of makes my heart hurt."

I laughed. "He's…" I said, then swallowed. "*Not* that this matters or anything but, he's a virgin."

"Oh."

"I don't want to corrupt him."

"How would you corrupt him?"

"I make sex complex," I said.

"What?"

"Well, I do."

"Jackson, do you want to have sex with him?"

I winced. "Yes."

His laugh was *loud* and shocked. So loud, in fact, Jesse turned to examine us. We both raised our finger to our lips. "Reed," I moaned.

"I wasn't expecting you to say yes, you *never* say yes."

"No, I know but my feelings are definitely developing. It's taken, what? A month and a half?"

"I don't know why I'd expect for that to be longer."

"What do you mean?"

"Well, *obviously* because of you I've researched demisexuality, a lot. I wanted to make sure I was somewhat educated, and when I read you needed your feelings to develop before you wanted sex, I assumed that was long term."

"How long did it take you to develop feelings for Quinn?"

"Like proper feelings?" he asked.

"You've just totally illustrated my point," I said. "But yes, proper feelings, like feelings of love or commitment."

"Oh, I guess it was by Halloween, so *yeah,* a month. We spoke for the first time in September. *Shit,*" he laughed. "Wait what do you mean?"

"The first time you looked at Quinn, what were your feelings?"

"That he was pretty," he said. "Okay, fine, I wanted to have sex with him, *because* I did."

"Exactly. *I* didn't. That wasn't my initial thought with Luca. Now, I'm still like I really like him, I think he's gorgeous but there's also a part of me that's like I want to kiss him and... do things with him," I sighed. "I've fell deep, and quick. But look at him," I whined waving towards Luca as he laughed happily at something Jason said.

"So why are you worried you'll corrupt him?"

"Because he'll have an expectation of sex. Like Charlie did and I won't be able to deliver it. I won't..."

"Stop assuming you know what's going on in Luca's

head," he shunned. "Stop it, because you don't know and all you're doing is internalising which will make everything toxic."

"Please don't tell me I should talk to Luca. That's all anyone's been telling me."

"Heed the advice?" he suggested. "I don't know, I'm not going to say Quinn and I are perfect. No way, we don't talk about everything. We keep things and whisper the things that embarrass us but I trust him. I trust him with everything and *know* that when we evidently talk about the things that bother us, whether that be hours or months later he'll listen."

"Because he's perfect," I mocked.

"Because he's my *boyfriend*."

"Ugh," I said. "He gets to meet Milo and Avory tomorrow."

"I wish him luck," Reed whispered before squeezing my knee. "Give him a chance before you condemn the relationship, hey?"

"How dare you make sense," I muttered.

"Are you two going to kiss? Should I leave?" We turned together. I laughed as Reed grinned at Felix.

"No way, he's kissing *him*," Reed told Felix, pointing towards the stage. They glanced towards Luca.

"Really?"

"Really," I sighed, fearing it sounded lovesick. *Apparently,* it did if Reed's snort was anything to go by.

"He's beautiful," Felix told me then they laughed. "But I guess that makes sense because you're also beautiful." They grinned as I gasped touching my chest at the compliment.

"Where's your brother?" Reed asked.

Felix frowned at him. "What?" they breathed.

"Where's Phil?" I asked.

Felix laughed lightly. "Backstage," they said. "I don't

know what he's doing but, that's where he is."

"That's what I asked," Reed mumbled.

Felix shook their head at me. "He talks so fast," they whispered.

"South African meets Scottish," I said then turned as I was called to the stage. "Good luck translating," I sang at them as I walked towards the stage.

Luca

"Relax," I whispered, before looking up and straight at Mateo. Xe raised xer eyebrows at me as I let out a long deep breath. "Just, relax."

"They're not going to hate you."

"Oh, I know *that*," I assured xem. "I know they're not going to hate me, but what if I say something…" I took a step closer, "that makes me hate myself." Another step closer, "and I think about that *over* and over." Another step so I was nose to nose with xem. "Until the day I *die*."

"Chaotic queer energy again," Xe told me.

"Oh, did you talk to Felix?"

"No." xem said rolling xer eyes.

"*What*? I kissed Jackson."

"Yeah, you did."

We turned together. I blushed instantly as Mateo laughed.

"Why hello, Jackson."

"I came to pick up my boyfriend, I've *never* been here before," he said. "Oh and this…" he came towards me, lifted my chin and kissed me.

"You've never been here?" Mateo asked, Jackson

shook his head as he stroked his thumb over my lip.

"No, surprisingly. It was very much Avory and Milo's place. Their thing," he shrugged. "Ready?" he asked me.

I nodded swallowing deeply before looking at Mateo. I widened my eyes, xe laughed smirking at me as I untied my apron.

"What was your end of the deal then?" Jackson asked.

Mateo sighed. "To talk to Felix about the whole…. HIV thing."

"Oh, you definitely should. They're very open about it." he said.

"I'm going to the clinic tomorrow, for them to give me medication. I'm not excited," Xe said.

Jackson hummed. "I can give you Felix's number, if you want?"

Mateo shook xer head although it got slower as I got closer to him. "I don't know. I don't think that's too good of an idea."

"*Okay.* What if, Jackson asks if he can give you Felix's number, and if Felix says yes… which I'm sure they will…" I said to Jackson who nodded.

"I'm sure," he agreed.

"I'll give you Felix's number."

"Okay fine," Mateo said raising xer hands. "Fine, fine. Now go, go meet Jackson's grandparents."

I whined. Jackson laughed as he watched me walk around the counter and pull out the cake tray, taking the last piece of cake from it and putting it into a polystyrene box.

"They already love you; this is just a precaution," he said taking my hand. I squeezed then nodded to Mateo.

"Stay chaotic, queer," Xe said as I left with Jackson. I blew a kiss back to xem.

We crossed over the road.

"Avory and Milo have always lived really close. They had a flat here," he waved towards a block of flats. "Then moved into an apartment when they adopted my mum. They've been there since," he told me, "walking distance of the café, and the club."

We stopped outside an apartment complex and he rang the buzzer.

"Hello?"

"It's your favourite grandchild," Jackson said. He glanced at me as the voice on the other end of the speaker laughed.

"Luca?" he asked.

I giggled as Jackson sighed dramatically.

"I told you," he said. "I told you they love you."

"I am very lovable."

"Yes, you are, Peanut."

I hit his shoulder as the door clicked. He pulled it open with a sigh then started me up the flights of stairs.

We went around, and around. I noted the lift on every floor until we reached the fifth. There were two apartments on each floor, both with wooden looking doors, and long rectangular windows that stretched the length of the entire door. The numbers on the wall next to them, a post box underneath, and a square light above. To me it looked like a hotel.

Jackson knocked on the door that said 5A.

Avory answered the door.

"Good afternoon," he said fondly as Jackson glanced at me. "I'm in the kitchen this afternoon." He nodded to us, telling us to follow him in.

"Really?" Jackson asked.

"Really," Avory sang as he let us through a door. I glanced at Jackson who sighed.

"Avory likes things spicy," he said.

"Now, as I don't think you've been properly

introduced. My husband, Milo."

"Hello," I offered.

"Hello Luca. I've heard a *lot*."

"I could say the same about you two," I said happily. "The makeup artist, and…" I curtsied, "the rightful Queen."

"Oh, you can keep *him*," Avory informed Jackson. "I was the rightful Queen," he told Milo who rolled his eyes as Avory laughed. "I need a word with you in the kitchen," he told me, "and as the Queen I request your presence now."

"I'd just got rid of his big head, Luca," Milo moaned as Jackson went over to him hugging when he did.

"It never went away," Avory informed him then beckoned me, so I followed. The kitchen was *far* bigger than I was expecting – *and* smelt amazing. "Jackson told me you had a gluten intolerance."

I nodded slowly.

"I just wanted to show you what we're having so you don't feel… worried."

"Thank you," I said. "I bought some cake for Milo, too," I added holding the polystyrene box to him.

"Oh, he'll be made up," he ginned taking it from me and opening it. "I'll let him thank you," he added amused as he placed it on the counter before pointing at a baking tray. "We're having Caribbean chicken with jerk sauce, coconut rice, beans, and corn cakes."

"That sounds amazing. Corn cakes?"

"Deep fried, I've made them with gluten free flour but if you're wary. Feel free to *not*…"

"No problem, you just hear cake assume wheat."

"Course."

"Where's the chicken from?" I asked. "I don't mean which supermarket do you shop in; I mean…"

"Jamaica," he replied. "It's a Jamaican recipe. One

from my grandma, that came from her Grandma before her."

"You're Jamaican?"

"Descendent. My Grandma's mum brought her and her sisters over here." He shrugged as he began to put the marinated chicken on the grill. "It was way back in the nineteen fifties, I think. I was born thirty or so years later."

"Wow," I said. "My dad found out he was of Melanesian descendant but that was *way* back, his family had been UK based for decades."

"Did they all find it out together?"

"No, he's adopted. Him and his twin. They were put up for adoption at birth. They just chose to do the test to find out, out of curiosity. I don't know much about it."

"Nor did I, at nineteen," he smiled. "I only really spoke to my grandmother about it later, when we were adopting Eloise because her descent was on the papers, her grandparents were also from Jamaica and we, Milo and I, thought it was perfect. It was like a part of me was in her." He waved his hand, "well, kind of."

"That makes sense," I told him. "Really. That's amazing."

"It kind of was, she made me look into my culture, into my families past. It was when I started cooking, because I wanted her to know, it just meant that I also learnt."

"Does Jackson know?" I asked.

"I take it you haven't met Eloise?" he said laughing. I shook my head slowly. "Yes, he knows."

"Are you talking about me?" Jackson grinned at me from the doorway as Milo also did.

"Of course we are," Avory said as he turned the chicken on the grill. "He hasn't met Eloise yet?"

"No, but he's met Dad, unintentionally."

225

"Definitely unintentionally. I almost told him we weren't having sex," I said then gasped, covering my mouth as Milo laughed joyfully.

"What?" Jackson choked.

"He asked me if I'd ever been to your bedroom when he wasn't there. I panicked."

"Oh, Luca," Jackson laughed as Milo shook his head.

"I love you, kid; you have no idea."

"He brought you cake, too," Avory said.

"You have been pushed down the pecking order Jacks."

"It was only a matter of time," Jackson said dramatically.

"You're still my favourite, darling," Avory added. "Now, set the table."

"It's a hard life," he told me then spun on the spot. "What do I know?"

"That your Mum is Jamaican."

"Oh yeah, I've known that since I was *born*. She has a very strong Jamaican accent."

"Always has," Avory commented as he placed the plates onto the table. "Take a seat, let's dig in."

"So, your makeup business was purely your own?" I asked.

Milo nodded laughing as he played with his drink. "I left school at eighteen, worked in Ahoy Matey's for a little while."

"Excuse me?" Jackson said laughing. "I didn't know you were a Sailor there."

"I was the *best* sailor," he cleared his throat. "Then I worked in a tailor. I was the person they called to book a suit fitting. I did makeup on the side and when I started earning more from makeup than answering phones, I left."

"That's amazing," I said.

"It was. I was comfortable, he was because Robin was a Queen by then. We were actually making more than we were spending and that was *massive*. We bought this flat. We adopted. It was perfect."

"Wow."

"I was lucky to be fair, I did some Editorials because my dad was a fashion photographer, and he took me along to the shoots every now and again."

"You worked your ass off, luck had nothing to do with it," Avory said shaking his head. "You're amazing."

"Yeah, I am pretty good," he agreed.

"Jackson did get your skills; Madison's makeup is always immaculate," I said. "I guess it took him too long to match his foundation though." I said.

Jackson's eyes widened as Milo shook his head. "What do you mean? I had Jackson matched from when he was six. When I started teaching him makeup."

"He had loads of foundations," I said. Jackson shook his head resting his hand on his forehead.

"I don't know why, he's Chai, well in the brand he uses he is, always has been. Avory's Sable. You've always known that."

"I really thought I was going to get away with this."

"What did you do Jacks?" Avory asked as he placed what looked like custard tarts on the table. Jackson sighed turning to look at me.

"The Rose Quartet has a vault. They've got everything you need to do drag in there."

"Yeah, I use the wardrobe most weeks," I said.

Jackson nodded then looked behind me at Avory. "They also have a room full of wigs, and makeup supplies. They update them periodically."

"Oh," Avory sighed.

"I was at your audition, remember. They asked you

loads, and you basically told them you hadn't done drag before, so I figured you didn't have makeup. I *mean* you might've, but I thought the precaution needed to be taken."

"I still don't get it?" I said looking between them.

"The makeup in the vault stops at Jason's shade. I think Jason's Golden?" he said.

Milo hummed. "If he's been in the sun, he's Golden," he laughed. "He's normally a Natural Beige."

"Thank you."

"I just didn't want the same thing to happen to you that happened to me," Jackson said. "When I started, I was sixteen and, *yeah* sure, I had my own supply of makeup. Milo gifted me with it all, but I still went into the vault, it was like Aladdin's cave. I'd been hearing about it for years.

"I loved the dresses, the shoes, the wigs of course but it hurt that there was *no*, literally *no* makeup for my skin tone and I mean, it's just not on their wavelength. They don't even think about it because they don't need darker tones. It made me feel weird and sad and I didn't want you to feel that way, *so* I got the darker foundations – in case you needed to be matched."

"That's like, one hundred pounds," I gasped.

"I *know*, but you didn't feel like I did. I worried about it with Felix and Phil, too. I spoke to Felix though and they didn't give a *fuck*. Genuinely. They were used to being the only black drag queens in their clubs, *then* they said well until this one."

"Wait, they're right," Avory gasped happily as waved his fork. "You realise that, right? Reed is the only white Queen amongst you. I *honestly* never thought I'd see the day and I love that club like, *that* club gave me everything.

"I adore Jesse, he's my best friend in *like* the entire world," he paused as he glanced at Milo.

"Did you, a sixty-two-year-old man, just state that Jesse is your best friend in *like* the entire world?"

"Yes, because he is," he stated. I laughed as Jackson did. "But they were definitely copy and paste Queens for a while. I'm so happy you're getting a fair chance on that stage."

"Jamie will *have* you for calling Blossom a copy and paste Queen," Jackson informed him.

"It wouldn't be the first fist fight I've got into with Jamie and surely not the last."

"I'm still on this whole spending that much money on me before knowing me, thing," I added.

"Really, we're still on *that?*" Jackson sighed; I shrugged nodding to him. "I *donated* my foundations to the club. Well, except yours and mine. I donated the rest to the vault."

"Well, first of all, I'll repay that money," Milo said.

Jackson turned to him. "No, I..."

"Case closed," He said. "Second, *I* can match you if you want."

"Yes," I gasped then cleared my throat. "I mean, Jackson already has. He said I was Spiced Rum."

Milo rose an eyebrow at me. "Not a bad assessment."

"Please match me," I said lifting my hands together then I paused. "*Wait* I'm supposed to be making a good impression," I said.

Jackson reached for my hand, squeezing tight. "I can assure you, you are," Jackson said.

Milo took me into the room at the end of the corridor. I was instantly taken with the various canvases on the opposite wall to the door. They all connected together like one big puzzle. They were mostly pictures, of Robin, of the Queens in the Rose Quartet. The centre picture was Queen Robin in the dress I'd worn of hers a few weeks back.

Milo was stood beside her maybe my age, maybe a little older, on his tiptoes, kissing Robin's cheek.

"I think you wore it better," Jackson whispered in my ear. I laughed in a loud cackly way. Milo looked at both of us, a smile playing on his face. I glanced back towards the wall. Interspersed amongst the pictures were drawings of makeup, as if they'd been designed especially for Robin. They were all signed by Milo.

"Take a seat," he offered, so I did. "What does Beau look like?" he asked as he ran his hand over his brushes then dropped a blender into water.

"What do you mean?"

"Does she have a particular style? Like a statement part of her makeup that someone would look at and be like *that*'s Beau May."

"No."

"That's okay," he assured me. "It took Madison a while to decide on false eyelashes."

"And red lipstick," Jackson intoned as he sat on the opposite end of the table. Milo rolled his eyes at me.

"I have so many gorgeous lipsticks, and *he* only wears red," he lamented then picked up a foundation bottle. "This is Spiced Rum." He turned my head painting a stripe onto my cheek. He hummed thoughtfully turning my head again, so I was looking his tabletop mirror. He turned on the ring light. "I think you could go a shade darker," he didn't look all too convinced, though. "Spiced Rum has rosy undertones; I don't think *you* do." I turned my head without him telling me to. He smiled as he painted another stripe across my other cheek.

"See?"

"Oh," Jackson said as I laughed.

"Don't worry, I saw it a lot and at least you're not way off like Avory was when I met him," he grinned then wiped both my cheeks with a wipe. "I'll do your makeup with Tiramisu. See how that looks."

I nodded. "I will literally allow you to do my makeup *any* way you say. I hope you know that."

Jackson took me back to his house after Milo had made my face possibly the most beautiful I'd ever seen it, *and* then persuaded me to wipe it off. It'd been a trial and multiple pictures had been taken, but I relented in the end.

It was dark when we started back to Jackson's. We played twenty questions to distract from the journey.

"I'd love to go to your uncles wedding with you," he said in a breath, when I'd used one of my questions to invite him. He definitely hadn't been expecting it, his surprise and stuttering proved that. "Oakley, I assume?"

"Oakley and Sky," I said nodding. "They've been engaged for so long, we're all kind of relieved its finally happening... They're getting married on New Years Eve."

"I love that. Yes, yes I'll definitely go to the wedding with you."

He said reaching into his pocket for his key and let us into the house quietly. The hall light was on but the rooms around us were quiet - it wasn't *that* late. Surely.

"I want to show you something," he said. "It seems only right, now you've seen Robin's," he added then led me towards the door under the stairs. He opened it to a basement.

"I was fully expecting a cupboard," I admitted.

"This was the requirement Jamie had when they bought the house. Enough bedrooms for his family and a basement for Cherry Blossom."

"What?" I whispered as he clicked the light on. I stepped past him on the stairs as the room exploded into light. "Oh my God."

"This… is Blossoms Lair. Every dress, every wig, every memory," He waved as I walked towards the rail. I wanted to reach out and touch, but I refrained linking my fingers together and chewing on my lip.

"This is incredible," I said as I turned on the spot. My eyes landed on Jackson as he sat on the chaise lounge that was against the far wall, underneath a big pride flag.

"This was my playroom," he said as I walked towards him. "Jamie said growing up if no-one could ever find me, it was guaranteed that I'd be down here. It was so inspirational to me, I just…" he waved his hand above his head as I sat beside him. "This is why I do drag."

"Thank you for showing me," I whispered. His smile was shy, so I kissed him and *that* was totally weird. Being able to just *kiss* someone and have them kiss me back.

"Oh, sorry."

Well until we were interrupted. I gasped turning away as Jackson laughed.

"Jamie," he said.

"Sorry, I was wondering where you were. How did dinner go?"

"Good," Jackson answered then squeezed my thigh, so I turned back to him. "Milo rematched Luca."

"He made me so beautiful," I told Jamie.

"Oh, I'm sure that wasn't too hard to do," Jamie said.

"Oh," I breathed. "Can you tell me about some of the memories in here?" I asked.

Jamie laughed fondly stroking his fingers over the dresses as he passed. "Really? Do you not want to use the sleepover time, to be…" he smirked, "alone?"

I almost choked as Jackson sighed. "Grandad," he said almost like he was a child. "Tell about when Dylan proposed."

"He interrupted Blossom's show."

"And you said yes?" I asked.

He laughed taking a seat on the other side of me to tell me the story.

Jackson

"Relax," I whispered, his eyes searched to meet mine. "Just, relax," I repeated as I unhooked the curtains that hung from the canopy above my bed. I drew the two sides before getting in the third and drawing it after me. "Just me and you, okay? No distractions, no interruptions…" I laughed as I stroked my thumb down his cheek. "No intentions."

"I just…" he sighed. "We need to talk about this I guess…"

I nodded, because I did fully agree. One of the things that had damned my relationship with Charlie was the severe lack of communication. He knew I was demisexual but he didn't at all know what that meant.

"I… when I develop deep feelings is usually when sex comes into play," I said. "I like you a whole damn lot and yes I think about having sex with you probably too much, but there will still be days that I don't want to do anything sexual.

"There might be days when I don't want you to touch me at all, but that's got nothing to do with you. It's me, all me."

"I understand that," he whispered. "I'm a virgin." He looked down. I bit my lip so I didn't tell him I already knew.

I mean, the likelihood of someone who had never kissed not being a virgin was slim.

"I'm not," I replied instead. "I was sixteen. Too young. It was with Charlie... we, at that point we'd been together two years and well, there wasn't a reason not to."

"Did you only do it once?"

"No," I whispered. "He told me we had to do it more. If we wanted to be in a real relationship, we had to have more sex. So, we had it at least once a week until he cheated, or at least until I found out he had. I... I was so stupid."

"No. You were sixteen. Don't berate yourself because you didn't know any better." He sighed, "have you only been with Charlie?"

"Yes," I whispered. "I want to be with you, sexually I mean. I want to touch you and make you come and have sex with you. Just not all at once."

He blushed. "I did research..."

I didn't dare interrupt him but I did move closer so the tips of our noses touched. He moved his head so our noses stroked against each other's.

"...Into foreplay because I didn't... I didn't even know that was a thing. I... anyway, I read about all kinds about hands and mouths and..."

"Okay. I'm down for hands," I said. "Like, I masturbate occasionally. I'm comfortable with that most of the time. I'm not here for oral sex though..."

"Would you be up for receiving it?" he asked.

"When do you get your braces off?" I asked.

"Soon," he murmured.

"We'll talk about oral sex after that."

"What about sex?"

"Fore play is sex."

"No, I know, I mean like... *sex*, like."

"Anal sex?" I asked. He nodded, his blush reappearing. "I've had it, I've enjoyed it. Again it'd be a day-by-day thing."

"Shouldn't sex be a day-by-day thing anyway? Like I wouldn't assume just because you said yes say, now, that you mean yes tomorrow, too."

"Screw like, I think I *love* you."

He smiled through his blush. I decided then would be a good time to kiss him. He obviously agreed as his hand rested on my cheek.

"Do you want to fool around now?" he whispered against my lips. "It's okay if you don't... I just... thought."

"Yes," I whispered, because I did and had wanted to most of the week. It had in fact been absolutely killing me and inconveniencing me as it made things... hard.

"How?"

"How about we touch ourselves..." I said. He looked down between us, knocking his head against my chin. "Would that be, okay?" He swallowed as he nodded. "Luca?" I whispered as he looked back at me.

"Yes." I smiled at him he laughed. "Are we... going to undress?"

"That depends..." I said.

He shook his head. "Not yet. I just... not yet."

"Not yet," I repeated as I leant my forehead against his, tilting his head down so he could watch as I slipped my hand into my bed shorts. He whined low in his throat.

"I'll be honest, I haven't done this in my pants for a long time," I whispered. He hummed, it almost sounded intrigued as I watched his fingers stroking around the waistband of his pyjamas. "I did when I first started doing it. I figured it made less mess, would be less noticeable. I was wrong."

He laughed. I kissed his forehead, smiling gently then biting my bottom lip as he slipped his hand into his pants.

"I didn't think it made any mess the first time…" he whispered back as his hand began to move under his pants. I copied his movements stroke for stroke. "All of my bed was covered, and it turned out, I'm also a screamer."

"You're a screamer?" I repeated. "Fuck."

He laughed, but his movements stuttered. "Fuck," he whispered back.

I lifted his chin. "It's okay. Okay?"

"I…" Luca said. I stroked his cheek, he kissed me, deeply. I felt my own hardness twitch against my hand. He moaned into my mouth. "Okay," he whispered, his strokes slower, more deliberate.

I was starting to think I wasn't going to last very long.

He groaned. "This isn't fair," he mumbled. "It's not you."

"Oh, I didn't think it was for a second baby."

He smiled back at me. I kissed him. "What's wrong?"

"I keep going soft."

"No, I mean…" I tapped his forehead.

He closed his eyes. "I'm nervous, and embarrassed."

"Embarrassed?" I repeated. "Why?"

"What if I make noises or, do it wrong or…"

"I hope you *do* make noises," I told him. "When you moaned into my mouth, I thought I was going come right there and then."

He narrowed his eyes at me, I did it back, he laughed.

"Want to try it a different way?" I whispered. "Can I touch you?"

His nod was quick.

"Still under the pants?"

"Please."

"No problem," I whispered, then stroked my thumb over his crotch. His eyes never left my face, so I continued to stroke him. Feeling as he hardened under my hand. "Okay?" I whispered, he nodded quickly so I lay next to him, my body facing his, I lifted his chin, kissing him softly as I slid my fingers under his waistband. His mouth opened against mine; a gasp caught in his throat as I wrapped my hand around him.

I nodded to him as I moved my hand slowly, he nodded back, resting his forehead against mine, his eyes only leaving my own when he closed them in a breath.

I let my hand get quicker, crinkling my nose at him, he mirrored me a small grin playing on his expression before he bit his lip, the bite deep. I pulled my tongue at him. He moaned.

"Jack...Jack... Jackson."

I shuddered, ignoring my own reaction as best I could as his hand weaved through my hair, grabbing the back of my head and tugging.

"I'm... I'm going to... Jackson..."

I swallowed down his scream in a kiss. His hands coming up to my cheeks holding my head in place as he came over my hand. I rubbed my thumb over his tip, feeling as his dick twitched. I knocked his head up with my own. He kissed me again.

"Can I touch you?" he whispered against my lips. I swallowed looking down between us before nodding.

He nodded back, his fingers slipping under my waistband and wrapping around my dick. He began to move his hand quickly, his grip loose.

I reached for his hand, wrapping my own around his settling his movements.

"Take it slow," I whispered as I turned to look at him, he nodded letting my hand guide his, although his expression was worrisome.

"You're good," I told him. "This is good." I let my fingers slip into his hair, wrapping around his tight curls as we got a little quicker. "Keep that up," I whispered lifting my hand from his and he did. A smile growing on his face that I watched until my eyes closed. We both made a similar noise when I came and then I laughed, knocking my head against his so he looked at me. A tentative smile on his face. "Good?" I asked. He nodded his smile growing in confidence until he was also laughing.

"We don't have to rush into anything, you know. We can figure it out as we go."

"Okay," he breathed. "Good."

I smiled and kissed his nose. "I'm going to take *off* my boxers..." I told him; he pulled a face, so I laughed as I stood from my bed, stepping behind the curtain so remove my pants. He did the same on the other side. He looked like he was thinking something over when I pulled back my duvet to get into bed.

"I'm sorry I'm so nervous," Luca whispered.

I shook my head. "Don't be. Sorry or nervous."

He laughed the rubbed his face. "I don't know what it is, I just always think I'm going to do something wrong or mess up in some way."

"There's no right way to do *anything* related to sex, you know?"

He shook his head, so I nodded back.

"It's about experimenting and having fun with the other person. It isn't about coming; in fact, it isn't about the end. It's about the *during*."

He nodded slowly his fingers weaving around mine until he cringed.

"I want to see you naked, for the record," he said. "I'm sorry, it's my own self-consciousness about my body. It's got nothing to do with yours."

"I'm not *ever* going to make you feel uncomfortable, Luca, but I do think you're perfect."

We looked at each other. "Perfect?"

"Definitely, as Luca *and* as Beau. One hundred percent. I envy Beau. She is stunning, I don't think I'll ever be as stunning."

He lifted my hand, kissing the back of it.

"I'm not going to be all self-righteous and tell you that you *have* to love yourself. I'd never be that person; it isn't my place. Some days I wake up, looking in the mirror and just think *not* today. Self-love is fucking hard."

"You can say that again," he whispered. "I'm still working on… this." He pointed at himself.

"Snap," I whispered. "I really like you though and if I waited until I was perfect, I might miss my chance."

He kissed me - with such force that I fell back onto my bed.

240

Luca

Text Message

Mateo: New meds don't agree with me at all 😣 I've been texting Felix none stop don't worry! I've asked Rory for the next few days off, hopefully I'll see you soon. Sorry for making you work with your Pa for the next few days. I owe you big time. 😅

I stopped, the food bag in hand on my way to Madison's dressing room. Texting back with one hand *but* also trying to hear who Jackson was talking to, or more aptly, shouting back at.

I walked a little closer looking around the door at Jackson as he held open the opposite door that led backstage, telling whoever it was to *get the hell through it and leave me alone.*

"Is that so your little boyfriend can come in, and you two can play happy families until he cheats on you?"

I stepped the rest of the way in, Jackson looked directly at me. I didn't falter.

"Get out," I told Charlie. He turned to me, genuinely looking surprised to see me stood in the doorway and then he scoffed, muttering *whatever* before leaving Jackson's dressing room. Jackson closed the door after him.

"Don't," he said lightly. "Thank you, but don't."

"I got you an iced coffee," I said. "And a panini."

"Thank you," he whispered. "Did you find something gluten free?"

"Yeah, they're really good with coeliac food," I said as we sat on his chaise lounge. He took a sip from his iced coffee. "So, does that happen with Charlie a lot?" I asked as I unwrapped my lunch.

He sighed. "I thought you weren't going to say anything."

"I didn't agree to that," I informed him. He looked at me as he bit the end of his straw. "Well?"

"Yes. He, tells me things like that a lot."

"I'm not going to cheat on you," I assured him, *although* that was unlikely the thing I needed to tell him. He glanced at me, "*and* he's a bully."

He shook his head as he picked from the contents of his panini.

"No, he's just..." he paused as if searching for a word. He obviously couldn't find one given how he shook his head. "It doesn't matter, Luca. I can handle him, can handle it."

I went to reply, he put his hand over my mouth.

"Luca," he repeated, so I closed my mouth. "Please," he pleaded, "let it go." He took his hand away. I pressed my lips together. He looked worrisome, so I kissed his cheek. He sighed; it sounded content as he lifted his hand to stroke my cheek.

I didn't let it go. In fact, I took it to Jason. *At* risk of making Jackson extremely angry at me.

"You have to understand it's complicated," Jason

242

said. I shook my head at him. He sighed as he fiddled with a pen on his desk. "Jackson's my godson. If I get rid of Charlie without evidence, without a reason, it could be seen as favouritism or…"

"To who?" I asked. "Who's going to see it as favouritism? I'm not, I can almost guarantee that Reed isn't. Jesse?"

"It's complicated, Luca."

"Isn't it evidence enough I heard him, isn't it *evidence* when they were shouting at each other, and Jesse had to break them up?"

"It's not enough, it'll just look like I'm firing my godson's ex-boyfriend. As I said to Jackson when he was unfaithful, I can't fire him for cheating."

"You can fire him for bullying in the workplace. You can fire him or at least put him on probation for harassment and inappropriate behaviour in the workplace."

"Luca," he sighed.

I shook my head. "He makes Jackson uncomfortable. In fact, he makes *me* uncomfortable."

"We moved him, so he's Felix and Phil's technician, you two don't need to have any contact with him."

"And yet he still finds his way into our dressing room at least weekly," I said. "I just don't understand…"

"I hear what you're saying. I will note it and will keep an eye on it from now on."

I laughed, it surprised both of us. "Do you know how many teachers I've sat opposite who have told me that," I said. "Teachers who didn't *really* listen to what I was telling them, who just nodded and hummed when I went quiet then told me they'll keep an eye on it. *They* were as bad as the bullies because they didn't care and they made me feel like I shouldn't tell anyone because it didn't matter."

"Luca, it's not…"

"I'm so tired of bullies winning. All my life bullies have won. Bullies made me cut my hair, bullies made me only enjoy Drag in my family, bullies hurt my uncle over and over. He moved between six schools, and when the words stopped affecting him, it became physical. All I've ever heard is *just ignore*, show them it doesn't bother you. they'll get *bored* but I don't want to make them *fucking* bored I want them to be punished.

"I want all the kids who made me go to the barbers whilst crying *non-stop* to be punished for that, to know the repercussions of what they did.

"Charlie is a bully. It's as simple as that, the things Jackson has told me about their relationship made me sick to the stomach. The things he told me that he says now is just *horrible* and what's worse is it's been so long; it's been a part of his life that now he thinks he deserves it. That he has to take it.

"You have the power to put a stop to it. You have the power to make a bully have a repercussion for their actions. Don't be scared of him Jason, please."

I went to Mateo's armed with soup after Pa had taken my Sunday morning shift and told me he'd close the café early so I could both check on Mateo and attend Sunday lunch.

I hadn't spent all too much time in xer flat, as xe barely resided there xerself. *Like* this morning.

Text Message

Mateo: Oh, sorry my love. I'm at Felix's. They stormed my flat telling me that they felt an obligation to look after me until I felt better.
Mateo: Sent an address.

Felix lived quite close to the Rose Quartet *and* by default the café. They lived on the fourth floor of an old looking block of flats. Nothing at all like Avory and Milo's, all white flat doors and welcome mats.

I knocked on the door, it opened as I did. Felix smiled at me.

"Sorry," they whispered, I frowned. "I feel like I've just come here and intruded on everyone," they said as they stepped back to let me in.

"Don't be sorry," I said. "It was me *and* Jackson that encouraged Mateo to talk to you."

They smiled at me, it was bright - and infectious.

"Well, I retract my sorry and convert it into a thank you," they nodded so I followed them. "Xe is okay. Tired and a bit grumpy but okay. The meds should equal themselves out soon." They sighed and opened a door. "Hello gorgeous."

Mateo laughed from within.

"I've got a drag queen here; says she knows you."

"Let her in," xe said. Felix looked back at me as they pushed the door open.

"Pa sent me with soup," I told xem as I walked into the room. Xe smiled at me sitting up in bed pushing xemself against the pillows. Xe definitely looked tired.

"Oh, Rory's soup, I must be sick."

I smiled as I walked around the bed to give xem it. "How *are* you?" I whispered.

Xe shrugged. "I've been better. It's quite something when the medicine is what's making me sick, huh?" Xe shrugged, "but apparently I have to have a positive mindset." Xe glanced at Felix so I also did. They smirked as they pulled on the string bracelet around their wrist.

"I'll go and get you a spoon," they whispered then left.

"They came and got me last night. After they'd finished the show. They sent me a message told me to pack up some stuff because I shouldn't be alone. They're sleeping on the couch for me."

I looked towards the living room. "They're quite a person," I said. Xe hummed so I looked back at xem. My expression must have done something given how xe rolled xer eyes.

"I am in no place to have romantic feelings for *any*one. Sexual interest isn't even a fleeting thought right now."

I smirked. I *knew* I did. Xe laughed.

"What?"

"I..." I began then shook my head. "I shouldn't kiss and tell."

"Come off it, Luca." Xe punched me in the arm, *amazingly* however tired xe looked xe still packed a punch. I rubbed my arm looking a little wounded. "Luca," xe shook me so I smiled.

"I fooled around with Jackson."

The noise xe made resembled a small bird more than a human. I rose my eyebrow at xem as Felix laughed from behind me.

"Not listening," they said as they passed the spoon to Mateo. "Carry on."

I shook my head, "you're okay. Xe isn't getting any more details than that."

Xe pouted at me as xe popped the lid from the soup.

"You and Jackson are like a real relationship? It isn't just sex?" Felix asked. Mateo choked on the soup. I punched xem in the thigh, it made xem laugh harder.

"Jackson's my boyfriend," I said, it sounding somewhat childish.

"That makes me happy in ways I wasn't expecting," they said smiling then sat opposite me on the bed.

"It was long winded," Mateo informed Felix.

"I honestly thought Charlie was with Jackson. Given the way he talks about him, at least."

"What?" I said quietly.

Felix glanced at me. "I'm not trying to cause trouble sugar."

I sighed. "No, I'm... don't worry. I'm just curious because he's been saying *horrible* things to Jackson and it's..." I wobbled my head looking between them, "discomforting to think he's only being horrible to his face."

"Oh," Felix said. "He talks really highly of Jackson. Compliments and almost swooning."

"That..." I shook my head, "that's what he means," I sighed. "When Jason says there's no evidence because Charlie's clever and careful..."

"What are you talking about?" Mateo asked.

I looked back at xe, shaking my head as I sighed. "I went to Jason. I told him what Charlie was doing, he said there was no evidence. He couldn't do anything about it."

"For real?" Felix asked.

"I'm surprised I still have my job, to be honest." I pulled a face, Felix laughed reaching out their hand to me.

"If he won't do anything you need to go higher up." they said.

I shook my head. "Jason's the highest I can go. There's no one above Jason."

"Didn't you tell me Jackson's grandfather was a Queen?"

I turned back to Mateo.

"Both of them, in fact?"

"Jamie," I said. "You think I should tell Jamie?"

"I think it wouldn't hurt," Mateo said. "And if he's as prolific as the prophecy foretells, I think he might get the ball rolling and *something* might actually come of it."

I looked back at Felix.

"Jackson's grandfather was Cherry Blossom?" they asked, I smiled as I nodded. "I am *not* worthy to be in his presence."

"If Queen Cherry Blossom hears what's been going on with a technician and his grandson..."

"He'll put a stop to it," I said as I squeezed Felix's hands.

Jackson

Text Message

Jackson: You told Jamie about Charlie????

Peanut😔: I couldn't let it go.
Peanut😔: I'm sorry 😞

Jackson: I haven't seen Jamie that angry in such a long time. He instantly went for Jason shouting and screaming at him.
Jackson: Charlie's been fired!
Jackson: How could you Luca? I asked you to let it go.

Peanut😊: I couldn't! you have to understand that Jackson, I was bullied loads as a kid. I couldn't see it happening to you. You shouldn't have to put up with it. I am sorry, so sorry but I'm also so glad he's been fired. He was tainting the thing you love.

Jackson: You didn't get to decide that.

Peanut   is calling...

Declined

I looked at my phone as it began to ring again. Shaking my head as I held the sewing needle between my teeth. The dress I was making for Madison, just *because*, was mostly done except a few embellishments. I glanced at my phone again as it lit up.

Peanut 😊: If you don't pick up, I will come over.

I sighed lowering my glasses to rub my forehead then I called him. He picked up instantly, he must've been holding his phone. When his face filled my phone screen, he was biting his thumbnail. An anxious look on his face.

"I don't want to talk right now," I told him, *that* made the anxiousness go away, but it shifted into sadness, and I hated that.

"Hear me out," he said. I looked at him, I *didn't* hang up. "I just kept thinking about it and it made me so mad, and so upset because you don't deserve that. You don't deserve for him to be a dick to you and to get away with it.

"I told Jason first. I thought he could do something, but he refused and that angered me further. He straight up refused, and I thought that was bullshit because you should move heaven and earth for the people you love, and I love *you*."

He took a breath as I gasped. "What?"

"What?" he gasped his voice high, his face flushed.

"Luca," I sighed.

He shook his head. "I didn't mean to actually say that. I mean, I do *mean* it, but I wasn't... I've said my piece."

"Luca, sweetheart," I sighed. He sighed with me. "I'm so mad at you," I added, he looked away from me.

"So mad, I can't even articulate. It wasn't your place to do that…" I shook my head, "but I also can't thank you enough for it, because I was too much of wimp, too."

"No, no Jackson," he said. "No you weren't a wimp. He was manipulative and horrible to you. I'm sorry. I'm sorry I just…"

"I was madder you told Jamie," I told him. "I mean, Jason's one thing, I get that, he's our boss first and foremost, but Jamie. Luca that was low."

"It was Mateo's idea," he mumbled. It took all my effort not to laugh. "He's really been fired?"

"As if Jason could get away with saying no to Jamie," I said. "It was on legitimate terms, bullying of a fellow employee. Charlie denied it, obviously, but there was *actually* evidence." I sighed. "Look, you crossed the line."

"I know."

I sighed. "But I do love you, too."

"You do?" he whispered looking up at me, I smiled at him. He grinned back.

"I do… still mad."

"I know," he sighed.

"But thank you."

He looked momentarily pleased, as if he didn't want me to catch him being pleased.

"How did you find out?" Luca asked warily.

"I was at Reed's rehearsal," I told him. "Mostly to do the final bits of sewing on his dress when Jamie made his grand entrance, like *only* Jamie knows how. He demanded he speak to Jason. Who was up in his office, so Jamie storms up there and we're all left standing there with our mouths open because *what the fuck.*" I sighed as I pulled my knees to my chin. "Jason came back down after about ten minutes, calls Charlie to his office. That conversation lasted about twenty minutes before Charlie left in a huff and Jamie returned triumphant."

He nodded along slowly so I looked directly at him.

"Jamie then turned to me and said, why did your boyfriend have to tell me about what's been going on with Charlie. He'd have preferred to hear it straight from well, me."

"Wow, not even discreetly betrayed," he murmured; my laugh was nasal.

"We talked for most of the night, until Jamie went to bed, and I came in here to pout," I wobbled my head, "and text you."

"I so wanted to stand up to a bully, *and* win," he stressed. "I'd never won before."

"Well, you won now," I said. "With the help of a over dramatic Drag Queen. Although, he did say in the car back, that I should keep hold of you."

"Yeah?" he whispered.

"Because *what* you did was something Dylan would've."

We looked at each other through the screen.

"I love you," I said.

"I love you."

The last show before the Christmas break was always a bit more chaotic than any other. There was far more glitter, far more alcohol and *far* more brightly coloured costumes.

Reed never commissioned me for Queenie's Christmas dress as he wished for me to be surprised *and* every year so far, he'd been successful in this.

She came to show off her outfit of choice as I did Luca's makeup. He gawped so I turned then laughed out in a shocked noise as I stood from the dressing table stool and walking towards Queenie.

"Oh, you are…" I waved my hands, "sensational."

252

She curtsied, before raising her arms so I could fully take in the red and white striped shift dress. She was *obviously* dressed as a candy cane. The neck high, with white fur around it and matching around the hem of her dress that rested comfortably on her thighs.

Her tights were white, her heels were red and so very high, she towered over me *far* more than *he* usually did. Her face was *of course* immaculate and glittering, her wig a blonde beehive with a striped red and white hairband.

"You wee Queens have to follow this," she stated blowing a kiss behind me to Luca. He grinned happily as I took Queenie's hand *because* at our Christmas Show, the Queen was on first. A turn in events for the Rose Quartet but primarily because of the tradition of doing a group number at end of the show. This year's was in homage to *that* Mean Girls dance which Jesse had sniggered through directing us in.

"I'm not worthy," I told her then kissed the back of her hand. She squeezed my fingers.

"Exactly, Princess," she whispered, then kissed the tip of my nose. She laughed gleefully before winking at me and leaving my dressing room towards the stage. I turned back to Luca. He smirked as he held a makeup wipe to me. Wiping the lipstick marks from my nose when I sat back opposite him.

Beau wore an Elf dress. An obscenely sexy thing that was a deep green apron dress with red fur lining around the hem, a big black belt and buckle. The skirt sat high on her thighs, and she looked extremely comfortable with this - which just aided with it being obscenely sexy. She had a little clip-on elf hat, clipped into her big natural afro wig and glitter on her cheeks.

We were both definitely gawping at each other - *but* I was still just in my shapewear.

"Why are you looking at *me* like that? Have you seen yourself?"

She made a noise like a squeak in my direction. I looked down myself then. "Wait, you like *this*?"

"Yeah," she said, her voice almost monotone.

"As Queen Jasmine taught me, be glamorous all the way down to your shapewear," I almost sang to her, opening my dressing gown further *definitely* teasing her. She threw the pillow from the chaise lounge at me.

"Get dressed," she said, I pulled my tongue at her unzipping my dress bag as I did.

I was a Nutcracker. Sporting a red leotard, with gold epaulettes and small blue toy solider hat on a hairband so it sat at an angle on my long shiny black wig. My heels high but not as high as Queenie's and black lace ups. Beau's eyes were trailing me.

"You didn't put many clothes on top," She informed me.

I laughed happily. "Is that a complaint?"

"Oh, definitely not."

I grinned at her then took her hand, pulling her to the side of the stage so we could watch Queenie.

Lemon and Lime were stood in the opposite wing, awaiting their slot to go on, *also* watching Queenie as she sang through a musical catalogue of Christmas Songs.

Lemon was a gingerbread, her dress - I'd made after a long message thread with Felix. It was a simple bouffant dress, gingerbread orange with white accents that looked like icing and green and pink bows as the buttons. Her hair was in dreadlocks, pulled back in a half-up half down style, and tied with a bow similar to those on the front.

Lime was a Christmas Pudding, strapless with a big puffy skirt aided by an equally as puffy underskirt. Her hair in long box braids. They both looked stunning. They caught our eyes from across the stage. Lemon blowing a kiss over to us. We both returned it with quiet giggles so not to disturb Queenies set.

Beau's set was before mine and I stood very close to being too far forward as I watched her down the runway. Her act had shifted *away* from mostly singing to a comedy act. Something that Beau had slipped into very comfortably and did well. The audience ate her up. She turned towards me at one point during a particularly long laugh, which I was very much joining in with.

She paused, a real smile on her face, crinkling her nose at me before winking and turning the rest of the way wishing her audience well and signing off with a song then running down the runway, reaching for my hand *and* pulling me from the wing.

She twirled me under her arm, swapping places with me so I was stood centre stage. Her expression playful as she blew me a kiss then waved at the audience leaving the stage. I laughed after her watching her go before I turned towards the audience, lifting my hand and clicking my fingers *so* the stage went dark except for a spotlight on me.

Luca

Jackson was stood outside with an umbrella, his suit folded over his arm in a protective bag, a backpack slung over his shoulder, in just sweats, a hoodie *and* his glasses.

"Good morning," he offered.

I smiled at him. "Good morning."

"Can I come in? It's quite cold."

I took a few steps back, letting him through the door. He shook off his umbrella holding it upside down as he searched for somewhere to put it. I took it from him putting it by the door. He followed me into the living room.

"I was kind of expecting a hive of activity," he said as he looked around my living room. Connor was sat on the couch, his PlayStation game loading onscreen. Dad was sat in the armchair, his third coffee on the arm as he looked at something on his phone.

He lowered it when he heard Jackson's voice, turning towards us and waving. Jackson waved back.

"The hive of activity was at Riley's this morning," Dad said. "They're having the ceremony now."

"And you guys aren't invited to the ceremony?" he asked looking between us.

I shook my head. "Small service. Just a witness each and their parents."

"We're just going to the party," Dad said. "You know what they say, small service, big party." He stood. "Coffee?"

"Yes please," Jackson replied. "I was fully expecting pre-show style..." he shook his head. "Or Pride chaos. You're all so chill," he said then turned as Connor began rapid fire on the TV. We both watched it for a few seconds.

"We've been sat here for hours," I told him. "Pa left for the ceremony and we've just been waiting since."

"I can guarantee though we'll be in a mad rush regardless and still possibly be late," Dad said as he brought the coffee to Jackson. He laughed as he received it.

"I'd be disappointed if that *wasn't* the case."

We'd slipped away to my bedroom when Connor's continuous gunfire transitioned from bearable to the most annoying thing on the planet. I let Jackson lead the way, shooting a look to Dad as we went up the stairs, *daring* him to make a joke about being alone in my bedroom.

He didn't make one but I could tell it was a difficult feat for him.

Jackson walked to my bedroom like he'd been here a number of times before. I walked around him to sit on my bed. He soon came and sat next to me. Picking up the cow - that I now called Milk - and stroking over her head.

"We've come quite far since our custody agreement," he said shaking Milk's head towards me. I scratched at her nose.

"Haven't ate a doughnut since," I replied.

He laughed looking up at me. "I still can't believe you

did that."

"Says the Queen who bought one hundred pounds worth of foundation for me."

"I liked you," he mock pouted.

"Ditto," I said. "It was stupid in hindsight."

"Liking me?"

I hit his thigh lightly, so he laughed resting his head on my shoulder. We swayed together.

"Yes, it was *very* stupid." He kissed my shoulder. We were quiet in our own thoughts - although I was pretty certain we were thinking about the same thing. "What you said, this week..." he began *confirming* that we were, in fact, thinking about the same thing. "Was it true?" he asked. "I mean do you still want to? Do you..." he looked up, I stroked my thumb over his forehead, watching as he relaxed.

"Want to have sex?" I finished for him because *somehow* the words weren't all that scary to me anymore. He nodded his eyes not leaving mine. I bit my lip. "Yes," I said. "But if you don't want to, I don't want you to feel forced."

"No, I don't," he said slowly, warily. "I don't feel forced, and if the situation were right, I *one* hundred percent would like to have sex with you."

"So, no?" I said.

"I never said that," he pointed out. "I just, can't tell you how I'm going to feel tonight *just* yet."

"That's..." I said then smiled, "fair."

He sighed, kissing my shoulder again.

"You won't be mad?" he whispered into my shoulder, I turned towards him, lifting his chin so I was looking at him.

"Never," I told him. "And I want you to *know* that for definite, okay? I'd never be mad, the only situation that I'd be mad is if I made you feel forced and *then* I'd only be mad at myself. I just…" I sighed. "I figured talking about it beforehand would be better than just springing it on you. At my uncle's wedding."

His laugh was definitely amused. "Let's see how the night goes," he said softly. "No intentions. No pressure. Deal?" he asked, I nodded.

"Deal," I whispered then turned towards my dad's shout. "Ready?" I asked, he nodded.

Oakley's dress code had been *come as you are*, neither he nor Sky wanted to dictate what any of us wore to their wedding. I knew they were both wearing light grey suits. Oakley with a baby blue waistcoat and Sky with a powder pink waistcoat, a nod to the others chosen hair colour.

Pa had also gone for a suit, a darker grey than Oakley's but with a baby blue bowtie to match him.

I'd gone shopping with Oakley, for his input but not his approval. I'd returned with a floral purple blazer which I decided to wear a white shirt underneath and black skinny slacks. Jackson wore red tartan slacks - which I kind of loved, with a navy-blue blazer, white shirt and a red bowtie.

"It was Reed who persuaded me to wear tartan," he told me as we started down the stairs, "because his formal wear is a kilt, and he thought it was really odd I wasn't brave enough to wear tartan."

"Did you start wearing it to shut him up?" I asked as I dropped my phone into my pocket.

"Mostly."

I laughed, then we both stopped on the stairs. Dad looked up at us, a smile on his face as he examined us. He wore a more traditional suit. Black blazer and slacks, white shirt but a waistcoat in the same colour as Pa's bowtie. Connor's was a dark blue pinstripe suit, his tie black.

I was disappointed with my family's flamboyance *until* we got to the reception and the sea of colour expanded before us. Friends of Oakley and Sky sporting every colour of the rainbow. Jackson gasped happily beside me, his eyes trying to see everything at once.

I watched him until my grandpa approached. He hugged me, cuddling me tight then taking a step back to examine me, as I also did to him *because* I had absolutely no words for how much I adored his powder pink suit.

"Your jacket is gorgeous," he told me, "as is your date."

Jackson laughed. "Your outfit is a Pinterest board wish of mine," he told Grandpa.

"The highest of compliments," he said, then, "if you don't mind though I need to steal your boyfriend as he is required in a family photograph."

Jackson waved his hand at us, as if saying he could have me. He did follow us when I began to walk led by Grandpa. I soon overtook him when I saw Oakley. Running past so I could hug Oakley.

"Hello beautiful," Oakley said. I took his hand, stroking my finger over the new golden band on his ring finger.

"You did it."

"I did it," he said almost as if it was a secret. He turned when a flute of champagne was held in front of him. "Isn't my partner good, bringing me champagne?" he teased taking the flute as Sky kissed his cheek.

"Smile."

We turned together, all smiling at the photographer. Flash after flash *until*, "Wait, wait," Oakley said. I looked at him as he left our line up walking towards the photographer taking Jackson's hand.

"You're as much a part of the family as any of us," he said then twirled him towards me. "Only be right you're in the photos," he added before lifting his flute. Sky knocked theirs against his. Them kissing over it as I looked over my shoulder at Jackson.

"I'm a part of the family," he whispered.

"There's no escaping now, Bennett."

He crinkled his nose at me. "I wasn't planning on it, May."

The party was alive from the moment we walked in, but my family had a history of knowing *how* to party and doing it with style. I sat and watched the dance floor as Jackson and the majority of my family walked the buffet. Watching as Oakley and Sky danced with Frankie and Sam. The laughter and joy evident on their faces *and* for the first time I wasn't envious of them. I didn't *want* to be them, *because* I was living my own fairy tale.

My eye drifted, a smile playing on my face as I watched Jackson reach the dessert portion of the buffet with Connor them both laughing at something. Pointing towards a particular cake that I couldn't quite see.

"Hungry?"

I jumped, turning to look at Grandpa as he stood beside me, smiling down at me.

"You're pretty fixated on the buffet," he added as he placed a plate on the table behind me, so I turned in my chair to examine it.

"I think you'll find I'm fixated on *Jackson*," I replied without even a little bit of shyness. Grandpa seemed proud of this as he sat beside me his own plate of food that matched my own. We both influenced the coeliac menu choice as Oakley had very *rightly* said he wasn't going to be eating it, so it didn't seem right for him to choose what it was.

It included a cake with rainbow layers that was a non-negotiable part of our menu.

"He's fit in well," Grandpa observed as he also watched Jackson and Connor. "Like he's been here all along."

I nodded. "I hope his family thinks the same with me."

"I'm happy for you, Peanut," he said gently, I smiled at him. "I believe Oakley booked you two a room to yourself tonight," he continued. "Thought that'd be better than making you share with your dad and Pa."

I nodded slowly. "That's good," I said then swallowed, as they started their way back to the table.

"Tonight the night?" he asked, neither of us looked at each other.

I shrugged one shoulder. "It might be. The jury's still out, could go either way."

"Make sure you're happy with your decision," he said so I looked at him. "*Just* because it's able to be done, doesn't mean it *has* to."

I nodded as Jackson sat beside me.

"I brought you some sweets," he whispered, I frowned lightly at him then smiled as he dropped a small drawstring bag of sweets into my hand. "There's loads on the table," he added looking towards it. I laughed freely so he grinned at me reaching into his blazer pocket and revealing a packet of love hearts. "These, too." He read the personalised packaging. and tore the top off, tipping the packet onto his hand and reading the sweet.

He appeared pleased with it, passing it to me.

Be Mine.

"I already am," I whispered.

The first dance was just before the countdown to midnight. The DJ cut the sound, welcoming Sky and Oakley onto the floor as the party cheered for them, clapping and whistling as they walked down the tables towards the dance floor.

It had been the thing Oakley had been dreading the most. The all-eyes-on-him-first-dance as he called it, because he fully believed he'd trip and land flat on his face *but* I knew Sky wouldn't let that happen. I knew Sky would keep hold of him and keep him upright *until* at least the attention had shifted and that's what they did, as they began to slow-dance together to Elton John's *Tiny Dancer*.

Grandpa and Grandad joined them first, after a verse or so. Grandad leading Grandpa to the floor. Grandpa winking at Oakley as if to say the pressure was somewhat off. Sky's parents were next to join and after them the dance floor filled up quickly, Dad and Pa, Enzo and Caleb, Frankie and Sam. I watched them all before turning to Jackson, smiling at him as he also watched a content expression on his face as his eyes tracked the couples across the floor.

"Do you…" I began, he turned to me, and I stuttered but his smile was gentle as I held my hand out to him. "Do you want to dance?"

He nodded. "Very much."

I stood, his hand slipping into mine then walking towards a space on the dancefloor. His arms slipped around my waist underneath my jacket, as if an instinct, his hands meeting behind my back as I held my own hand over his shoulders.

There was far too much space between us. We took a step in together, I stepped on his foot. He began to laugh, soft and happy as he moved closer to me again. His hands stroking my back, somehow successfully soothing me as we rested our foreheads together.

I closed my eyes. Listening and moving to the music.

"Hey," Jackson whispered.

I opened my eyes. He smiled at me, I grinned back

then he kissed me, delicate and soft kisses that we didn't stop when the DJ announced midnight was approaching *and* that we'd be celebrating with fireworks.

The room began to clear out behind us. He kissed me one last time, knocking his forehead against mine then taking my hand and walking out into the courtyard with the rest of the party.

Jackson

We sat outside a little longer than was actually necessary. The fireworks long over, our bones feeling the cold. I'd have given him my suit jacket if he didn't have his own.

He looked back at me as I examined him this thought in my head. He smiled at me a little apprehensively, his brace catching the streetlamp that was behind us.

"I was just thinking about how I'd be all romantic right now and give you my jacket…"

"I have a jacket," he informed me.

I almost cackled. "I know, that's why I was staring at you."

"I thought you were having second thoughts."

"No," I said lightly, a slight inclination to my voice that obviously made him not believe me.

"We don't have to do this."

"I know. It's a choice, it's always a choice," I shrugged, "and I have confidence if I told you to stop, if I requested that of you, you would."

"Always," he nodded. "I think Riley would disown me if I didn't," he added almost as an afterthought, I smiled.

"We don't have to even go to the room now, we can go back to the party."

We turned together, the party was still alive, the energy not faltering one little bit whether that was people bringing in the new year or celebrating Oakley and Sky, that wasn't all too clear.

"I don't want to go back to the party," he said quietly. He didn't turn from watching it. "I want to go to the room," he said. I nodded reaching for his hand stroking my fingers over his. His was freezing. He still didn't turn to me as he turned his hand so we could hold hands.

"I want to get warmed up and talk and... if it happens it... does." He looked back at me, "because it's okay if it doesn't happen tonight."

I nodded. "I saw an ice cream vending machine by reception."

He rose his eyebrow at me.

"That sounds amazing," he hummed. "Let's go get the key," he added, so I stood pulling him up with the lightest of tugs. He pulled me closer to him, wrapping his arm around me, not letting go of my hand.

He spun me out of his cuddle as we approached our table, keeping hold of my hand but walking in front of me.

He stopped at his dad. "You're heading up early," Rory said looking from Luca to me. I nodded meekly, trying not to draw attention to myself.

I feared my face shouted about the potential of sex and most of Luca's family would be able to decode that.

"Don't be too loud. You're sharing with us remember," Alistair said.

"What?" Luca replied, he didn't sound as if he was even considering entertaining the joke.

"Alistair," Rory said simply. Alistair sighed sounding defeated as he reached into his blazer and retrieved a key card.

"Five fifteen," Alistair told Luca, passing the card over and squeezing his arm. I jumped when I felt a hand on my shoulder.

"Are you going to bed?"

I looked up. Riley smiled down at me squeezing my shoulder lightly.

"We're heading that way," I told him he nodded rubbing his hand down my back.

He dropped something into my jacket pocket. I thought it wise not to fish it out right away. Instead, I looked at him, he winked at me before his hand went into Luca's hair. They spoke quietly, Riley kissed his cheek, wishing us both a goodnight.

Luca turned to look at me, nodding once so I did back.

We walked the corridors, neither of us in any rush.

"What did Riley say to you?" I asked as we rounded towards the reception. He sighed lightly as he searched his pockets, he found a pound coin then, he started on my pockets.

He laughed lightly as he pulled out what Riley had dropped into my jacket.

"He said to not let anyone pressure us," he whispered as he lifted the condom out. "To be safe and to talk to each other. He said he wanted me to make sure it was our decision and not anyone else's influence. And to have fun."

"To have fun," I repeated, he smiled then continued through my pockets until he found a second pound.

"Phish food?" he asked.

I nodded, "And Chunky Monkey."

"You have good taste."

"I thought you already knew that," I teased lightly; he bit his tongue his amusement clear as he watched the machine dispense the ice cream.

The hotel wasn't too hard to navigate so we ran, hand in hand through the corridors, following the numbers until we reached five fifteen.

He tapped the card against the door, turning to me almost impressed when it opened first time, before letting me in and turning on the lights. Our two backpacks were already on the double bed that sat as the main feature of the room.

"I guess there wasn't any twin rooms left," I teased. He turned to me the smile big on his face, so I laughed reaching for his hand and squeezing gently before shrugging my blazer off. Lying it over the chair I was stood in front of. He followed suit, *then* followed me into the bathroom.

"I guess you no longer have an issue sharing the bathroom with me," I said as I undid the button of my pants. He laughed.

"No. But I can leave though, if…"

"Hey, I told you last time, don't worry. I'm quite easy…"

"You know that's not true," he deadpanned. I gasped dramatically touching my chest. He sniggered sounding far more relaxed so I proceeded to go the toilet. "You're making me need to go."

"You're very welcome to join me," I said, as I took a step closer to the wall. He did after some hesitation. I gasped in an overly dramatic fashion; he narrowed his eyes at me. "I saw your penis," I whispered as I stepped away from the toilet. He laughed as I washed my hands. I left the bathroom as he did. Unzipping my backpack and rifling through it until I found my shirt and bed shorts. We changed either side of the bed, tossing our backpacks away from the bed.

The ice creams piled on my bedside cabinet, still cold

but likely now soft enough to eat. I climbed onto the bed. He lay opposite me, his hands under his head as his eyes examined me.

"Can I kiss you?" I whispered. He looked taken back for a moment before nodding *but* I was well aware that he was extremely in his head, he wasn't *fully* comfortable with the situation and although I didn't believe it to be *me* or the fact, we were sharing a bed, I still wanted to tread carefully. In case it was.

I placed my hands on his cheeks, knocking my nose against his then kissing his smile. His hands stroked down my side, playing around the hem of my shirt but never touching skin. I grinned when his hands found their way around my shorts, until he was playing with the bow I had tied in the front of them.

"Luca," I whispered, he looked down between us, watching as he twirled the string around his fingers.

"I don't think I want to have sex," he whispered, my smile didn't falter, *but* I did make it slightly softer, lifting my hand so I could stroke through his hair. "Tonight," he added. "I mean, I definitely do. I definitely want to have sex with you but... not tonight."

"Okay," I whispered.

"Okay," he repeated, then he exhaled.

"I hope that wasn't stressing you out, gorgeous."

"No," he whispered back. "Gorgeous." I pulled a face at him, he laughed. "It wasn't stressing me out, I was just really thinking about it."

"That's all I ask of you," I said. He shook his head a laugh quiet in his throat. "That your decision is what you want."

"What do you want?" he asked. "Do you want to have sex? In any capacity."

"I want to *kiss* a little more," I answered. He nodded. Apparently, he agreed with that, "and sleep next to my boyfriend *after* we've…" I turned reaching for the ice cream pots. He gasped happily taking the Phish Food from me. "Eaten ice cream. Or we can go back down to the party." He looked up at me as he held the little wooden stick that acted as a spoon in his mouth. He crinkled his nose at me.

"I'd so much rather stay in here with you."

"Okay, try saying that again *but* this time make sure you're looking at me and *not* the ice cream, yeah?"

Luca

I am a Drag Queen. *This* was especially prominent of a Sunday morning when my makeup was still on my face - and on my pillow even after we were sure we'd wiped it off in the dim afterglow of the show. I was yet to be successful with the *whole* wiping my makeup off after a show thing, but it made me laugh every week, a soft thing that was mostly memory of the evening before. My phone rang whilst I was moisturising my face in the bathroom after my shower.

"Hello," I said softly. Jackson laughed so I actually looked at him, smiling as he was also moisturising - because he didn't clean his make up off well, either.

"I just wanted to confirm with you," he started, I nodded as he rubbed his hands together. "So, lunch is at two?"

"Three," I corrected, he frowned at me, "my shift finishes at two."

"Ah," he said. "Is Mateo your relief? Or is xe still sick?"

"Xe said xe's feeling better but not by much. Still thinks xe is on the wrong medication as does Felix, but xe has a nurse review this week."

"Yes?" he asked.

"Yes. Mateo is my relief."

"Cool, cool, do you want me to meet you at the café?"

"You can, Oakley usually picks me up to take me to lunch, I'm sure he'd be happy to take you, too."

"Well, I'll go visit Avory and Milo. Go to café with them when they're ready."

"Deal," I said.

"I'll see you later, I'm nervous but prepared, I think."

"Don't be nervous," I said quietly. "You don't have to speak if you don't want to, and it's purely a feel-good thing. We're not in the game of pressuring."

He nodded slowly. "Okay! I will see you later. Enjoy work."

"I will try," I almost sang back at him as I picked up my toothbrush. He blew a kiss to me, I did it back.

I sat on one of the tables opposite Mateo as xe sat on the nearby chair. The café was empty, we'd had a few coffees to go, or someone coming in for a slice of cake, but it was quiet. Quieter than normal, at least.

I'd been trying to get information about Felix from Mateo but xe wasn't biting, I changed tact in the end.

"How are you feeling?" I whispered.

Xe sighed but nodded. "Fine, I guess. I'm shattered, like I always feel tired no matter how much sleep I get but nothing too bad. Felix said I should stay off longer but I just, I couldn't. I was getting bored, and I go back to uni next week." Xe shook xer head. "I can work through fatigue. That's fine, and it's not as if we're rushed off our feet here or anything."

"True," I said quietly, xe smiled, xers eyes tracking something behind me, but I didn't turn.

"I do like Felix," Xe said, the bell to the café door

rang, "and that's all you're getting."

I moaned going to make a move off the table but stopped. I smiled at Jackson, he grinned right back before lifting my chin and kissing me as a greeting. I glanced behind him as Avory stopped at the counter. Mateo standing to serve them.

"Quiet today," Milo commented as he started towards his regular couch. I nodded as I sighed.

"Been like this all morning," I told him. "Mateo and I have been rushed off our feet."

"I can tell," he laughed as he took his seat.

"You know now, because we're family," Mateo said as xe set the tray.

"We're family?" Avory asked

Mateo nodded. "Duh, my baby is dating yours," xe explained, Avory laughed deeply but nodded as if asking Mateo to continue. "Can you..." xe changed xer attention to Milo, "draw our menu?"

Milo beamed. "I haven't done that in so long," he told Avory. "Look at me, I'm a legacy."

"Jackson could do it," Avory said. "You know if his big head puts him off-balance."

Milo looked mildly wounded, Jackson laughed quietly beside me.

"You draw?" Mateo asked.

Jackson nodded. "I draw, I sew, I'm a catch."

"Ah, the big head's genetic," Avory said, he sounded mildly resigned. Milo and Jackson shared a smirk.

"You can do it this time," Jackson said as if he was providing Milo a service. "I have to be somewhere." Milo snorted lightly as he sliced this week's cake with his fork.

"Am I interrupting?"

I turned then leapt from the table running towards Oakley as he let the door swing shut behind him. He grinned, catching me in the hug.

"How was your honeymoon?" I asked. "I love your tan," I added as we moved away from the hug.

"We had the best time," he sighed happily. "Didn't want to come home, but Sky *reminded* me they had a youth club to run." He pulled a face, I laughed. "Are you ready for lunch?"

"I am," I told him. "Jackson's coming, too."

"Oh, baby," Oakley said. "Are you prepared for this?"

"I survived your wedding, didn't I?" Jackson said as I took off my apron.

"Oh good, a bit of sass will get you through this," Oakley teased as I hugged Mateo.

"Text me what happens with the nurse? Okay?"

"Of course," xe said softly kissing my cheek. "Tell me if he survives lunch," he whispered. I laughed turning to look at Jackson as he laughed with Oakley.

"Of course."

I hugged Sky over the driver's seat when I got into the car, them laughing and cuddling me back, kissing my hands before putting the car into gear. They spoke mostly of Cannes and their exploration of the South of France. Until we pulled up outside of Grandpa's.

"I assume Luca has already told you about Vent It?" Sky asked.

Jackson nodded slowly. "He has, I've been racking my head all week for something to... say."

"Riley will never make you speak," Sky said, a slight laugh in their voice. "He's the most empathetic and understanding man I've ever met, and my dad was a therapist."

"I think that's saying something," Oakley added, Jackson laughed beside me.

"If you've got nothing, he won't push," they said. "I don't even think we've got something this week."

"That's the beauty of being a couple, you can deliver shared news," I said. "You can piggyback off mine if you want?"

He laughed. "No, I got this," he said.

I grinned at him. Sky and Oakley got out of the car. We followed.

"If you need me to cause a distraction say something like, pass the gravy," Sky said to Jackson.

"Got'cha," he laughed then stood back as Riley opened the front door and nearly picked Oakley up with the force of the hug. *His* hug wasn't nearly as committed to me, but it was still a cuddle as he looked over my head at Jackson.

"Ah, coming back for more," he said.

"I'm a glutton for punishment," Jackson replied. Riley sniggered, his fingers threading through my hair as he did.

"You're growing it out," he commented as he straightened one of my curls in his fingers.

"Yeah..." I said slowly. "I thought *why* not."

"Brilliant, your hair was - well, always is, but was so gorgeous when you were small."

He kissed the side of my head.

"Vent It is open," Kieran declared this week lifting his wine glass happily and taking a sip from it. We all raised our own glasses back to him.

"You can start if you wish to," Riley told Kieran; he shook his head.

"I haven't got much; I'm just *officially* retired now. I left the school before Christmas and left the club this week. That's it," he shrugged. "I've kind of really loved staying in bed with you late into the morning," he added to Riley. They kissed. We all cooed back at them in an overly teasing way.

"My parent's love aside," Pa said, they both laughed as he grinned at them. "Alistair and I…" he began.

"If you finish that with, are going to have another baby, I'm going to be *really* upset," Connor said. Dad squawked as he laughed, almost choking on his wine as the rest of the table *tried* to suppress sniggers.

"That isn't *actually* possible anymore, son," Dad said although he still sounded as if he was choking.

"Yeah, they had you and thought *never again*," I added.

"What *were* you going to say?" Riley nudged.

"It's a bit lacklustre after *that*, but we're finally getting a new car."

"Finally," Kieran sighed.

"I had a few particularly well-paying jobs, so we figured we could afford to do it," Dad continued. "We also figured that *if* you wanted it, you could have our current one, Luca."

"Really?"

They both nodded. "At least to learn in," Pa said. "It's a bit…"

"Shit," Kieran offered. I glanced at him. He grinned and drank more wine.

"You get a car, and I don't even get a baby brother," Connor murmured beside me. Kieran reached for his shoulder squeezing gently.

"Figured it'd help as well…" Dad said waving his hand at me, so I took the bait.

"It would help," I said, "as I'm moving out."

"What?" Oakley said. "Where?"

"When?" Riley asked.

I quietened them with my hands. "I'm twenty *real* soon, and I've never really been able to afford it before, even though the café wage was amazing. Now, with the club's wage on top I'm in a pretty solid place to move into a flat of my own. I went through all the numbers with Frankie," I said as if it was a defensive to Oakley, he nodded slowly, "and he said I was in a good position if it's what I wanted and I so do."

"I didn't know that," Jackson said beside me.

I looked at him. "I told you; you could piggyback on my news if you wanted," I reminded him. He shook his head gently. "I mean, it'd make sense because I wouldn't say *no* to a roommate."

"Oh," he laughed then he blushed. I touched his arm.

"You don't have to make any decision now. At all. I've been thinking about this for a long time. *I'm* moving out regardless," I explained. He nodded as I rose my eyebrow at him, "and apparently getting a car."

"Winning," he said.

"And you'd still be allowed over for sleepovers," I said, the rest of the table got *pretty* loud. "You've all got the filthiest of minds." I told them, as Oakley laughed sliding down his seat, and Riley knocked his fork against his wine glass. My Dads were the only two shouting about how I was an innocent little virgin. I glanced at Jackson raising my eyebrow at him.

"You really want to be a part of this chaos?"

"Every minute of it."

Jackson

I was a Drag Queen. It was embedded deep into my DNA at this point as much as I was gay, as much as I was demisexual, as much as I was an artist, or a dressmaker or surprisingly good at maths. I was a Drag Queen right down to my bones *and* I loved every glittering moment of it.

I sat with the Queens of the Rose Quartet on the floor of my dressing room. A sandwich platter between us because it was Luca's turn for the sandwich run and he'd prepped in the café. There was sandwiches, cakes, and crisps although they were all almost gone by now. Luca's own little tray completely empty as he sat back on his hands laughing as he watched the theatrics from Felix. They were fully engrossed in a story they were telling about *this one time back in London*, the laughs and egging on the story loud, almost unruly.

This was proven when Jason came knocking.

"What on earth is going on back here you shrieking Queens?" he laughed looking around us all before landing on the remaining sandwiches in the tray. Reed took the tray and held it too him.

"You all need to start getting ready," he said. "Queenie is, of course, closing the show. Lemon and

Lime, you're opening followed by Madison, then Beau."

"Ha," Luca said. I turned to him. "I'm a higher billing than you now."

"You *know* it's decided on a coin flip," I said.

He gasped dramatically. "I love going on after you," he told me, "because it means I can rip you to pieces in my set."

I touched my hand to my chest. "True love." I gushed.

"Move Queens," Jason urged. Felix and Phil did, standing and leaving my dressing room with *little* to no urgency. I blew a kiss to them on the way out as Felix reminded Luca to text them.

Reed knelt next to me to cuddle me. Kissing the top of my head and reminding me that tomorrow we were due to watch Guys and Dolls, and I was on the takeaway. I also blew a kiss to him as he left.

"Jamie's here," Jason said. I frowned at him. "He came around for a coffee this morning, I said he might as well come with. It's not like he hasn't been here before."

"No," I laughed.

"He wants to do your makeup."

"Really?" I whispered, smiling.

"Can I watch?" Luca asked. "I want to see Queen Blossom at work, that'll be…" he chef-kissed.

"You'll have to get direct consent from HRH Blossom, she's a bitch," Jason said.

"She is," I whispered.

Jamie took the time to absorb my dressing room when I'd finally allowed him to come in. Luca and I had agreed we should both be tucked and shaped when he joined us, so we didn't have to usher him out when we had to get ourselves ready.

We'd gotten distracted as I now had the knowledge that Luca liked my shapewear - and that he was easily wound up so we'd both bolted into our tracksuits and acted like the epitome of innocence when he came in. I sat myself on my dressing table stool, *him* on my chaise lounge. Jamie pulled a chair from the hallway, setting it in such a way that I couldn't look in the mirror, *but* that was okay because I trusted him. There was no doubt in my mind that I trusted him.

I didn't trust that he could look directly at Luca though. That worried me.

"It was strangely difficult coming here without Dylan," Jamie told both of us. I didn't turn away from him even though he wasn't actually looking at me. "I hadn't expected that, because you *know* this was my thing, my place. I knew Dylan had a presence. Of course, he did, he built so much of this room."

"Wait, what?" I whispered.

"Oh yeah. We underwent a *big* renovation when the original lights blew on the stage. They replaced the lights with the LED strips that are there now, but we also decided to do the bar up, to repaint the stage. You know, freshen everything up."

He began to cleanse my face.

"The dressing rooms need some life, too, so he made all the vanities with Parker's help of course, but he was made up. I still have a video on my computer somewhere of when he tested the lights the first time. The delight on his face when they turned on. If I didn't love him already, I would've fell in love with him then."

"Grandad," I said softly.

"He's everywhere in here. It was stupid of me really," he admitted then began on my foundation. "Anyway, I said yes to Jason because I didn't think and then I got here, and Dylan practically slapped me in the face."

"So, makeup," I said softly.

"So, makeup. To ground myself," he exhaled. "And

so I can look at your beautiful face for an extended period of time." He smiled at me; I smiled back. "Maybe teach this boyfriend of yours a thing or two," he teased; Luca gasped behind me.

"Jackson does my makeup," he told Jamie, who rose an eyebrow at me.

"He was nervous for Beau's first show, so I did his makeup *then* he just kept appearing in my dressing room."

"I did," Luca confirmed.

Jamie laughed. "I like him," Jamie informed me whilst dabbing concealer under my eyes with his little finger.

"I know."

"You'll have to come and endure a family dinner soon," Jamie said to Luca. "Can we bring Rosie back just so the *entire* family's there."

"He'll be there," I said, he met my eyes. "We won't stop talking about him, in fact we'll talk about him so much he'd have told us to shut up and talk about something else."

"Too right," he said softly his eyes jumping over my face as he ran my brush through the blusher. I glanced at Luca, he winked at me then openly laughed when Jamie held my chin, so I'd face him again.

We sat opposite each other on my chaise lounge, *both* of us fully dressed. Beau's skirt covering my knees because she wished to be a Princess tonight. I'd told her she looked like the Amazing Miss Maisel, and she'd *rightly* taken it as a compliment.

Now she used a glue gun on her heels to stick rhinestones onto the stiletto - it was *shockingly* effective and made my Sandal heels feel basic. I didn't tell her that though.

"I'm at Jason's tomorrow afternoon, but I can go

home with you tonight," I suggested.

"That could work." She cleared her throat looking up at me, "you can help me unbox tomorrow morning then go to Jason's. He's here in the morning, anyway, isn't he?"

"Yes," I said. "Shit."

She rose her eyebrow at me.

"Piano lesson with Jesse."

"You could still come home with me tonight," she said. "I'd like that, most of my flat is in boxes but the bed *isn't*."

"Oh," I teased; she bit her tongue.

"I didn't mean that, but also, *that*."

I laughed. "I'll come home with you tonight, help you unpack as many boxes as I can before I leave, deal?"

"Deal."

"Then I'll return to your abode on Monday because I usually stay at Jason's."

"That sounds like a plan," she said nodding then held her heels to me. "What do you think?"

"They're incredible," I told her, "genuinely. You've just done some kind of magic."

She winked at me before putting them on. We looked towards the knock on the door.

"Madison to the stage," Chandler almost sang.

"I'm on my way Chandler, darling." I told him then took Beau's hand, standing her with me and taking her to the stage. I kissed the back of her hand before letting go and walking onto the stage.

I was stood in the middle of the runway when the lights came back up. I waved with my fingers.

"Hi," I said, the audience replied so I giggled, "let's get started," I requested and the music started around me. A loud poppy song I requested everyone join me on their feet for, the vast majority of the audience did.

"Oh, you're all eating out of the palm of my hand, aren't you?" I purred at them, the audience sniggered, one of them whistling at me so I blew a kiss in the general direction and then I began to sing.

They were *also* eating out of Beau's hand when she walked onto the stage. Her laughter starting before she even spoke a word.

"You are *rowdy* tonight," she said. "Good. Madison's lovely, isn't she." She purred turning to look back at me, I rose an eyebrow at her from where I leant on the wing. "A bit..." she trailed off as she made some sort of gesture in front of herself so I couldn't see it, *but* I still laughed when the audience erupted in giggles. "She and I are a *thing* see, partners..."

The audience erupted into wolf whistles and whoops. Beau waved her hand as if telling them to settle down.

"She passed me backstage see, and do you know what she said?" she continued as she walked the stage. "She tapped me on the shoulder and went, *Beau* my one true love Beau, beautiful Beau."

The audience whistled again; Beau chuckled deeply.

"She said, did you pop the dishwasher on before we left? Because I don't want to go home to dirty dishes *again*."

The audience shrieked.

"Apparently, romance truly is dead. I was expecting a break a leg, or I hope you don't bomb out there, some loving words of support but *no*," she continued. "And the real kicker is that I *didn't* put the dishwasher on." She paused, "shit." She turned so she was looking back at me, she winked. I smiled back. "Sorry, Madison," she called back to me before looking over her shoulder. "It's a good job she loves me, huh?" She turned all the way, "in fact, it's a damn good job I love her."

I sighed contently as I buried my head between Luca's chin and shoulder. I kissed his neck gently, smiling when the glitter that I'm *sure* Beau hadn't been wearing shimmered on his neck. I ran my finger down his neck. He shivered.

"That tickles," he whispered, so I laughed.

"You're sparkling."

"Always," he informed me turning himself, so we were lying face to face. He ran his finger down my nose. "You're also sparkling," he said a laugh playing on his voice. "I feel like glitter will be embedded into the walls by, hmm, next week?"

"Oh, by tomorrow," I stated.

"Only if the two of us are here."

I rose my arm.

"We are."

"I mean..."

"Long term?" I suggested. He nodded slowly, I ran my finger down his neck again.

"Have you thought, you know, thought anymore about it?"

"I have. In fact, it's all I can think about."

"And?"

"Show me where I can make dresses," I whispered as his eyes met mine, "and you've got yourself a deal."

"For *real?*" he whispered.

"I want to live with you, Luca."

He kissed me. I laughed against him, holding his head in my hands.

"Does that mean..." he whispered against me; I closed my eyes. "That we get your canopy bed?"

I coughed out a laugh. "I see your priorities, Luca."

He nuzzled his nose into my neck, kissing me gently. I threaded my fingers through his hair.

"You really want to live with me?"

"Yes," I whispered. "I really do. Why, don't you want to live with me?"

He blew a raspberry against my neck.

"One thing though…" I said. "Don't you *ever* forget to put the dishwasher on."

"Deal," he said kissing deeply, then stroking his nose against mine. "I really do love you; you know. I wasn't just saying that for comedic effect."

"I know," I whispered. "And I really do love you. Almost as much as drag."

"Don't lie to my face," he teased, tickling my sides.

"I'm not lying," I shrieked at him trying to capture his hands. I didn't succeed.

"Really? Because I think I love drag more." He gasped; I gasped back. "There's just more glitter," he continued. I pushed him onto his back. He kept hold of my hand. Laughing as he flattened my hand on his chest. His heartbeat was a little quick. "Have I ever actually told you how I fell in love with drag?" he asked turning his head to look at me.

"You actually haven't," I said shaking my head.

He stroked his fingers down the back of my hand. "Well, I've *always* wanted to be a Drag Queen…"

SRL Publishing don't just publish books, we also do our best in keeping this world sustainable. In the UK alone, over 77 million books are destroyed each year, unsold and unread, due to overproduction and bigger profit margins.

Our business model is inherently sustainable by only printing what we sell. While this means our cost price is much higher, it means we have minimum waste and zero returns. We made a public promise in 2020 to never overprint our books for the sake of profit.

We give back to our planet by calculating the number of trees used for our products so we can then replace them. We also calculate our carbon emissions and support projects which reduce CO_2. These same projects also support the United Nations Sustainable Development Goals.

The way we operate means we knowingly waive our profit margins for the sake of the environment. Every book sold via the SRL website plants at least one tree.

To find out more, please visit
www.srlpublishing.co.uk/responsibility